PRAISE FOR

DETACHMENT FAULT

"Action-packed."   —*Tucson Weekly*

"*Detachment Fault* should be read twice: once to discover who-dun-what-and-why—and then a second time, slowly, relishing Miller's evocative and knowledgeable descriptions of Arizona natural history and landscapes."

—Wynne Brown,
author of *More Than Petticoats: Remarkable Arizona Women*

"Absorbing. . . . Well-developed characters, a lyrically drawn sense of place, a budding romance, and the importance of family and friends distinguish this mystery series."   —*Booklist*

"Full of sensory detail, [*Detachment Fault*] brings to life the flavor and multicultural heritage of southeastern Arizona. Fast-paced, it is intertwined with natural history and plenty of murder and mayhem."   —Sharman Apt Russell,
author of *Hunger: An Unnatural History*

DETACHMENT FAULT

SUSAN CUMMINS MILLER

BERKLEY PRIME CRIME, NEW YORK

THE BERKLEY PUBLISHING GROUP
Published by the Penguin Group
Penguin Group (USA) Inc.
375 Hudson Street, New York, New York 10014, USA
Penguin Group (Canada), 90 Eglinton Avenue East, Suite 700, Toronto, Ontario M4P 2Y3, Canada
(a division of Pearson Penguin Canada Inc.)
Penguin Books Ltd., 80 Strand, London WC2R 0RL, England
Penguin Group Ireland, 25 St. Stephen's Green, Dublin 2, Ireland (a division of Penguin Books Ltd.)
Penguin Group (Australia), 250 Camberwell Road, Camberwell, Victoria 3124, Australia
(a division of Pearson Australia Group Pty. Ltd.)
Penguin Books India Pvt. Ltd., 11 Community Centre, Panchsheel Park, New Delhi—110 017, India
Penguin Group (NZ), Cnr. Airborne and Rosedale Roads, Albany, Auckland 1310, New Zealand
(a division of Pearson New Zealand Ltd.)
Penguin Books (South Africa) (Pty.) Ltd., 24 Sturdee Avenue, Rosebank, Johannesburg 2196,
South Africa

Penguin Books Ltd., Registered Offices: 80 Strand, London WC2R 0RL, England

This is a work of fiction. Names, characters, places, and incidents either are the product of the author's imagination or are used fictitiously, and any resemblance to actual persons, living or dead, business establishments, events, or locales is entirely coincidental. The publisher does not have any control over and does not assume any responsibility for author or third-party websites or their content.

DETACHMENT FAULT

A Berkley Prime Crime Book / published by arrangement with Texas Tech University Press

PRINTING HISTORY
Texas Tech University Press hardcover edition / 2004
Berkley Prime Crime mass-market edition / March 2006

Copyright © 2004 by Susan Cummins Miller.
Cover design by Pyrographx.
Interior text design by Kristin del Rosario.

ISBN: 0-425-20893-1

BERKLEY® PRIME CRIME
Berkley Prime Crime Books are published by The Berkley Publishing Group,
a division of Penguin Group (USA) Inc.,
375 Hudson Street, New York, New York 10014.
The name BERKLEY PRIME CRIME and the BERKLEY PRIME CRIME design
are trademarks belonging to Penguin Group (USA) Inc.

PRINTED IN THE UNITED STATES OF AMERICA

10 9 8 7 6 5 4 3 2 1

For Marjorie Jean Miller,
Michael "Skook" Eckman,
William R. Daily,
Mary Elizabeth Williams,
and Jan Schmidt Marmor—
who brought laughter, storytelling,
and poetry to my world,
and who left it too soon.

ACKNOWLEDGMENTS

I HAVE EXERCISED ARTISTIC LICENSE IN MY DESCRIP-tion of people and establishments in and around Tucson, Douglas, Sonoyta, and Puerto Peñasco. Foothills Community College exists only in my imagination, as do La Roca, CZ-Storage, and Tía Miranda's Arte Folklorico. The Eclectic Cafe, the pistol range, the churches, and Sabino Canyon, on the other hand, are real. You will not find Spiny Hollow listed on any maps of the Santa Catalina Mountains, but if you follow the well-worn mountain trails you will find many spiny hollows, and just as many dry hiding places amid the rocks and cacti and packrat nests.

Unless otherwise noted, epigraphs are taken from Julia A. Jackson, editor, *Glossary of Geology,* fourth edition.

Although many people provided insight, answers, and expertise as this story unfolded, any errors are mine alone. I would like to thank, in particular, geologists and equestrians Eleanor and Frank Nelson; Wynne Brown, who demonstrated the care and gentle training of horses, shared a research trip to Douglas, introduced me to "Charley's ranch" in the Chiricahua Mountains, and listened patiently to my geologic monologues as we hiked in the Santa Catalina Mountains; Hedley Bond, a mad mountain trail runner, who ran from the top of the Catalinas and through Bear Canyon to the entrance of Sabino Canyon Park, just to see how long it took to cover those twenty-five miles; Robert Wm. Wagner, retired police lieutenant from Chicago, who taught me about guns and police procedure; the helpful staff of Desert Trails Gun Club and Training Facility, Tucson; Logan and Jordan Matti, who composed poetry with me from magnetic words on the refrigerator; Randal B. Arriola, Robert W. Brunken, and Sharon S. Bart, who shared details of their border-crossing experiences; Bear and Hollie Pitts, who introduced me to Native American healing cards; Dr. Stephen M. Richard, who helped me put metamorphic core complexes and detachment faults into layman's terms; Dr. Karl A. Taube, University of California, Riverside, who introduced me to the history, provenance, meaning, feel, and magic of Olmec blue jade; and Richard D. Mandell, who allowed me to examine blue-jade celts. Because many years have passed since I played college volleyball, I am grateful to University of Arizona volleyball coaches David Rubio, Charita Johnson, and A. J. Malis, and to the 2001 women's team, for discussing and demonstrating the finer points of today's game. My heartfelt thanks go to Wynne Brown, Lynda Gibson, Leesa Jacobson, Dr. Douglas M. Morton, Robert Powers, and Robert Wagner, who offered constructive comments on the text. And I deeply appreciate the generosity of Amanda and Mike Tevis, who awarded me a fellowship—"a gift of time"—to work on this manuscript at the Djerassi Foundation Resident Artists Program in Woodside, California, during April and May 2002.

A proverb says that wild ducks and deadlines come without calling. I wish also to thank Judith Keeling, at Texas Tech University Press, for her valuable critique of the text and for setting reasonable deadlines; and to Virginia Downs, also at TTUP, and John Mulvihill, copy editor, for their careful attention to detail.

Lastly, I'd like to thank the Athens jeweler who many years ago sold a young, ignorant American student a synthetic alexandrite ring. Though the ring itself had little value, it triggered this story. And for that I am grateful.

Detachment Fault (décollement): A shallow dipping to subhorizontal fault or shear zone. Typically, faults or folds in rocks above and below the décollement do not extend across it. Rocks above a décollement commonly are either shortened or extended whereas those below the décollement are not.

PART I

Saturday, October 11
Columbus Day weekend
Sonora, Mexico

Fishing: Attempting to recover, by use of specially pre-pared tools, a piece or pieces of equipment (such as sections of pipe, cables, or casing) that have become broken or been accidentally dropped into the hole.

CHAPTER 1

1:30 P.M.

WE WERE OFF CHOLLA BAY, SEVENTEEN MILES OUT in the Sea of Cortez, when our fishing lines became tangled with a rope-bound package. During the previous night someone else had gone fishing. He'd used Jorge as bait.

My younger brother Jamie, his girlfriend, Carla, and I shared the boat with a family of three from St. Paul. Our skipper, Chuy Desierto, a Seri Indian with leathery skin, mischievous black eyes, and compact body, had been guiding our family fishing trips since I was a child. He remembered me, he said, though I'd been away twelve years.

The sea was calm, the swells as gentle as an unbaffled waterbed. High-altitude haze created a halo around the sun. Throughout the morning there had been just enough breeze to keep us cool, not enough to make big waves. For five hours Chuy had led us from fishing spot to fishing spot, using small squid to coax triggerfish, rockfish, and flounder onto our hooks. Our final stop was his favorite, marked by an old buoy—and by Jorge.

Shock, dismay, and anger flashed across Chuy's face as

he looked from the water to me. "*Mi hermano* . . . Jorge," he said.

Oh God, I thought, his brother. I felt helpless—and nauseous. Innumerable biology labs hadn't prepared me for the remains of Chuy's brother. Right then, I longed for the clean objectivity of rocks and fossils.

I shouldn't have been able to identify the body. I'd seen Jorge only twice before, and there wasn't much left of the man: a portion of his bloodless torso and upper arms, partly covered by a tattered plaid shirt. But I remembered the shirt. And the rattlesnakes tattooed above his left elbow. Now, the distal humerus seemed an extension of the rattles.

The back of the head was covered in coarse black hair that drifted back and forth with the waves. The face was gone. Somehow, the heavy gold chain with its sunburst medallion still clung to his neck—a most effective lure. Small fish nibbled at what was left.

The St. Paul family promptly lost their lunch over the side of the flat-bottomed skiff. I chewed furiously on my cinnamon-flavored gum. Carla Zorya dropped her pole, moaned something unintelligible, and curled up in a prenatal ball in the bow of the boat. I covered her with my jacket.

Chuy cut the weighted line that held the body just under the surface. Then, with Jamie's help, he gingerly hauled what was left of Jorge aboard and wrapped it in a tarp at Chuy's feet. Jamie, who'd explored his share of cadavers in medical school, returned to his seat in silence, his windburned face a study in control.

Chuy opened the throttle with shaky fingers. The skiff had a big, fast motor, but it still took forty-five minutes to get back to Puerto Peñasco. When we reached the beach, a crowd gathered around the boat, sensing something amiss by the looks on our faces. Two boys ran off to get the police as Jamie lifted Carla out. We left our catch in the boat. So did the Minnesotans. None of us felt like eating seafood.

Back on solid ground now, Carla was coming around. But she still looked dazed.

"What do you think, Frankie—do we stay for the rest of the weekend, or do we head for the border?" asked Jamie.

"I want to go home," said Carla.

We were on the road in thirty minutes, some kind of record, even for MacFarlanes. We just wanted the comfortable cocoon of home. It never occurred to us that our departure might be interpreted as the flight of the guilty. That was our first mistake.

Jamie offered to drive my Jeep. Carla stared straight ahead, unmoving, unblinking. She seemed to be on some other planet. Jamie slipped in a CD to cover the silence. While I tried to adjust my six-foot frame to fit the short rear seat, Eric Clapton sang "Tears in Heaven."

It took us another seventy-five minutes, driving the speed limit, to reach the border at Sonoyta. Three lanes were open. The car in front of us was waved through. A border guard in khaki uniform, automatic rifle over his shoulder, tapped at Jamie's window. He rolled it down. The guard ordered us to pull off to the right and park. He looked all of seventeen. Two other guards closed in, one at Carla's window, one at the back. My stomach plummeted through the floorboards.

CHAPTER 2

"NOW, *POR FAVOR*, SEÑORITA MACFARLANE." *AGENTE de policía* Gallegos-Martínez stood by a scarred desk in the middle of the scantily furnished room. "Tell me what you saw last night, and today. *Todo*. Everything. From the beginning."

He pointed to a brown metal folding chair in the middle of the room. He seemed to be a secure man without nervous habits—no pacing, no chain-smoking, no jerky movements. Meekness wasn't normally a part of my repertoire, but I wasn't up to confronting anyone right then. So I sat and focused inward, clutching the edges of the chair seat, the metal biting into my fingers as I relived the grisly discovery and how we came to be there . . .

Jamie, Carla, and I had left Tucson for Puerto Peñasco, a small fishing village on the Sea of Cortez, at midmorning the previous day. I was a last-minute addition when another couple canceled. We arrived at Uncle Mitch's beach house around two, after a brief stop at a Corona outlet for a case of beer.

While Jamie and Carla went off to visit the tide pools, I strolled the beach. I'd planned to prepare the midterm exams for my geology students, but the textbooks stayed in the car. This was the first break I'd had in three years.

The sea had a shallow, sandy, ripple-marked substrate, the kind you scuff along in to alert the skates and rays to your presence. Crabs scuttled across the asymmetrical ripples. Minnows darted around my feet, feeding on the organic feast I kicked up. Tendrils of red, golden-brown, and green algae clung to the foam at the water's edge. I found a dead sand shark, wings spread, mouth displaying two small knobby plates perfect for crunching crustaceans. The sun was warm, winter still two months away.

"I am not interested in what the sea looked like, señorita," Gallegos-Martínez interrupted. I must have smiled, because he frowned. *"¿Qué?"*

"It was nothing, señor. I'm just hungry, and very, very tired."

"Continue, then. Tell me who you met, where you went, who you saw."

We ate dinner at La Roca, Carla's choice, a noisy, cheerful restaurant I remembered from childhood. The noise was provided by a mariachi band playing on a raised stage at one end of the largest room, and by two busloads of American tourists. The food was great, the beer was cold. On walls the color of oyster shells, the same dusty sombreros from twelve years ago hung beside woven rugs, sequined shawls, and velvet paintings of Elvis, Mother Teresa, and Spanish dancers. I spotted two new posters, of a bullfighter named El Tarrés and a guitarist called Alessandro, but the other decorations were older than I. Hand-painted garlands and trellises of roses and bougainvillea encircled arched doorways. The floor was inlaid with uneven Saltillo tiles that showed, here and there, the handprints of their makers or a dog's pawprint. Amber globes enclosed candles on every table, turning the room to gold.

The noise limited conversation, so Carla walked to the stage to make a request. The bandleader smiled, nodded, and leaned toward a guitarist sitting a little apart from the others, in a dim corner of the stage. He wore the standard uniform: white shirt, short black jacket, black pants and boots. Shoulder-length dark hair, a mustache, and a goatee obscured his face. When he turned his head to the conductor, I saw he was wearing dark glasses. I wondered if he were blind.

The rest of the band left him alone on stage, where he waited, motionless, for the crowd to quiet. His fingers delivered a haunting homage to Spain, from the hill country of the north to the riverbanks of the south. I recognized "Asturias," by Albéniz, and the adagio from Rodrigo's "Concierto de Aranjuez." The last note faded away into silence. He looked up at our table, breaking the spell. The audience began to clap and wouldn't stop. He nodded his head, raised one eyebrow, and seemed to beckon Carla. She shook her head. The owner brought a pair of thick-heeled shoes to our table. "All right, all right," she said, "but only if you dance with me."

Carla spoke English with a faint accent. She'd recently returned from living with her mother's people in Spain, she'd told me. Laughing, she slipped off her sandals and strapped on the dancing shoes. She stood, looking tiny and delicate next to the barrel-chested restaurateur in his plain black pants and loose white guayabera. She was wearing a soft black shawl over a sleeveless white blouse and simple, cotton skirt. Retying the shawl around her hips, she stepped lightly onto the stage. He followed. The crowd had swelled to standing room only, but they were silent now, waiting.

The guitarist returned to Albéniz. The amber light seemed to dissolve. I felt myself surrounded by the heat-drenched, red-tiled roofs of Andalucía, watching fla-menco dancers stamp out their furious rhythms in a smoky bar at midnight. The soulfulness of "Sevilla" slid imperceptibly into "Rumores de la Caleta." The slow, measured beats took on a life of their own, gathering the shadows, the passions, the cries of lovers and of hunted, wounded animals on moonlit nights. Heels tapped, hands clapped, fingers snapped. Carla's back arched over her partner's arm. Her red skirt swirled, dark hair flew, eyes sparkled like desert pavement after a storm. Every man in the room fell in love with her; I could see it in their eyes. But she didn't notice. She was lost in the dance, lost to us and to time and place.

When the dance was over, the owner passed the hat. Laughing, Carla added her tennis bracelet to the collection and gave it all to the guitarist. He accepted with a tiny smile, bowed, and left the stage.

Conversations resumed as she sat down. It wasn't possi-ble to ask about her training or if she'd danced here before. That could wait until later, when we were back in the quiet of the condo.

"And had she?" asked Gallegos-Martínez, startling me out of my reverie.

The drab, bare room felt cold and alien. I shivered. "Why don't you ask her?"

"I am asking you, Señorita MacFarlane."

"Then yes, she danced there before she went to Spain to continue her training, she said. But only once or twice since she returned."

Gallegos-Martínez jotted down a note. "What happened next?" he said.

"We ate," I said, mentally escaping from the cold inter-rogation room into the warmth of last night . . .

I was halfway through my burrito verde and my second

Corona *con limón,* when a Mexican—a local, I guessed—
entered. He was conspicuous in his loud yellow-and-
brown-plaid shirt, canary-colored polyester pants, and
gold, sunburst medallion. He wove his way between the tables to talk to a man sitting alone in the corner, a stocky
man with heavy features and a well-trimmed, graying mustache and beard. I recognized Canary-Pants as the vendor
who'd sold us trinkets on the beach earlier in the day. He
tugged at the sleeve of the mustached man, who brushed
him off and resumed his meal. Canary-Pants turned away
and looked around. He bypassed a table of Americans and
came toward us. He leaned over Carla, putting his hand on
her arm, revealing a tattoo of mating rattlesnakes above his
left elbow. I could smell his pungent body odor and tequila
breath from across the table, but the surrounding clatter
drowned out his words. Carla's delicate nose wrinkled; her
eyes were wary. He captured her hand in both of his. She
tugged her hand away, murmured something, and leaned
toward Jamie. A wavy curtain of hair obscured her oval
face. Jamie pushed back his chair and started to rise. In the
corner, the man with the mustache was watching us. He
turned back to his food when the manager hurried to our
table, apologized, and hustled sweating, protesting
Canary-Pants outside. That's when I heard the victim's
name: Jorge had been alive and kicking eighteen hours before we found his body.

"It was the same man? You are sure?" asked Gallegos-
Martínez.

"Yes," I said, and went on.

We stepped from the dim restaurant into a dirt parking
lot bathed in the blue light of a full moon that I hoped
boded well for fishing the next day. The cacophony was
muted here, and I asked Carla what Canary-Pants had
wanted.

"Money," said Carla. "I could not help him."

This morning we'd gone fishing at eight. "That's all," I said, looking up at Gallegos-Martínez.

He was staring out the narrow window. He couldn't see anything but his reflection; the sun had set while he interviewed Jamie. The single sixty-watt bulb in the ceiling emphasized the lines around his heavy-lidded eyes. The face was strong, intelligent. Grooves, like large parentheses, enclosed his nose and mouth. The thick brown-black hair curled tightly above a high forehead.

"What did you do last night, after dinner?" he asked, without turning around.

"We went back to the condo, played cards, went to bed."

"You did not go out again?"

I shook my head.

"What about your brother and Señorita Zorya?"

"I don't know."

"Perhaps they went for a walk on the beach later?"

"You'll have to ask them."

"How long have you known Carla Zorya?"

"I met her yesterday morning," I said.

"And Jesús García Desierto?"

"Who?"

"Your fishing guide."

"Oh, Chuy. About twenty years."

"Who arranged the fishing trip?"

"I did. Last evening, on the way to dinner."

"Did you know his brother, Jorge?"

"No. Chuy never spoke of his family. We didn't know him that well."

Gallegos-Martínez took photos from his left jacket pocket and handed one to me. It showed two men. The swarthy, powerfully built man, wearing sunglasses, a navy knit shirt, denim jeans, and deck shoes, looked vaguely familiar. His face was out of focus, as if he'd moved just as the camera clicked. Standing next to him on the dock was a

short, muscular, grinning man in wrinkled pants, an unbut-
toned Hawaiian shirt, and flip-flops. A gold medallion
made a circle of light against his chest. Hanging between
the men, suspended from a pulley, was a ten-foot hammerhead shark.

"Jorge," I said, pointing to the second man. "He was
still wearing the medallion when we found him this
morning."

"And the other?"

"Something about him, the way he holds his head, perhaps, or the shape of his beard, reminds me of a man who
was eating in the restaurant last night. Jorge spoke to him."

"*Gracias,*" he said, handing me the second photo. "And
this man?"

I studied the picture of a man, in profile, again slightly
out of focus. His hands gripped the steering wheel of a
boat; the open sea was in the background. He had a clean
line to his jaw, a straight nose in proportion to the rest of
his tanned face, nicely shaped ear, unsmiling lips. Sunglasses hid his eyes. His dark hair was pulled back into a
ponytail at the nape of his neck. Mid-thirties, I guessed—
the hairline seemed to be receding a bit.

I was hungry and exhausted. I wanted to end this little
guessing game. "Antonio Banderas?" I said.

Gallegos-Martínez was not amused. His shoulders stiffened. He waited, watching me from under those hooded
eyes. A junior officer tapped lightly on the door and handed
Gallegos-Martínez a manila folder. He took his time studying it, flipping through the pages. I saw a subtle change in
his stance, a sharpening of focus. He glanced up at me only
once, but it was enough to tell me that the file was mine.
He's misjudged me, I thought, as he put the file down at the
edge of the desk. He's going to apologize for the inconve-
nience and let us go . . . As usual when it came to interpret-
ing people's reactions, I was mistaken. I'm so much better
with rocks.

"Do you recognize the man?" he asked again.

"No, señor, I don't. And no, señor, I don't know if I've ever seen him. It's a blurry profile, for heaven's sake, and he's wearing sunglasses. I can't even tell what color his eyes are."

"It is important?" he asked softly.

I stared at the floor, thinking, sensing the answer was vital in some way I could not understand. I was out of my depth, and he knew it. "Some people never look at eyes," I said at last. "They can know you for years, but not know the color of your eyes. I always look at eyes first. They're more important than anything else."

"And why is that, do you think, Dr. MacFarlane?" His voice was softer than before.

I lifted my head. He was facing the window again, his right hand resting on the sill. "The title will only apply if you let me go home to submit my dissertation."

He didn't rise to the bait. He just waited, watching my reflection in the dirty glass.

"Because eyes tell me who I can trust . . . and who I can't."

He seemed to weigh my answer forever. "And what color are my eyes?"

The question changed the tone of the interrogation. It became almost intimate. And I became more wary. I knew he was testing me, and that my answer meant everything—possibly even my freedom.

"Your eyes are hazel, señor . . . honey gold, flecked with green and brown, with perhaps a hint of blue. They are wide spaced and quick. They miss little. You stand, while I sit, so you can look down at me, reading my eyes while screening your own with your lashes."

He smiled for the first time, a quick ironic lift of his lips, then turned and met my eyes squarely for the space of a dozen heartbeats. "I think, Señorita MacFarlane, that I would not like to be your enemy."

"I have no enemies," I countered in surprise.

He tapped the manila folder with his index finger. I felt the ground shift. *"Es verdad,"* he said, acknowledging the truth of my statement. "They are dead, are they not? All three."

His words hit me like body blows. I saw two corpses—one lying in the Nevada dust, one in a raging torrent . . . "There were two," I said, "just two."

"You forget about your Señor Travers."

"A suicide, they told me."

"Perhaps."

It wouldn't do any good to protest my innocence. I couldn't prove that I was working alone, finishing my dissertation fieldwork in Nevada when Geoff died last May. The time of death was approximate. His body hadn't been found for three months. By then, they'd used dental records to identify the remains . . .

"Geoff was not my enemy," I said at last. "A former lover, nothing more."

"Who died under . . . questionable circumstances."

"That's the first I've heard of it." I didn't beg him to believe me. He would or he wouldn't. It was out of my hands.

He studied me for a long moment. "That is all for the present. You may wait outside."

I stood on rubbery legs; one foot had fallen asleep. He accompanied me to the doorway.

"Some day," he said, in a voice so low that I could barely hear him, "when this is over, you and I will talk again . . . about your Señor Travers."

Over my dead body, I thought, but shrugged and said, "As you wish," making sure he could not see my eyes. But I wondered, all the same, what it was about Geoff's death that would interest a Mexican officer.

Gallegos-Martínez called Carla's name, then stepped aside to let me pass.

"Carla?" Jamie sounded as if he'd just awakened.

Forgetting to watch my size-eleven feet, I tripped over the metal threshold. Gallegos-Martínez leaped forward to catch me. He missed. When I looked up, Carla was gone.

CHAPTER 3

THERE HAD BEEN AN OFFICER WORKING ON A LAPTOP at the corner desk. He was missing, too.

"Where is Señorita Zorya?" Gallegos-Martínez asked Jamie.

"I don't know. I fell asleep," Jamie said, rubbing his eyes. He stood up, towering over our interrogator. "She probably went to the restroom."

"Stay here," said Gallegos-Martínez, and left us alone.

"You okay?" asked Jamie, hauling me to my feet.

I nodded. I hadn't enough air in my lungs for speech. A minute later, two guards arrived. They had side arms in holsters, rifles slung over their shoulders. Hands on hips, Jamie stared over the guards' heads, searching the hallway for inspiration.

"What happened?" I asked him.

"Last thing I remember," he said, sitting down beside me, "I was lying on the bench. The officer was typing up a report or something. Carla was beside me, next to the door."

I reached for the hand of my little brother, who was ten months younger and six inches taller. We'd shared troubles for twenty-eight years. In the last twelve years most of his troubles had been of the female variety. Jamie was an absolute moron when it came to relationships. He was a warm, outgoing, positive person, with an athlete's physique and a scientist's intellect; a fledgling pediatrician with a soft spot for big-eyed children and helpless women. The women tended to ignore the intellect.

But the problems in his relationships weren't one-sided. A few years back he had described his ideal mate: a woman who was intelligent, played at least one sport well, knew the rules of basketball, volleyball, football, and baseball, and could bait a hook and gut a fish. Not necessarily in that order. Unfortunately he kept getting sidetracked by fragile types in ruffles and lace, who didn't know a buttonhook from a lateral pass, or a perch from a brookie. I doubted that any of the women had had personal experiences with angleworms. So his female acquaintances had three strikes against them from the start.

Jamie's mind knew what he wanted. It just wasn't in sync with his body yet. He periodically swore off romantic entanglements. I think four weeks was his record dry spell. I had hoped, for his sake, that Carla was different.

We sat there, saying nothing, each trying to puzzle out what had happened to Carla. Belatedly, I realized this couldn't be the main border station, or even the local police station. It was more like borrowed accommodations. The one-story stucco building was divided by a hallway. The two rooms on our side were unfurnished except for dilapidated wooden benches lining one wall and the gunmetal-gray desk under the window. The place had all the atmosphere of an inner-city bus station. Gingerly I sat squarely in the middle of the bench and rubbed my bruised knees and scraped hands. No one offered to fetch me ice from the noisy cantina across the street.

Gallegos-Martínez returned, looking grim. Behind him was the young officer who'd been at the desk. He gave me one terrified look before fixing his eyes on the floor.

"Nothing?" Jamie asked. Gallegos-Martínez ignored him. "If your men have hurt her in any way—"

"My men have done nothing. Señorita Zorya left the building alone. We are searching."

"Have you called her family?" Jamie asked.

"A phone call is premature."

"I'd like to use the restroom." I stood up. "And get some food."

"The food will wait. But Leo will accompany you to the facilities. I do not want any more of you to disappear." We stepped forward together. "One by one, if you please."

I went first. The restroom at the end of the hall gave a whole new meaning to *pit stop*. The frosted window was cracked, rodent droppings littered the floor, and the place smelled as if it hadn't been cleaned in a year. Daddy long-legs gathered in the corners, and a twenty-five watt bulb seemed to absorb more light than it gave off. But the toilet flushed, and the sink had cold running water to bathe my wounds. On second thought, I decided against putting water on abraded flesh. All I needed now was a case of Montezuma's revenge.

"Take your rosary," I said to Jamie as he took his turn in the restroom. My stomach rumbled in the silence.

"We will eat after we find Señorita Zorya," Gallegos-Martínez said.

Jamie scowled and brushed something out of his hair when he came back. A cockroach scuttled off to a dark corner. Jamie walked into the inner office without being asked. I felt a sense of loss as the door closed behind them. The night yawned before me like an endless tunnel. I heard Gallegos-Martínez making phone calls—short phone calls. I dozed on the bench. An hour later, Carla still hadn't reappeared.

At ten o'clock the activity at the cantina heated up and spilled into the street. Over the din I thought I heard shouting. Moments later a man ran directly to the inner room. I couldn't follow the rapid Spanish. Gallegos-Martínez left, and the two remaining officers again blocked the door. Jamie sank down next to me and slumped against the wall, eyes closed.

"They found something," he said in a controlled monotone. "But not Carla." He ran his hands through his thick brown hair. He'd cut it short recently, and it now looked as if he'd had a close encounter with a Hoover upright. I reached for his hand.

Except for finding the body, nothing linked us to Jorge's murder. So why had Carla disappeared? Or had she been taken? What did we—even Jamie—know of her, after all? What did we know of Gallegos-Martínez? He wasn't border police or even local police like the men at the door. They wore khaki uniforms with insignias; he wore a charcoal suit.

Gallegos-Martínez returned thirty minutes later, empty-handed. He went into his office, reached for the phone, then went back and kicked the door shut. I didn't blame him. I wouldn't have liked to explain to my superiors that I'd lost a suspect—an American, at that.

Jamie and I waited in silence for the next event to unfold. A frowning Gallegos-Martínez opened the door ten minutes later. He stopped abruptly on the threshold; a look of surprise crossed his face. I followed his eyes to a point under the bench on which we sat. He strode over and picked up a Mexican hand-tooled leather purse with a long strap.

"This is yours?" he asked me.

"No, Carla's."

He handed the purse to me. "Open it," he said. "Tell me what is missing."

"I can't. I didn't know her that well." I seemed to be saying that a lot lately.

"*Por favor*. Try. That is all that I ask."

I carried the purse to the inner room and spread the contents on the scored surface of the desk. No drugs, thank God. No contraband. No fake lining. Just a handful of Mexican and American coins in a plastic film container, a brown leather wallet, a few business cards in a matching brown leather case, a key chain with seven keys, a plastic bag of hand-painted note cards she'd bought at the La Roca gift store the night before, her passport, a jar of Carmex, a red lipstick, a small comb, a container of birth control pills, a plastic container of Tampax, two condoms in foil wrappers, a packet of clean tissues, and a second plastic sandwich bag containing baubles. I felt ashamed of invading her privacy.

Gallegos-Martínez took the second bag from me, emptying it out a little away from the other things. The lot contained a cheap Aztec sun pendant carved in yellow onyx; three pesos; a bracelet woven from varicolored embroidery floss; a silver ring with inlaid mother-of-pearl; a sand dollar wrapped in a piece of tissue; two wave-smoothed basalt pebbles, one crudely carved into a head; and a few turban and olive shells. There were a couple of postcards, color photos glued onto heavy paper. One was of a stone mask, the other of a jade celt, a kind of ceremonial axe head worn and traded by the Olmec. Carla hadn't had time to write jaunty messages and send them off to her family or friends.

"You know where she got these things?" Gallegos-Martínez asked.

"At the beach yesterday," said Jamie. "A man was going from tourist to tourist, selling things from his satchel. She traded him for these."

"It was Jorge García Desierto?"

"Chuy's brother?" Jamie thought for a minute. "I suppose it could have been. I wasn't paying close attention."

"No? And what did she trade for these trinkets, Dr. MacFarlane?"

"A bracelet," said my brother. "It kept slipping off as we walked along the beach."

"Can you describe it?"

"Heavy silver, I think, with greenish blue stones. She told me she'd picked it up in Hawaii, and the stones were plastic."

"They looked like jadeite to me," I said. "Alternating square blocks and carved masks. Definitely not Hawaiian."

Gallegos-Martínez put the pile back in the plastic bag and handed me her wallet. It contained an American Express card, a Discover Platinum card, a Costco card, a AAA card, a couple of gasoline credit cards, and seventy-six dollars. Nothing incriminating. I thought he looked disappointed.

"I'd like to call her family now," said Jamie, as I stowed Carla's things back in her purse.

Gallegos-Martínez thought it over, then nodded. "As you wish," he said, and turned to me. We stared at each other. He was trying to decide what to do next—what to do with us. He motioned me to resume my seat in the metal folding chair. It seemed to be even less comfortable than before. This time, Leo joined us. He sat at the desk, opened his laptop computer, and waited.

"Describe for me what she was wearing when she disappeared, *por favor*."

This time it was a request. He let me search his eyes. He needed help. I rested my hands loosely in my lap and stared at the floor.

"An ankle-length red skirt and sleeveless white blouse—like a short Mayan *huipil,* decorated with machine-embroidered flowers around the neckline; simple brown leather sandals with cork soles . . . that's all I remember."

"Jewelry? Polish on her fingernails?"

I concentrated, pictured Carla riding in the Jeep, so quiet and distant, as if in a trance. "She wore clear nail polish, and a gold watch on her left wrist. On the right, a heavy gold-link bracelet with a pendant dangling near the clasp—a circular disc of jet or black serpentine, I think, about two centimeters across. It was carved with a bird-god motif. Quetzalcoatl, perhaps. The disk was encased in gold with latticework edges. A similar bird shape was cut like a stencil in the back . . . Around her neck was a fine box-link chain with a small pendant . . . a Mexican coin, I think, set in a gold frame."

"Earrings?"

"Pendants—coins—that matched the necklace . . . There were gold rings on her second toes, and an anklet on her . . . right ankle."

"Rings?" he said softly, as if afraid to disturb my train of thought.

"Just one. On the ring finger of her right hand . . . an alexandrite in an antique gold setting." I looked up at him then.

He raised a questioning eyebrow. "Alexandrite?"

"A rare gemstone, señor—much rarer than diamonds and rubies, emeralds and sapphires."

He examined me in silence, taking in the gold class ring on my right hand, the sturdy, inexpensive silver-and-gold-toned watch. My thick black hair was twisted up in back and secured by a plastic butterfly clip. There were simple pearl studs in my ears. I wore no makeup except a neutral lipgloss that I'd reapplied while they were searching for Carla. I had on a turquoise tank top under a pale aqua camp shirt, tucked into black jeans. I wore dark gray Teva sandals, but there were no rings on my toes or chains about my ankles. I would have looked overdressed and garish. I was as different from Carla, in every way, as night is from day. And he knew it. But all he said was, "You are certain of these things?"

"I'm a geologist," I said. "It's what I do. Observe, measure, take notes, make judgments, interpret what I see. My mind takes snapshots . . . It's cluttered with information, with photographs I can't erase, no matter how much I try." Like Jorge in the water this morning, I thought, but kept it to myself. I slumped in the chair. "Enough," I said, "I need food." I closed my eyes. I heard the chair behind the desk scrape back, the door open, orders given. I let my mind drift into safer channels.

A little while later, when Jamie carried in the food, I was alone.

"From the cantina across the street," my brother said, handing me a burrito wrapped in yellow waxed paper. He sat on the floor next to the chair. "How are you holding up?"

"Okay. He has what he needs." I talked with my mouth full, forgoing manners. "Did you get hold of Carla's family?"

"Tía Miranda, who's a bit wacky at the best of times, Carla says. Took her a while to understand, and then she lost it. But she said Carla's brother or father would call me back. That was nearly an hour ago. I'll try again after I eat."

Gallegos-Martínez came in, carrying Carla's passport. "What do you know of her family?" he asked us. I looked at Jamie. My mouth was full.

"Carla's father bought the property next to ours last summer," he said. "And by 'ours' I mean my parents' place. Frankie and I are house-sitting while they're on sabbatical in England. The Zoryas haven't been particularly sociable, but then I'm at work most of the time. Frankie and I met Carla's father when he asked if he could stable his horse at our place while they're renovating theirs, but I've only seen him from a distance since. And as I told you before, I met Carla two weeks ago. A friend introduced us after I saw her dance."

"When you are finished eating, you may go," Gallegos-Martínez said. "Someone will contact you if we need more." He looked down at the passport. "De la Frontera . . . *la gitana*," I thought I heard him say, as if, having dismissed us, we were already gone. I caught a note of condescension in his tone.

"You go ahead," Jamie said as I stood up and brushed

crumbs from my clothes. More food for the rodents and cockroaches. "I'm staying till they find her."

I looked at my watch. "They close the border soon."

"I can't leave her, Frankie. If you were in my shoes, you couldn't either. Don't worry about me. I'll take the bus home tomorrow. Monday at the latest."

"All right," I said, hugging him. I picked up my purse and looked at Gallegos-Martínez. I didn't say that it had been a pleasure; nor did he. "I wish you luck, señor."

"Uno momento," he said, as I reached the threshold.

I knew he'd let me go too easily. When I turned, he was looking down, fingering the edge of my manila folder. "Why did you drive to the border instead of staying in Puerto Peñasco?"

Why did we do something that would make us look guilty, he meant. I gave him the simple truth. "Carla was our guest. She wanted to go home . . . And I was afraid. Interrogations in Mexico, even of the innocent, can be very . . . unpleasant, and take a very long time."

"Gracias. Adiós, Señorita MacFarlane," he said. I sensed that it was more prayer than polite convention.

PART II

Wednesday, October 29
Tucson, Arizona

Twinning: the formation of twin crystals. "Twin crystals are those in which one or more parts regularly arranged are in reverse position with reference to the other part or parts. They often appear externally to consist of two or more crystals symmetrically united, and sometimes have the form of a cross or star. . . . Repeated twinning of the symmetrical type often serves to give the compound crystal an apparent symmetry of higher grade than that of the simple individual, and the result is often spoken of as a kind of pseudo-symmetry."

—EDWARD SALISBURY DANA
A TEXT-BOOK OF MINERALOGY, THIRD EDITION

CHAPTER 4

**Campus of Foothills Community College,
5:30 P.M.**

"FRANKIE MACFARLANE?" THE BRITISH ACCENT HAD
undertones of impatience. It obviously wasn't the first time
the music director had called my name.

I was sitting in the front row of the music hall, waiting
to audition for the newly formed college chorus. I stumbled to my feet, dropping the newspaper and stepping on
the article about a car bombing at the Tucson Convention
Center. The stairs up to the stage echoed, but not loudly
enough to cover the giggles and whispers of other audi-
tioners. My right Birkenstock tangled with a black cord
loosely taped to the floor. I arrived breathless at the piano
with the cord trapped between toes and sandal bed. Louder
giggles.

"Provided you can carry a tune, have you considered
musical comedy?" Gavin Plinkscale asked.

I'd introduced myself, one faculty member to another,
when I first arrived. So, though my dignity lay in shreds
on the stage, I fixed him with a withering stare. He ig-

nored it. "Do you need a moment to collect yourself?" he asked.

A moment? I'd need a decade. I took a deep breath and shook my head.

He gave the faintest twitch of a smile. "You sing alto?"

"Second soprano."

His left eyebrow arched high enough to touch the thatch of shaggy brown hair as he made a note on the yellow sign-in sheet. "Right."

I sang scales, following his lead on the keys. When I hit an A below high C, about the limit of my range, what I heard was a scream—a sharp high C. I stood there, mouth open, while Plinkscale, with a bemused expression, tried to match the peculiar pitch on the piano. Plink, plink. Maybe that's how his ancestors got their name. Maybe the piano was out of tune. I closed my mouth. The scream faded away into an awkward silence.

A short figure ran in through the open side door, babbling in high-pitched Spanish.

"A body," said one of the male students. "She found a girl's body. Come on." He punched the shoulder of the young man next to him, and they loped outside. Plinkscale and I weren't far behind.

Twilight cloaked the gravel path that connected the hall with a sandstone amphitheater built into the slope leading to Sabino Wash. The woman pointed to where the students waited solemnly beside a janitor's cart, a wheeled affair that held cleaning supplies and a trash can. It was parked on a little rise in the path. When I joined them I saw we had a clear view of the amphitheater floor.

The semicircle faced south. In the far distance, tinted rose by the setting sun, the Santa Rita Mountains marked one edge of the Tucson basin. The setting was serene, simple, intimate—a place for storytelling, stargazing, and Greek comedy. Not a place for murder.

I looked down at the woman sprawled dead center on

the circular floor. She wasn't moving. Glossy black hair, white blouse, red skirt . . . Carla?

On my left, Plinkscale looked from the janitor, to the body, and back to me. Definitely not the decisive type.

"Call 911, Gavin," I said, and went down to check for signs of life.

CHAPTER 5

I TOOK THE STEPS FOUR AT A TIME, PRAYING THIS was just another early Halloween prank like the horde of red-spotted toads I'd found in my desk drawer that morning.

She lay on her side. Blood oozed from a small wound at the base of her skull to pool on the stones. Gently, I lifted her hair away from her face and touched the side of her neck. No pulse.

The pale fingers were tipped with clear polish. She wore a ring with an antique gold setting on the fourth finger of her right hand. A row of tiny gemstone earrings ran down the outer edge of her ear. Dangling from the lobe was a silhouette of a black cat with arched back and rhinestone eyes . . . It wasn't Carla. It was Angelisa Corday, one of my students.

Plinkscale peered over my shoulder, his face matching the color of her hand. He gave a little moan. I led him to the lowest tier and pushed his head between his knees. The evening breeze flowed down Sabino Canyon, whispering among the mesquite and paloverde trees nearby. Something or someone crunched fallen pods underfoot . . . a javelina, rooting for dinner among the litter of the bosque? Or was it the murderer? Had he stayed to watch, taking pleasure in his handiwork?

Campus security arrived, followed closely by two sheriff's cars and a fire truck. Deputies ordered us out of the amphitheater and cordoned off the area. A crowd gathered, staring down.

"Dr. Plinkscale?" A bull-necked fiftyish officer in black slacks and a tan plaid blazer strode rapidly to where I sat, a little apart from the others, on a bench beside the path. I pointed to Gavin, who seemed to have recovered his composure. At least he was upright.

"Frankie?" said a woman's voice behind me, a smoky voice that tugged at my memory. I stood up and turned. She had large blue eyes behind rimless glasses, and thick tawny hair that hugged her head. Hers was a familiar face in unfamiliar clothes—navy pantsuit, pale blue blouse, sensible shoes. She wore a badge on her belt. And a gun.

"Toni? Toni Navarro?" I shouldn't have been surprised. Despite Tucson's large population, it's still a small town. Every day I encountered people from my past. Toni and I had attended the same schools, played on the same teams. I'd lost track of her after high school. She'd joined the Marines; I'd gone to college in California.

A hug would have been appropriate in other circumstances. Instead, I shook her hand. It had a scar running across the back of the right wrist, as if a bullet had furrowed the skin.

"You haven't changed," she said.

"Older and not so wiseass."

"That'll be the day. Mom said you were back in town. Sorry I haven't called."

The older detective joined us. Apparently Gavin hadn't had much to say.

"Frankie MacFarlane, this is my partner, Scott Munger," said Toni.

I shook his hand, too, which seemed surrealistically civilized. Below us, the forensic team took over. Portable lights turned night into day.

Toni jotted down my contact information in her notebook. "Isn't that your old address?" she asked. So I told her about house-sitting for my parents. "And what were you doing before you found the victim—"

"Angelisa," I interrupted. "Her name is Angelisa Corday. She was my student."

Toni and Munger exchanged looks. Munger went over to the janitor. "Let's go inside," said Toni. "It'll be quieter."

We sat in the red plush seats at the rear of the auditorium. It was comfortable, soothing, warm—so unlike the scene of my Mexican interrogation.

"Your student?" Toni asked. "What class?"

"Introduction to Geology. The Tuesday-Thursday section. Ten to eleven-thirty, with a Thursday afternoon lab."

"Do you know anything about Ms. Corday? Single? Married?"

"Single, I think. And she's—she was a freelance journalist. Mostly travel pieces and human-interest stories. I don't know which papers. She wanted to learn about earth science to add fresh imagery to her articles, she said . . . and to her poetry."

"Any idea why she was here tonight?"

"I know she sang. We talked about it a few weeks ago. Maybe she was going to audition."

"Okay. Let's go back. Tell me what you did before you found Ms. Corday."

I went over the afternoon's events. My geology lab ended at four. I'd locked up and headed over to the student union to meet Jamie for pizza. It was supposed to be his night off, our first chance to have dinner together since he'd returned from Mexico two weeks before. He'd been working constantly, trying to take his mind off of Carla. I got there about four-thirty. Jamie'd already ordered. About twenty minutes later, his pager went off and he left for the hospital. I finished dinner and walked over to the music center. I was early—the auditions didn't start until five-thirty.

"The hall was open?"

"Yes. I came in through the front. Gavin Plinkscale entered through a backstage door a few minutes later."

"You hadn't met him before tonight?"

"Hadn't even seen him."

"Did you notice anything unusual about his behavior—did he seem nervous? Rushed?"

"He seemed a bit distracted, but that may be normal for him. And speaking of distracted, I'm sorry we disturbed the crime scene."

"How, exactly?"

"I brushed back her hair and touched her neck, looking for a pulse . . . I thought she was someone else."

"Who?"

"Jamie's girlfriend, Carla Zorya. She disappeared in Mexico a couple of weeks ago. You probably read about it."

"Cézar Zorya's daughter?"

"Yes. From a distance, they're physically alike—small, slight build, dark haired . . . Carla was wearing a similar outfit when she went missing . . . and then there's the ring Angie's wearing. Carla had one like it."

"How like it?"

"The settings seemed identical. But there wasn't enough light this evening to tell if it was the same kind of stone in Angie's ring."

Toni gave me a sharp look. "Maybe you'd better tell me what happened in Mexico."

CHAPTER 6

I GAVE TONI THE SHORT VERSION, LEAVING OUT THE grim details.

"But Carla never turned up," Toni said, when I finished.

"No. Jamie stayed a couple of days and then came home . . . alone. He had to get back to the hospital. That was a little more than two weeks ago."

"Could they be related?"

"Carla and Angie? I don't know." I told her about the Zoryas buying the place next door. I wished now that I'd looked at the family pictures in Carla's wallet. "Jamie mentioned an aunt, Tía Miranda, and a brother, but not a sister or cousins. And I talked to Carla's father only once, when he arranged to stable his horse at our place."

"I'm going to have to talk to Jamie," Toni said.

Poor Jamie. Just what he needed. But I gave her his phone numbers. Munger walked up as we finished. The two of them moved back into the lobby, the doors swishing shut behind them. Silence settled like a voluminous old cape over the auditorium. I assumed I was alone until something moved backstage. Someone was watching me between the heavy black curtains. I felt it. The same person who was in the bosque?

I heard soft footsteps on the wooden floor followed by the metallic sound of a door bar being pushed. The curtains at stage left billowed out before the door closed with a thunk.

Toni was back to hear the tail end of the noise. "Who was that?"

"I have no idea. Someone was backstage. They just left."

Toni ran down the aisle, vaulted up on the stage, and went out through the same door.

"Missed him," she said when she came back a few minutes later. "Frankie, I need you to stick around until they bag her. Sorry," she said, looking at my face. "I forget sometimes. Anyway, I want you to look at that ring again."

"How long will it be?"

"Another hour, hour and a half. Maybe more."

I'd go crazy if I had to sit here for ninety minutes. "Would you consider a compromise?"

"What kind of compromise?"

"I want to go swimming."

"Here? On campus?"

"The gym's next door. I . . ." I struggled to find the right words. Finally shrugged. "It's what I'd planned to do after I auditioned." I didn't say I felt tainted, or that the events had resurrected memories I'd rather forget. I'm sure she read it on my face.

She was silent for a moment while she studied me. "One of the security officers will escort you over. I'll send someone to fetch you when we're ready."

"Thanks, Toni." I struggled to my feet, feeling old, though my twenty-ninth birthday was only a few days away. I picked up the field bag I use as a purse. It triggered a memory. "Did you find Angie's purse?"

"It wasn't with the body. What's it look like?"

"Big black leather affair. She could practically live out of it." I started up the aisle.

"Frankie?" she said as I reached the swinging door. I turned back to face her. "Don't talk about this to anyone."

"Talk about it? Toni, I just want to wash it away."

The campus security guard's name was Spock. He didn't have pointy ears, but was just as taciturn. So I looked around as he escorted me to the gym.

Since the late 1800s, the college site had been, in succession, a cattle ranch, a sanatorium for tuberculosis patients, a dude ranch, and a boarding school. An elderly real estate tycoon, a Scotsman who'd made gazillions in Arizona and California, had bequeathed the land to the county for a college campus. Like Andrew Carnegie, Simon Selkirk's passion had been education and lifelong learning. He'd had his favorite architect design the campus with an eye toward conserving the environment, even to the point of minimizing light pollution. With few exceptions, the outside lights went off at 10:30 P.M. The windows were treated to reduce glare, and all offices and classrooms were equipped with blinds. Only low-lying, dim-wattage groundlights lit paths after lights-out.

The campus had accumulated an eclectic assortment of architectural styles over the years. The original adobe dormitories had been converted to classrooms for fine arts, social sciences, and humanities. The territorial-style science building, remodeled for the math and computer sciences departments, contained a state-of-the-art computer lab. A gymnasium had been built on the east side of the complex, between the open-air Olympic-size swimming pool and the new music hall. Spock left me at the front door.

The gym smelled of new paint and waxed floors and chlorine. Ernie was on duty at the gym cage. He was in my geology class, MWF, 8–9 A.M., with a lab on Wednesday afternoons.

"Evening, Dr. MacFarlane. Gonna do laps?" Ernie held out a white towel large enough to dry my face.

"Uh-huh. Anyone else in the pool?"

"It's all yours. Water polo and diving teams finished a little while ago."

"Would you turn out all the lights except the one in the diving well? I don't want to bang my head, but I'd like to see the stars."

"Sure thing. Anybody complains, I can always turn them on again." Ernie flicked a couple of switches on the wall. "Just remember this at grading time."

The night air was dry as an ocotillo in June. It smelled of rosemary, as if someone had tramped through the newly planted beds that hugged the western wall. The temperature was still around seventy, but I knew that it would have dropped five degrees by the time I finished.

I swam in lane one, freestyle up the lane, backstroke return. Face down, face up, not fast, just steady. I swam for distance, turning my head every fourth stroke in the freestyle, inhaling, then exhaling slowly, evenly, watching the bubbles flow past my face. The water temperature was around eighty, cold enough to make the hair on my body stand up. The stars were clean and sharp in the black rectangle of sky. The groundlights gave off just enough light to see the black lines on the bottom, not enough to dim the starlight or the waxing sliver of moon. The quiet was broken only by my breathing and by my body cleaving the water. I let the rhythm carry me away, a form of self-hypnosis. Subconsciously, I measured the distance, knowing instinctively when to turn, but I didn't count the laps.

Other shadows joined me from time to time, swimming in lanes eight or six, never closer. One by one they came, some aggressively faster than I, some slower, some male, some female. The males displaced more water, sending swells crashing against my face. Eventually I was alone again. I kept swimming. A body can travel a long way fueled by adrenaline and pizza.

I tried to concentrate on the good things: being employed, finishing my dissertation, having the freedom to build a curriculum without interference, walking at dawn when the desert animals are active, the silky feeling of water against my skin . . . But Angie intruded, a woman who'd never feel again . . . The black lane line curved away like a snake into the depths. I reached the end, turned over on my back. The stars blurred; the moon had a halo . . .

Someone had joined me in the pool, swimming in lane two. I felt hemmed in by his bulk. He displaced a lot of water, half of it toward me. At the deep end, we flip-turned to a backstroke. I slowed to let him surge ahead. Instead, though he was longer than I by inches, he matched his strokes and speed to mine. I saw goggles on a long angular face above a serious swimmer's body. I focused on the North Star where it hung above the Santa Catalina Mountains, while I struggled to regain the rhythm and the quiet place I'd found before. I concentrated on my breathing, hearing it, feeling it flow in and out, and was there again. Or maybe we both were there, sharing the night and the water and the rhythm.

My toes cramped. I pumped my left foot and pushed on, but slower now, as if I were swimming in sand. The body in lane two eased back on the throttle, keeping pace. This time, when I touched the wall, I stopped. So did he—crouched, like me, to keep his shoulders under water. Pulling myself a few feet to the left, I collapsed on the lowest step and took off my goggles. I was light-headed, and my legs felt like lead. I watched him remove his goggles, but his face remained in shadow, his back to the lights in the diving well. He ducked under the lane line and stood, hands on hips, angled so that the light slid across his chest and fell on my face. The evening breeze was picking up; I felt my skin tighten and prickle with cold. He didn't seem affected by the temperature.

Ernie poked his head out the door. "Everything okay? We close at ten. Fifteen minutes."

If I'd been on the bottom of the pool since I last spoke to him, I'd be dead by now. "Just resting," I said.

"No problem," said the man.

I knew the voice, even after thirteen years. And I knew why I hadn't recognized him: a man's body changes a lot between twenty-two and thirty-five. He was carrying more muscle in the shoulders and chest and thighs; probably weighed about two hundred.

He slowly reached out his right hand and tugged the nylon cap from my hair. The sopping black strands felt cold on my shoulders. "Toni didn't tell me you'd cut your hair."

"I thought you were dead," I said.

CHAPTER 7

"**IT COULD HAVE GONE EITHER WAY,**" **SAID PHILO** Dain, shifting so I could see his face. "I got lucky." His smile hadn't changed. "I'm surprised Kit or your parents didn't mention it."

"I've been in California for twelve years . . . out of the loop." I rubbed my hands together, trying to warm them. "And I was so absorbed by my work that I just assumed . . . you know, the worst."

Philo climbed out and tossed me a towel. "Come on, Frankie. Toni asked me to walk you back."

In the dressing room, I quickly rinsed off the chlorine, patted myself dry, and dragged on my black silk camp shirt and stonewashed jeans. With my wet hair combed back into a ponytail, I looked like the tall, angular sixteen-year-old I'd been the last time I'd seen Philo. But the image in the mirror lied; inside, I felt old as a bristlecone pine.

At the cage, Philo was shooting the breeze with Ernie as if they were old friends. Maybe they were. Everyone, everything, seemed to be interconnected tonight, as if a time warp had opened. Philo and I exchanged looks, sizing up each other, noting the changes the years had wrought. His dark blonde hair was shot through with gold and gray. He'd been almost homely the last time I'd seen him, a nose like a hawk's beak dominating his face. Now there was a harmony about the features, a comfortable cragginess, from the fan of lines around sea-green eyes to the deep vertical clefts that scored each cheek.

Philo had been a schoolmate and close friend of my eldest brother, Kit. They'd both attended the U of A, Philo on an ROTC scholarship. He'd gone into the service the summer after he graduated. The last I'd heard, he'd been missing and presumed dead after a helicopter crash in a South American jungle. That was ten years ago.

Ernie was fidgeting. The clock showed 10:05. "I'll drop your lowest grade before I average the rest," I said. I didn't tell him I did that for all my students.

"I'll take it," he grinned, and locked the door behind us.

The night air chilled my wet head, the temperature dropping rapidly as the day's heat escaped into the dry atmosphere. I wished I hadn't left my jacket hanging over the back of a chair in my office. Without saying anything, Philo settled his sport coat around my shoulders. *"Por nada,"* he said when I thanked him.

His legs were about the same length as mine; the extra four inches in height was in his torso. But I noticed he had a slight limp.

"Did you pull a muscle?" I asked. "Or is that from the helicopter crash?"

"Neither," he said. His eyes were as shuttered as a house in a gale. He ran a hand down his right thigh, then paused for a moment, meeting my eyes. He'd always had a rare ability to focus his energy and attention into stillness. It was even more pronounced now. "Just an old injury. It acts up when a front moves through."

I looked up. Clouds were ambushing the night sky,

pushed by a southwest wind that tightened the skin of my face. "I usually have the same trouble with my left hip. But not tonight, for some reason." I started walking again. "Well, I'm glad you made it back in one piece. How do you happen to know Toni?"

"We met in the service. She was an MP. Escorted a friend back to the barracks one night. They got married a few months later."

"I didn't know she's married. We haven't had time to fill in the blanks."

"Past tense. She's been married a couple of times. We co-own a fixer-upper in the Sam Hughes neighborhood. I bunk in the main house, which is a shambles. She has the guest-house out back. It works. We don't step on each other's toes."

"So she just calls you anytime she needs a witness escort?"

He laughed. "Not exactly, though I occasionally work for the county when their investigators are overloaded. Toni's short-handed tonight. There's a double homicide over on Silverbell Road. She remembered I teach a course here on Wednesday evenings . . . and she thought it would be easier on you if I came."

I didn't have a chance to ask him what he taught because we'd reached the music hall. The crowd was gone. Now it was just a windswept crime scene.

"Frankie?" Toni's voice called me to the back of a coroner's van. She faced me across the body bag. It was halfway unzipped. Toni's flashlight picked out Angie's oval face, wide-set, closed eyes, the red highlights in her hair. I could see no traces of blood on her face, no signs of terror or surprise.

"She's our age, Toni. She hadn't even started living. It's just plain wrong," I said, as she handed me a pair of latex gloves. I put down my purse and tugged them on.

"It's always just plain wrong, Frankie—even when they're eighty-five."

"Well, this one's personal. And whether you like it or not, I'm going to help you find who did this. Call me an unpaid consultant, a volunteer, whatever."

"There'll be paperwork, a background check."

A background check would turn up the same things that were in the Gallegos-Martínez file, and Toni would learn more about me than I wanted her to know. "Fuck the paperwork. Do you have a match or a lighter?"

Looking guilty, as if one of the nuns at our high school had caught her smoking in the restroom, Toni pulled a Bic from her pocket. She didn't ask me what it was for as I flicked it on. I appreciated her trust. There was so little of it left in the world.

I lifted Angie's right hand, turning the ring so the stone caught the light from different angles. The flawless stone changed from emerald green to fiery red. "Guard this ring with your life," I said, handing back the lighter. "It's a genuine alexandrite. Only the second one I've ever seen."

"It's that rare?"

"It's that rare. I doubt I'll see another one in my lifetime—at least of this size and quality."

"And you still think it looks like Carla Zorya's?"

"A dead ringer," I said, and turned away as she zipped the bag.

CHAPTER 8

ALL BUT THE GROUNDLIGHTS WERE OFF AS PHILO and I walked to the north parking lot. The air was filled with the rustling of nocturnal animals. Coyotes called from nearby ridges, their barks and yelps echoing from the canyon walls. But we saw no one and nothing except a banded gecko clinging to a classroom window, silhouetted by the interior light, waiting for its dinner to land.

Philo shined a tiny flashlight beam into the back of the Jeep as I unlocked the door. No one lurked behind the seats. "You okay?" he asked.

The question was an echo of Jamie's that night in Mexico. "I'm fine," I lied. The adrenaline had worn off and my hands were trembling. I gripped the wheel so he wouldn't notice. "I'll see you around campus, then."

"Probably not. It was a short course. Tonight was the final exam."

"You never told me what you teach."

"A primer for private investigation. It's a good recruiting tool. I always find at least one person, usually a mother, who wants to work part-time. And women make the best operatives. People trust them." He closed my door. "You're sure you're fine?"

"Of course—"

"Because you forgot this back at the van." He handed my field bag through the window.

"Silly of me," I said.

"I'll follow you home."

"As long as you don't mind stopping at a store. I'm out of breakfast things."

"I don't mind," Philo said.

My parents owned a little more than ten acres, much of it untouched desert. The two-bedroom main house had an attached guesthouse. Nearby were three corrals, with stables; a spacious tack room; one large and one small ring for training horses; and a bunkhouse.

When I turned into the narrow graveled drive, the Jeep's headlights picked out the Halloween decorations I'd put up the previous night. Trick-or-treaters rarely ventured this far off the paved road, but it was the principle of the thing. Because my own decorations were in storage, along with my household things, I'd raided the box of odds and ends accumulated by my family over the years. Like Christmas ornaments, each had a history. The white crib sheet had become a ghost with felt-penned eyes after Jamie graduated to his own bed. I'd been almost three, but I remembered helping my mother outline and color in the eyes, faded now. Every year we'd made a ball of quilt batting and used a rubber band to hold the stuffing inside the sheet. It hung, suspended from a mesquite tree to the left of the front porch. Spider webs, festooned with plastic black widows, draped the porch. A twenty-year-old cardboard skeleton danced across the front door, one arm lifted in greeting. Plastic snakes coiled on the steps.

The motion lights came on as I climbed stiffly from the

Jeep. Jamie's MG was parked by the attached guesthouse. A bicycle wheel protruded from the narrow well of the backseat. In the shadows, something moved. Was it a trick of the light, or wind blowing the paloverde branches? Now that my hair was dry, the night air felt mild. It was still in the mid-sixties, Indian summer. A night to celebrate, not a night for death.

"Déjà vu," Philo said, stepping down from his truck. He followed me into the kitchen, carrying one of the bags of groceries.

"Coffee?" I asked.

"I can't stay," he said, setting the bag on the counter. On the kitchen stoop, he handed me his card, home phone scribbled on the back. "Call me if you need me."

There were sounds of a commotion in the backyard. Philo stepped in front of me. A crash. Loud voices. Swearing. The wind carried the fragments away. Philo held a gun in his left hand. Pulled from his boot? His fanny pack? He caught my look, but all he said, in a voice so low I barely heard it, was, "Expecting company?"

"Only Jamie. He lives in the guesthouse."

"Not the bunkhouse?"

"Teresa's staying there."

"Teresa?"

"Black. Charley and Rosa's daughter."

"The skinny, quiet kid who beat me at archery?"

"She's twenty-eight—same age as Jamie. She's caring for the twins' horses while they're in South America." My twin brothers, Matt and Luke, were wilderness guides and climbers.

"What are they doing this time? Guiding rich Americans up the Amazon?"

Apparently Philo had kept in touch with the rest of the family since he left the service. "Up Aconcagua, actually. Three stockbrokers. And then they're descending the Amazon."

He shook his head. "I'm in the wrong business."

We walked quietly through the passageway between the main house and the guesthouse, touching white-washed adobe walls still warm from the sun.

"Shit," said Jamie, as we emerged into the backyard. "Shit, shit, shit, shit, *shit*." He was sitting barefoot on the flagstone patio, rubbing his shin. There were tears on his cheeks. Teresa stood next to him, hands on hips. Lights on the encircling wall reflected off broken glass and an overturned wrought-iron table. Philo put away his gun.

"Hi, Frankie. Philo." Teresa didn't take her eyes off of Jamie. "Your brother's an idiot, Frankie."

This didn't strike me as something a therapist was supposed to say.

"He just keeps swearing," Teresa went on. "All he told me is that he got a phone call at work—something about Carla—and found a sub for his shift. He saw me in the parking lot, fixing a flat on my bike, so he offered me a ride. Soon as we got here, he grabbed a bottle of wine from the house and promptly tripped over the table." She shook her head and looked up at me. "I've never seen him like this. Do you know what's going on?"

"You tell her, Philo." I picked up a broom and dustpan from the corner of the patio.

Philo related a succinct version of the night's events. At least I think it was succinct—I was concentrating on finding all the tiny shards. This was barefoot country.

"You're sure it wasn't Carla?" Jamie asked me.

"Positive. It was one of my students."

"Who just happened to be wearing an identical ring," said Jamie.

"I could be wrong."

"Not about something like that," he said. A backhanded compliment at best. "It still doesn't solve the problem of where she is." I hadn't heard that note in his voice before. He was on the edge, looking into a deep, dark place.

"No," Philo said, "but at least you'll have more police resources looking into it."

"Go ahead and get some sleep, Frankie," Teresa said. "I'll keep Jamie company for a while . . . Oh, by the way, Dad's here."

"In Tucson?"

"In the bunkhouse. Mom's staying at Abuelita's for el Día de los Muertos. But it was so noisy at the tamale-making that Dad ducked out."

Charley and Rosa Black were my godparents. Charley wasn't Catholic, so a proxy had stood in for him at the baptism, but we all considered that a technicality. Charley was Apache. He and Rosa lived on a small ranch in the Chiricahua Mountains, the ancestral homeland of Charley's people. Rosa's parents had emigrated from Mexico just before World War II. The Day of the Dead celebration on November 2 was a time of reunion for them. But Charley wasn't comfortable picnicking on family gravesites, so he usually escaped to the relative peace of my parents' home.

"Tell him he's welcome, of course, and I'll see him tomorrow?" I said.

"Will do."

Philo and I cut through the house to the front door. Stepping out, his head brushed the fake spider webs hanging above the porch. He paused at the edge of the gravel drive, stared up at the ghost dangling from a branch of the mesquite tree. "You can't go back, you know, Frankie. None of us can."

Philo, I thought, saw too damned much. I heard the kitchen door open. Teresa rounded the corner and jogged off toward the bunkhouse. Jamie must have sent her packing.

"*Hasta luego,*" Philo said.

"Good night, Philo." I watched the truck taillights grow smaller until the black night swallowed them altogether.

In the kitchen, a subdued Jamie was putting dishes in the dishwasher. "You weren't surprised to see Philo," I said.

Jamie's hands stilled, and he turned to look at me. "I take it you were?"

"I thought he died ten years ago."

"Well, you haven't been home much. I guess we took it for granted you got the news. He and Kit are still tight, and Philo sometimes house-sits for Mom and Dad when the twins are gone." He gave me a sheepish smile. "I've been so busy at the hospital that I forget to pay the bills," he said.

Jamie was a resident in pediatrics at UA hospital. It's all he ever wanted to do . . . except for when he was four and wanted to be a garbage collector.

We lapsed into a comfortable silence as we put away the groceries. At the bottom of the last bag was a white prescription sack from the pharmacy in the store. He handed it to me.

"It's not mine," I said, taking out an amber plastic bottle. "The bagger at the store must have put it in with my things."

"Digitalis," Jamie said, reading over my shoulder. "It's Cézar Zorya's."

"That's for a heart condition, isn't it? He might need it tonight." I dialed the phone number on the label, the number of the man whose daughter was missing . . . and perhaps as dead as Angelisa Corday. Cézar answered, speaking formally and with a faint accent.

"I hate to call so late," I began, then explained about the mix-up at the store.

Cézar reassured me he'd be okay tonight. He'd get the pills when he exercised his horse in the morning.

"Okay?" asked Jamie. I nodded, and put down the phone. "Sorry about earlier," he said. "Don't know what got into me."

I ruffled his hair. "Don't worry about it. You've been on an emotional seesaw since Carla disappeared."

The kitchen door opened and Charley came in, a book in one hand and a cup of tea in the other. He handed me the tea. It was strong and sweet, with some aftertaste I couldn't identify. I grimaced. "Just drink it," he said in his soft, slow drawl. "And you," he said to Jamie, "get some sleep."

Jamie smiled. "Teresa talks too much," he said. But he went.

Charley settled into my father's favorite chair and opened a book of Simon Ortiz's short stories. Light from the reading lamp shone on his thick straight blunt-cut hair, the color of perlite. I couldn't tell what he was thinking as he looked at me over the top of his bifocals.

"You'll live," he said. He was never much on pampering.

Sometime in the early morning hours I started to dream in Technicolor. I was swimming in warm seawater. My even breathing through the scuba gear sent intermittent ribbons of bubbles floating toward the surface thirty feet above. Schools of fish approached as single units and then parted, like liquid curtains of color, to flow around me: teal, indigo, crimson, and silver flashed in the muted light. I swam through curtain after curtain until they vanished, suddenly, as if responding to a secret signal.

I glanced up. The sunlit surface was a golden oval framed by my mask. In the center was a rectangular shadow, too small to be the boat. Curious, I swam slowly toward the light, stopping when I saw long, streamlined, anvil-headed forms approaching the shadow from either side. Hammerheads. Their broad mouths opened and grabbed, ripped and tore at the shadow. Pieces of pale brown and ivory and pink drifted down like snow.

I had nowhere to go. I was alone in the pale green water—except for sharks that were twice my length. There were three of them now. I tried to look inconspicuous, knowing that my heartbeat was sending seismic waves through the water. I reminded myself to breathe. Another shark brushed by me, heading for the feast. The tooth-hard cones embedded in its skin scraped my bare hand as it passed.

I looked around, but saw no more sharks. So I eased gently, carefully, away from the site. Another, larger shadow joined the first one. The boat. I'd almost reached it when my eye caught a flash of gold in the water. Not fish, this time. A black cat's paw, ignoring the sharks, dipped into the water and toyed with a medallion, a stylized Aztec sun. I tried to yell, to make the cat stop, but the seawater absorbed all sound. The gold chain broke, and the medallion drifted past me, spinning and flashing, the Sun God smiling, down into the darkness.

I didn't sense the shark approach from behind. Through the wet suit, I felt the strong, muscular mouth clamp down on my shoulder. The great head moved violently in short, sharp jerks, and I flapped in the water like Raggedy Ann. I screamed, but the sound came out as a whimper, muffled by the mouthpiece of my scuba tank . . .

"Wake up, child—it's a dream." Charley let go of my shoulder. His black eyes were solemn as he sat down beside me on the couch where I'd fallen asleep.

I squinted in the sudden light. A bright handmade quilt was twisted around my body.

"It was so real, Charley. Jorge, the sharks, the cat . . . What bizarre Apache herbs did you put in that tea?"

"Just something my mother used," Charley said.

"Well, if it was meant to be soothing, it missed the mark by a mile."

"Maybe. But night is a good time to talk." He gently tweaked the ponytail draped across my shoulder, an old, familiar gesture. "And ours is long overdue."

And so I told him everything—about what had happened in Nevada last summer, about Geoff, about Carla and Jorge and Mexico, and about last night. It took a long time. But then Charley's a very patient man.

When I finished, the sky was still black. Through the picture window, I watched dry lightning lance the peaks of the Catalinas. It would be dawn in a couple of hours.

"You'll sleep better, now," said Charley.

Right. I felt like Pandora after she'd lifted the lid on the golden box. I wondered if she'd ever slept peacefully again after that willful act . . . And I wondered what the cat in the boat was trying to tell me.

PART III

Thursday, October 30

Bomb: volcanic bombs—balls of lava which took shape while whirling in the air, and solidified before falling to the ground.

—WILLIAM HARMON NORTON
THE ELEMENTS OF GEOLOGY

CHAPTER 9

I AWOKE WITH A STIFF NECK WHEN THE FIRST, FAINT light tinted the sky. I took my coffee to the front patio where I stood for a moment, testing the air. Quail coveys scavenged between the prickly pear and cholla. Gila woodpeckers called raucously from the chimney top. A phainopepla chirruped softly over a breakfast of mistletoe berries, while a cardinal snagged fruit from the fan palm. Above me, a flock of mourning doves flew low and straight toward the eastern sky, wings whistling. That way lay the spring-fed pools of Agua Caliente Park.

Smells, I read somewhere, trigger memories more easily and far longer than the other senses. That was true this morning. Mixed in with the pungent scents of verbena and lantana, I recognized the sweetness of crushed mesquite beans, the muskiness of late-blooming desert willow, and stable smells—dust and manure and hay. Some things that ground us don't change in twelve years. I bent to smell a rose, then walked toward the dust cloud in the arena, where a man was free-longeing a horse.

Cézar Zorya was a small man, lightly built as a jockey. He looked tiny next to the mare. The dapple gray was nearly seventeen hands high, with powerful chest and leg muscles. She was in a playful mood, shaking or dropping her head, sidestepping, bumping a barrel with her shoulder, kicking up her heels. Cézar waited patiently for her to settle down.

I'd met him the morning after I'd returned home in August. He was renovating the old Baker place next door, he said, and could he use one of our empty corrals until the new stable was built? I said yes, of course. Since then, there'd been only a nod and wave if he was about when I went to work. He walked the path between our properties and rode his dapple gray along the wash behind the house. He was a quiet man, so I refrained from interrupting his solitude. But this morning he was expecting me.

I saw his hand move. The mare stopped, still as a standing stone, at the edge of the arena. I heard a whistle like a curve-billed thrasher, and she trotted around the ring. Cézar's body, the hub of the wheel, turned slowly so that he always faced her. Another whistle, musical as a canyon wren, and she broke into a canter, her lines clean and crisp as the morning air. The training whip in his right hand never moved. I could sense her eagerness for the next step in the drill, but I missed the silent signal. She suddenly galloped past me—two, three, four times around the ring, stopping so abruptly her front hooves pawed the air and dust rose in a plume. To the clicking call of a cactus wren, she dropped her forelegs, arched her neck, and sidestepped first left, then right, angled left, right, her steps precise and perfectly timed. She tossed her head and charged him. I held my breath as thirteen hundred pounds of horseflesh bore down on a man who weighed no more than one-thirty. He didn't flinch. When the dust settled, they were standing nose to nose. She bowed. Releasing her with a word, he kissed her forehead, caressed her neck, ran a hand down her nose, combed her forelock with his fingers, whispered in her ear. She nudged his pocket until he fed her the apple she knew was there.

I must have moved, for he saw me then, standing next to the gate. His eyes changed color as the morning brightened, like tiger's-eye quartz with its shifting golden band—arresting eyes, which held mine. He walked to the iron-barred gate, the horse trailing after.

"*Buenas días,* Ms. MacFarlane." His hands were golden brown, long fingered, and fine boned. He rubbed them on his pants and shook my hand. His palms were calloused. He might be rich, but he hadn't stopped working. "Meet Alba," he said. She poked her nose over his right shoulder.

"Dawn," I said, running a hand down her nose. She backed away.

"The time of heartbreak."

As if on cue, the sun's rays, lovely enough to break anyone's heart, poured through Redington Pass. The shadows seemed to draw back. Pale citrine light made Alba's coat glow.

"So it is," I said, and thought I understood. "She's beautiful."

"An unusual breed," he said. "Friesian/Andalusian. She is not registered, of course. Friesians are always black, and their owners wish to keep the line pure. But I wanted a dapple gray, a horse that would sooner die than give up . . . Unfortunately, her dappling will fade. In time, she'll be more white than gray."

"How old is she?" I asked.

"Only seven. But the spots have already begun to disappear."

"A pity," I said, setting down my mug on the fence post.

"One of the prices we pay for living long enough to grow old." He looked at his hands for a moment. "I have something to ask you." When he raised his eyes, I saw pain there. "About my daughter."

"I wish I could help you, but I only met her that weekend," I said. "She danced for us the first night."

"A talent that came from her mother, who was just as lovely . . . They say in the old country that a beautiful wife and a white horse bring much grief to a man." He paused. "I like to think that Carla received her mother's looks but her father's temperament."

I looked at his small frame, golden brown eyes, beaked nose, close-cropped silver curls. Except for the fine bone structure, he and Carla couldn't have been more different. "I hope to get to know her better when she returns," I said. "Have you heard anything?"

"No, although I pursue it daily. They claim to know nothing, say she vanished like a dust devil." His right hand circled like a twister ascending to the clouds. "But you were there. Would you be kind to an ailing man and tell me what you saw that night? I have spoken to your brother, but he says he was asleep when Carla left."

"I can't help you, Mr. Zorya. I was being interrogated in the next room. I'm sorry."

He was leaning against Alba, his arms wrapped around her neck. "There is no need to apologize." He dropped his arms and faced me. "I have learned what occurred earlier in the day . . . but can you tell me how she behaved?"

I didn't want to go there again. Now he could see the pain. "Please, I am not what you would call a good man. I have made much money, many enemies, and few friends. Perhaps, if I had spent more time with my family . . ." He gave a little shrug. "Please," he said again. "I lost my wife. I cannot bear to lose my daughter also."

It was a standoff, my pain against his. I leaned my forehead on the rough weathered wood of the fence and focused on Carla. "She was fishing from the bow. It was her line that snagged on . . . Jorge. She dropped her pole—"

"I know that part. It is in the police report," Cézar rescued me. "But what did she do next?"

"Nothing. She collapsed on a pile of rope and seemed to withdraw. Her body was there, but she didn't speak or move . . . I thought she was in shock. I checked her pulse, but it was very slow and steady, as if she were in a trance. Her eyes were open and her skin tone was normal, so I just covered her up and helped the Minnesota couple. When we reached shore, she seemed to come out of it. She said she wanted to go home."

"And so you and your brother drove to the border and encountered more trouble than you could have imagined."

"I'd prefer not to repeat the experience."

He laughed, the action transforming his face. "I think you are a very strong young woman, Ms. MacFarlane. Very different from my Carla."

You have no idea, I thought. But something in his eyes said he understood. I wondered what his own story was.

"You have told me what I needed to know. I thank you for that." He settled a red felt saddle on the mare's back, stepped up on the cottonwood stump by the fence, grabbed a handful of mane, and vaulted like a young man aboard the mare. "I am lunching out on Saturday. Would you care to join me?"

From the corner of my eye I caught movement at the edge of the stable. A woman, a stranger in a long black dress and brightly colored Guatemalan vest, stood in the shadow of the stable's far side. She drew back as I watched. I wondered who she was and how long she'd been there. Ten yards behind her, blending into the darkness of a mesquite trunk, was Teresa. She gave the slightest shake of her head. I gave no sign I'd seen them.

"I'd like that," I said. We settled on the Eclectic Cafe at one o'clock.

The woman in black was gone when I closed the gate after Cézar. He rode down the dirt drive between the stables, heading toward Soldier Wash. As he passed the corrals holding the twins' horses, the mare sidled toward the geldings.

"The slut of the stable," Teresa said from just behind my right shoulder. I hadn't heard her approach. But then, she was her father's daughter, taking after the Apache side of the family more than the Mexican. She'd been the main reason that Charley and Rosa's children always won when we played cowboys and Indians—a game they initiated, though they were outnumbered five to three. Technically, it could have been called Indians and Indians, since my brothers and I were one-sixteenth Lipan Apache. But our Lipan great-grandmother had been raised by the white MacFarlane family, so we were relegated to cowboys or cavalry.

"He rides like an Indian," she said.

I watched the retreating figure turn right at the wash and cut through the mesquite trees toward his domain. There, hammers, saws, and cement trucks had begun the day's work. "Who was the woman by the stable?"

"Someone from next door. A relative of Zorya's, I think," Teresa said.

Carla's aunt, Tía Miranda? I wondered, as Charley pulled up in an electric-blue three-quarter-ton GMC pickup with a cab-over camper.

"A business expense," he said, not in the least apologetically. "I'm probably the only doctor you know who still makes house calls." He was both a traditional healer and a licensed counselor. "You slept?"

"Enough."

Charley looked at Teresa. "I'm going your way."

"I shouldn't. The race is less than a month away . . . El Tour de Tucson," she said, when I looked puzzled. "My first time doing the full circuit."

El Tour de Tucson bicycle race takes place each fall. The full circuit is 108 miles, though racers can compete at shorter intervals. I took in her olive-print camp shirt and khaki skirt—not your basic cycling gear.

"Oh, what the hell," she said, putting her bike in the camper.

The yard seemed very quiet after they left. It was only seven, but warming quickly. When I slipped off my fleece vest, I felt something in the pocket. "Shit," I said, pulling out the small white bag. I'd forgotten to give Cézar his prescription.

CHAPTER 10

THE ORIGINAL RANCH HOUSE NEXT DOOR HAD BEEN
built when Apaches still raided for cattle and horses in the
late nineteenth century. In those days, the homestead was
eight miles east of Camp Lowell, fifteen miles east of
Tucson. Water came from wells, though the quarter section included the confluence of two intermittent
streams . . . intermittent being the operative word. Flowing water was a seasonal thing. Spreader dams had redi-
rected flow to a kitchen garden and fields of corn, squash,
and beans.

During the Apache Wars, family after family had been
wiped out, their stock taken. Until the tenacious Bakers arrived. Lucinda Baker, their last descendant, was still in the
house when I was a child. But she'd whittled away at the
property over the years, selling off ten-acre parcels whenever she needed money. When Old Lady Baker had died
last year, her holdings had been reduced to twenty acres,
with ranch house, corrals, and outbuildings that were in

complete disrepair. But in the present real estate boom, the land alone was worth millions. The neighborhood gave a collective sigh of relief when Cézar Zorya bought the place for his private use. It could have been rezoned for another condominium complex.

There had never been a fence or wall between the two properties; there had been no need. One was being built now, I saw, as I drove the short distance between our driveway and Cézar's—an eight-foot-high straw-bale wall that would be aesthetically pleasing when it was plastered and painted, but now looked like the end of haying season before the bales were stashed in the barn. The wall had been completed on the street side, along with a straw-bale guardhouse attached to the left-hand interior side of the entrance gate. The gate was a double wrought-iron affair that would be impregnable once the wall was finished.

A guard, built like a silo, stopped me at the gate. When I tried to hand over the prescription, the guard shook his head and phoned the house. A second guard, small and spry as Jackie Chan, hopped in a golf cart and escorted me up the gravel drive and into a beehive of activity. Two long wings had been added to the ranch house, forming an inverted U. In the center was a blue-tiled fountain. An iron-studded double door, massive enough to accommodate an eighteen-wheeler, connected the two wings and enclosed the courtyard. The doors stood open now, as workmen came and went with flagstone, tile, lumber, adobe bricks, and pipes.

Only a man who owned a construction company could get so much work done so quickly. Behind and off to the side of the house, workers were finishing a new barn with a corrugated iron roof. The old barn was being converted into a garage with at least ten bays, two large enough to accommodate RVs or buses. A greenhouse adjoined the

southeast corner of the house. Workers were installing so-
lar panels on all the roofs. And there were three parallel
seventy-by-fifteen concrete strips with adjacent hookups
for water, sewer, and electricity. Pads, I surmised, for mobile homes. The place could accommodate an army. I wondered if the guards would hand out candy to any
trick-or-treaters brave enough to venture near tomorrow
night, or shoot them on sight.

I got out and followed the guard around to a small patio
on the north side of the house. Beds of herbs, vegetables,
and flowers flanked the floor of sandstone slabs. The guard
pointed to a glass-topped table where someone had been
having coffee and reading the paper. It was open to an article on Angie Corday. "Mr. Zorya will be out in a moment,"
said the guard before he trotted off.

I set Cézar's medicine on the table and wandered
through the herb garden—rosemary, thyme, oregano,
sage, dill, cilantro, chives, five species of basil, seven different chilies. A glazed statue of Saint Teresa of Avila nestled among the rocks. A separate garden contained
Saint-John's-wort, with its red-spotted white flowers,
members of the mint family, and other plants I couldn't
identify. Saint Francis of Assisi guarded the plot. Un-
painted terra-cotta birds, rabbits, lizards, and snakes sat at
his plaster feet.

"My sister-in-law takes great pride in her gardens," said
Cézar behind me. "In the greenhouse she grows vegetables
and flowers all year."

"It's very peaceful," I said. A rock-bordered path led to
a grotto of angular basalt. Light flickered inside. "May I?"

"Of course," he said. "I will just go and put my medicine away. Take your time."

The shrine, roughly ten feet in diameter, was shaped
like a traditional Pueblo oven. *Ristras* of red chilies,
shaped like crosses, hung on either side of the oval door-

way, while bunches of drying plants hung from hooks set into the domed ceiling. On the simple main altar, candles of all shapes and sizes surrounded statues of Our Lady of Guadalupe, Our Lady of Fátima, and the Infant of Prague. Rosaries of crystal and carved beads drooped from the rough wall behind it.

A smaller altar on the right blazed with as many candles as the main altar. It was dedicated to Saint Anthony, patron saint of lost objects . . . or people. A mirror-framed photo of Carla stood beside the statue. I smelled no incense, but the shrine was redolent of beeswax, flowers, and herbs. A vase of white roses sat on the main altar; another, with gold chrysanthemums, on Anthony's. To the left stood a marble-topped table with fresh candles and a Day of the Dead display. The small skeletal figures went about their daily tasks in a village built from scraps of wood and miniature clay bricks. Tables held tiny blue-glass bottles, wine glasses, and hand-painted vessels with offerings of glazed fruit, bread, and paper flowers. A skeleton sitting in an open grave seemed to have my face and hair. I chalked it up to my imagination until I noticed that the gravestone marker had my initials . . . I shivered. A draft of air made the candles flicker.

Taking a used fireplace match from a metal bucket of sand, I lit three candles, placing one on each altar. The light from the entrance was eclipsed. I saw Miranda's reflection in Carla's mirrored frame, but she did not speak. After observing me for a moment, she glided silently away.

I turned to the entrance, where niches contained two additional statues, one on either side of the door, each with a tiny votive candle. The candles had given out. I lit two homemade ones that smelled of cinnamon. I didn't recognize the saint on the right, and couldn't read the inscription in the plaster base. On the wall beside her hung a framed copy, in Spanish, of "The Martyrdom of Saint Eulalie," from Federico García Lorca's *The Gypsy Ballads*. The statue on the left was the Archangel Gabriel, wings unfurled as if he were appearing to Mary. I could use a revelation or two, I told him as I replaced his candle with a fresh one.

Miranda had not gone far. She was hovering over a flower bed, dropping plucked dead blossoms into a blue plastic bucket. Her pale green eyes were puffy. I supposed she was missing Carla.

"Good morning. I'm your neighbor, Frankie MacFarlane," I said, as if I hadn't seen her earlier. I held out my hand. After wiping her hand on her apron, she touched mine. Her skin was cold as a pool in winter. I wanted to snatch my hand back, but it was as if she were imprinting my palm on hers. Definitely not the person I'd choose to raise my children.

"Señorita MacFarlane." Her voice had an odd, sibilant quality that reminded me of Gollum and his Precious. "I am Miranda Xeres de la Frontera."

"You have a lovely garden. There are a few plants I don't recognize. This one, for instance." I bent to touch the purple blossoms.

"It is pennyroyal, from the mint family—well past its normal blooming time," she said proudly as she led me to the table. Cézar was there, reading the paper. Miranda had already poured me a cup of coffee that steamed gently in the golden air. "Cream?" she asked.

I sat down and took the cream, but declined the sugar. A fly buzzed the surface for a moment before landing. I picked up the cup to brush him away, but saw he was already dead, floating on the margin.

"Something wrong, my dear?" asked Cézar.

"A fly in my coffee."

He looked sharply at Miranda, who looked away. He

took the cup from me and tossed the contents in the closest rock garden, splashing the plaster robe of my patron saint. I wondered how many innocent bugs would die at his feet in the next moment or two.

"Miranda will get you a fresh cup," he said.

I stood up. "I can't stay. But thank you for the hospitality, Mr. Zorya."

He didn't ask me to call him by his given name. "Thank you for bringing my medicine. I shall see you for lunch on Saturday?"

"The Eclectic Cafe," I said, shaking his hand. "One o'clock."

Out of the lion's den, I thought, sighing with relief when I reached the street. There's a fine line between a folk healer and a *bruja*, a witch. That wasn't something healing she'd put in my coffee.

There was no direct route from my parents' suburban ranch in the northeastern corner of the Tucson basin due west across the foothills of the Santa Catalina Mountains. Few bridges cross the arroyos that carry surface runoff from the mountains. Though dry, sandy channels most of the year, they can course with roiling muddy water from the male thunderstorms that mark the summer monsoon season or the steady, female rains of fall and winter. These washes curve and coalesce, joining forces to carry floodwater north to the Gila and Salt River system. Every year, people underestimate the flash flood's power. They dare to cross inundated washes and intersections. The lucky ones lose only their cars.

In order to reach the campus, I headed south on Old Soldier Trail toward Tanque Verde Road. Before me, the shadows drew back from the valley as Tucson stretched and awoke. In twelve years the Old Pueblo had spread like a flood basalt over the landscape, erasing geomorphic features and the raw desert that I loved. Ridges of Tertiary sedimentary rock had been planed flat for developments. Condominiums, apartments, and houses sprouted like pampas grass. Thank heavens for road cuts that exposed the geology, I thought, until I remembered that many road cuts had been covered by fake rocks designed to stabilize slopes and beautify the roadbeds. I'd been home less than three months and had yet to adapt to the changes, the ceaseless construction that overlay the former slow pace of life in my hometown.

Most of us hardly notice change when it happens around us and to us. We adapt, move on, or die. But I felt a sense of dislocation and detachment coming back to a place that had destroyed many of the landmarks of my childhood. I'd changed, too. And the new me couldn't slip back into the carapace I'd sloughed off twelve years ago . . .

A man in a white Miata, phone glued to his left ear, pulled off the dirt strip beside the road and cut in front of me. I slammed on the brakes. The man never even looked. He drove slowly and erratically, forcing oncoming traffic on the two-lane road to swing wide into the dirt. When his right hand lifted the blue baseball cap on his dark hair and resettled it, I wondered who, or what, was holding the wheel. I braced for the worst. He pulled off the road again to finish his conversation, and I started to breathe. Glancing in the rearview mirror, I saw sunglasses, tanned skin, clenched jaw, white knuckles. Then he threw the phone onto the passenger seat and ripped back onto the road. He passed me in a no-passing zone, just as a yellow school bus came over a small rise. I laid on the horn, yanked the wheel, and slammed on the brakes. The Jeep stopped in a cloud of dust and pebbles. The man in the sports car ignored me, accelerated, and disappeared into the distance.

I wrote down the license number—just in case we met again—then massaged the indentation on my palms from where I'd clutched the wheel. Definitely not the old Tucson I knew and loved. Only time would tell whether it would be a temporary haven or the place where I sank my taproot.

CHAPTER 11

CONVERSATION AROUND THE COFFEE URN STOPPED abruptly when I stepped into the science office at Foothills Community College. I surmised they'd been discussing Angie Corday. I said hello, collected my mail, and left them to their gossip.

The new physical and life science buildings had ten-to-fifteen-foot-high ceilings and small patios outside each office. Mine had an unobstructed view of the mountains and enough floor space to accommodate a cot, now stowed in a locker. I sometimes spent the night when I worked into the wee hours, which I'd done frequently of late as I finished writing and drafting my dissertation. It was all over but the shouting. I'd sent the three-hundred-page tome off to my advisors yesterday. My dissertation defense was scheduled for early December, which left me five weeks to prepare the presentation. Plenty of time, I'd thought, until now.

I'd just finished brewing coffee in my office when Hector Ortiz, a chemistry teacher, stopped by. He had mail and a newspaper tucked under his arm, a coffee mug shaped like a skull in his hand. "Do you have a minute, Frankie?"

"Can it wait? I'm getting ready for a field trip this afternoon."

"I guess . . . okay . . . Could I bum some coffee?" I nodded and began collecting compasses and topographic maps for the students. I heard him fill the mug, stir in sugar, then clear his throat. I looked around. "How about an early lunch after your first class?"

I couldn't avoid my colleagues forever. "Meet you here," I agreed, reluctantly.

I'd lied to Hector. I didn't need time to prepare for the field trip; I needed solitude. The events of the last sixteen hours, including my run-in with Miranda, unsettled me. I took my mug of coffee and a beaker of water out to the patio, watered the potted *Echeveria* and geranium in the corner, and plopped in one of the white plastic chairs.

A cactus wren poked among the detritus of the mesquite and cactus garden a few feet away. An Anna's hummingbird sipped from salvia blossoms; a cardinal gathered seeds from dying lantana. Mourning doves splashed in a puddle formed by a broken dripline. Such beauty . . . it pissed me off that Angie Corday would never see it again.

"Life's a bitch," I'd said to her when she missed one question on the last quiz.

"And then you die," she'd replied with a smile. She'd meant it ironically.

The south flank of the Santa Catalina Mountains rose like a wall in front of me, so close I could follow Sabino Creek north into the yawning canyon; so close I couldn't see the more than one hundred square miles of blackened forest burned last summer by the Aspen fire, or the scars of the rockslides that had closed Sabino Canyon during the monsoon rains of August. The forest would take a long time to heal. I was glad the scars were hidden from me.

These mountains, and the three other ranges that ringed Tucson, were my classroom. They held all the geology lessons I could teach beginning students: the rock cycle, the major rock types, folding and faulting, fossils. Weathering and erosion had carved deep canyons into the Catalinas, exposing the belly of the range. At its core was a granite heart, cut by crystalline dikes and sills, surrounded by a broken carapace of stretched and thinned and deformed rock.

As a child, I didn't know that the mountains had a history spanning two billion years, that an ancient sea once covered the place where I stood and left its fossils in the limestone rocks of these mountains. I didn't know that dinosaurs later walked riverbanks and lakeshores, while, nearby, volcanoes spewed ejecta into the sky and lava flowed like viscous syrup, cooling so quickly in some places that rocks were filled with glass shards. I wasn't alive for the last great quake of 1887 that tumbled boulders and split the desert surface. Had I seen an aerial photograph of the fault-scarred hills, I wouldn't have been able to identify the alluvial fans of eroded debris spilling from canyon mouths, or the striped minarets of foliated gneiss. I didn't know the secrets the rocks could tell me. I only knew that the mountains were a place to escape the heat, to gather firewood, to hike, to swim and picnic, to scale granite cliffs while attached to a rope held by my parents or brothers. I knew that, in the streambeds, garnets collected in the lee of gneiss boulders. We called them sand rubies.

From my patio chair, I couldn't see the granite heart of the range. I could only see the metamorphosed forerange that had been arched into an anticline, broken and bounded by faults. Running along the foot of these mountains, less than a mile from where I sat, was the trace of a low-angle fault plane. The thin, rocky skin of the mountains had wrinkled and cracked and separated from the core along a zone of dislocation, a detachment fault . . .

I flashed on Carla, sitting in the front seat of the Jeep,

detached, staring into the shimmering Sonoran Desert . . . Where *was* she?

My ten o'clock was Angie's class. The students, ranging in age from eighteen to seventy, were trying to make sense of the news. They pelted me with questions to which I had no answers. I didn't know if it was safe to walk the campus, but I suggested they use the buddy system for a few days. I didn't know if the killing was random or whether someone had had a grudge against Angie. I didn't know if this was the beginning of a murder spree or was an isolated incident.

Ginger, a young redhead straight out of high school, handed me a withdrawal slip. "I'm sorry. My parents are scared . . . I still live at home," she added, as if it explained everything. "I'll re-enroll next semester."

Cathie, a mother returning to school now that her children were out of the nest, had brought a bouquet of flowers. "Would it be okay," she asked, "if we put the flowers where Angie died? It might make the younger students feel better. I know it'll help me."

We talked quietly as we walked under soft blue skies. The floor of the amphitheater had become an impromptu memorial site littered with candles and flowers, the wordless, universal language of mourning. Students were sitting or lying on the sandstone tiers—not studying, as they would have been on a normal day, but staring forlornly toward the valley or down at the stage. Some were crying. Gavin Plinkscale was sitting by himself on the top tier, eating a doughnut. And a camera crew was recording the scene for the noon news.

We were halfway back to the classroom when the buildings shook. Not an earthquake. It sounded like a bomb.

•

CHAPTER 12

SMOKE FILLED THE COURTYARD. FIRE AND CAR ALARMS blared. The students fled to the safety of the parking lot. Fire trucks and ambulances were already there. Most of the windows on that side of the building had blown out or cracked. I could see the gaping hole where Hector's office used to be. Smoke and flames billowed through the opening. No one could have survived that blast. I prayed Hector had been somewhere else.

I looked at my watch. I knew Hector's schedule. He didn't have a ten o'clock class. He might have been in his office. Sitting under a desert willow at the edge of the parking lot, I waited for news.

It came thirty minutes later, after the flames were out, after fifteen injured bystanders had been carted away in ambulances: A man had been sitting, alone, at the desk in Hector's office. There wasn't enough left of him to put a name to, not yet. But I knew it was Hector.

The news spread like a soft murmur through the milling crowd. Near me, a reporter broadcast live to a local news station. I stared at the mountains, wondering what to do. I felt I had to act, to do *something* for my friend and fellow instructor, but my legs refused to move. Shock does that to me. So I took deep, reassuring breaths, while my mind sorted through the options.

Hector had no family, as far as I knew. I'd have to find out. In the meantime, I could focus on Angie, pull her file, see if I could find a thread that might lead somewhere. I couldn't accept that she was just a random victim. I pictured her the last time I'd seen her alive: perhaps five feet tall, in Levis, a long-sleeved purple top, and denim vest, carrying her overloaded purse. She'd always worn pants to school . . . But last night she'd been wearing a skirt. Had she been meeting someone special? And where was the purse? It hadn't been with the body. Had it been stolen by the murderer?

Some of my students were Hector's as well. I offered comfort and a shoulder to cry on where I could, but they'd had enough for one day. I canceled the afternoon field trip and sent them home. It would be hours, I was told, before I could go back into my room. Maybe not till tomorrow. The fire marshal had to check the building; insurance adjusters had to assess the damage; structural engineers had to do a safety check . . .

To hell with that. I circled around until I reached my patio door. No one stopped me. My key was in the lock and I had the door closed in a twinkling.

The place was a disaster. The sprinklers were off, but there were puddles of water everywhere. Broken glass from beakers and graduated cylinders littered the floor. No electricity. My desktop computer . . . I'd have to dry it out and see if it still worked . . . Most of my dissertation work was at home, thank heavens—maps, cross sections, columnar sections, and backup copies of the text. But my slides and digital photos were here.

I looked at the file cabinet with my class notes. Most of

the materials inside were dry. Hector's newspaper, soggy now, lay on top . . . He must have forgotten it when he got his coffee. When I picked it up to toss it into the recycling bin, a diskette and a set of keys fell to the floor. Three keys. They weren't mine.

Behind me, the door handle turned. I heard the *snick* of the lock unlatching. I was trapped with no place to run, except through the open connecting door into the lab/classroom . . .

"Thought I'd find you here," said Philo.

"Holy shit, you scared me," I said, putting my rock hammer back in the desk drawer. "How did you get in?"

"Picked the lock." He slipped a tool into a small leather case and pressed the Velcro patches together.

"I thought that was illegal."

"No more than what you're doing. Does Toni know?"

"Haven't seen her. But I'll apologize when she calls me on the carpet." In the parking lot outside, a car backfired. I ducked.

"Pathetic." Philo looked at me as I brushed off my denim skirt. "This has got to stop."

"I'm open to suggestions," I said. He didn't offer any. "What brings you to campus?"

"Had to turn in my final grades. I heard the commotion—just thought I'd see if you were okay."

"I'm okay." I picked up the last bunch of books from the shelves and set them out to dry on the patio.

"You knew him?"

"Hector? Not well, but better than I knew the other faculty. We teach—taught—together."

"Are you going to leave or stay?"

"I'm going to clean up. I want to keep busy."

He looked around at the mess. "Do you need a hand?"

"How are you with a mop and broom?"

"I've mastered the fine points."

We scrounged cleaning supplies from the janitor's

closet. "And where are you going?" he asked, as I grabbed the disk, my class and research files, and headed to the door.

"I'll let you know when I get back."

"Sometime today, I trust?"

"Give me twenty minutes."

"I'll set my watch," he said, picking up the broom and dustpan.

The smell of smoke was still strong in the air as I put the files in the Jeep and walked across the courtyard to the department office. I was determined to copy Hector's personnel file, if I could get by Smaug. Smaug was my nickname for the dean's assistant, who, like Tolkien's dragon, guarded the files as if they were treasure. Security officers blocked the office entrance, but they were there to keep out the media. Inside, an army of janitors swept up glass from the shattered windows. Smaug was at her desk, fiercely fielding phone calls. Perfect.

I casually checked my mailbox and Hector's, then found and copied Hector's file in the back room. I wished I could have copied Gavin Plinkscale's, as well. Something about him bothered me . . . I slipped out again, moving on to the Admin building. Because Angie was in my class, I could legitimately ask for her file. Unfortunately, someone had beaten me to it. I hoped it was Toni.

The computer center, though unaffected by the blast, was almost deserted. The unmarked disk I'd found in my office had one file, created by Hector Ortiz that morning. It was an architectural plan of a building, or rather a complex of buildings, all connected. But he hadn't included an address, or city. I printed two copies.

Philo had done an amazing amount in a short time. The glass was off the floors and counters, the window cracks were taped, and he was busy with the mop. "You're hired," I said.

"I work for food," he said.

"Dinner?"

"You're on. So what did you find, Sherlock?"

"Hector's file." I showed him the photocopy. "Degree in chemistry, with honors, from Stony Brook. Ph.D. from Columbia. Dissertation on synthesizing organic compounds. He worked for Averry Pharmaceutical until December 2001. There's a handwritten note in the margin that says he left his native New York City and moved west after losing his wife in the World Trade Center attack . . . But I didn't find a letter of recommendation from Averry."

"I have a friend who did some work for that firm," Philo said.

"Small world."

"Becoming smaller all the time, thanks to the Internet. Want me to pick her brains?"

"Your friend's? Absolutely." I looked out the window. "They're towing away Hector's Lexus."

"It had already been stripped," he said. I raised an eyebrow. "What? I just happened to overhear a conversation between a couple of deputies. The deed was done while everyone else was focused on Hector's office."

"If someone wanted to kill Hector, why use a bomb? And why in such a public place?"

"Because they wanted to destroy whatever was in Hector's office at the same time. Evidence, presumably."

I looked back at Hector's application. "There's a one-year gap between when he left his pharmaceutical job and accepted this one. He was living in Las Vegas when he applied."

"Can you think of anything that would trigger this—a motive?"

"As I said, I didn't know him that well. We taught a class together . . . and we went out once. He took me to one of the casinos." I wrinkled my nose. "Not my thing. The odds are in their favor, and it's too noisy to think or talk."

"I suspect that's the idea. If you're thinking or talking, you won't bet as much. Did you win anything?"

"Two hundred dollars. Hector lost a bundle. The more he drank, the more he bet. I quit early and took a cab home."

"Did anybody in the department dislike Hector?"

"I don't think so. Hector was what he appeared to be— a quiet nerd who took his classes seriously and occasionally drank too much. I knew he was widowed. I thought he was still in mourning for his wife."

"No one is ever what he appears to be," said Toni from the doorway. "Take Philo, for example."

"I rather like my Mr. Fix-it persona. It comes in handy with desk clerks and administrators."

"I don't want to know," she said, and turned to me. "I don't remember clearing you to be here."

"I'm sorry. I didn't think this was part of the crime scene. I needed to restore order. It bore fruit, though." I handed her the disk and a copy of the printout, explaining where I'd found them. "By the way, did you ever find Angie's purse?"

"It wasn't at the scene. And it wasn't in her car or at her apartment, either."

"That's not all that's missing. Admin couldn't find her file."

"I know. I tried to get it this morning. Someone removed it before she was killed," Toni said.

For the next thirty minutes she questioned me about Hector's private life, teaching load, whether I could recall any unusual activities, how he looked, whether I'd noticed any strangers in the building lately. What time had he dropped by this morning? Did I know his friends? Did he fit in? Were there any disgruntled present or former students?

"He was sweet, Toni. And a good teacher. The students liked him. I liked him."

"Sounds like an epitaph," she said.

CHAPTER 13

JAMIE WAS ON THE DOORSTEP READY TO HAND OUT
candy to ghosts and goblins when Philo and I got home.
"Halloween's not till tomorrow night," I said, taking the
bowl of candy from him and setting it on top of the refrigerator. "Or was that supposed to be dinner?"

"Sorry. The days seem to be running together. Hi,
Philo."

"Hungry?" I asked.

"After all that candy?"

I opened the huge old refrigerator, looking for inspiration. Eggs, bacon, jack cheese, blue-corn tortillas . . .
"Huevos rancheros okay?" I asked Philo. It was a rhetori-
cal question. "How do you want your eggs?"

"Over hard."

"I wish my cholesterol level would let me indulge like
this every day," Philo said minutes later as he spooned guacamole and salsa onto the eggs and bacon.

"Where's mine?" asked Jamie.

I cracked two eggs into the pan and handed him the

spatula. "Do you know what I missed most when I was in the field last summer?" I asked Philo, as I took a seat at the old oak table.

Philo stopped chewing and just looked at me; his eyes crinkled at the corners.

"No, not that. Spices. Mexican, Szechwan, Thai—anything but the bland fried food they served at the local cafés. My deprived palate went dormant."

"Beats C rations."

"By a hair. Do you still play baseball?" I asked him.

"City league baseball, some slow-pitch softball. How about you?"

"Before I went back for my doctorate, I played slow-pitch. My mitt's in one of the boxes I have in storage." I focused on my food for a minute, savoring the tang of homemade salsa. "But volleyball's still my first love."

"Toni and I play sand court. Let me know if you want to join the roster."

"I'm rusty."

He gave the lopsided grin I remembered. "I'll bring the oil can."

It was there, between us, on the scarred table—the emotion resurrected in the pool last night. Now he'd thrown down the gauntlet. But I didn't have to pick it up. "We'll see," I said at last, and searched for a safer topic. Jamie joined us as I related my morning visit to the Zorya compound.

"What do you know about the family?" Philo asked Jamie.

"The Zoryas? Not much. Carla and her brother Michael are close. Their mother died just after Carla was born, and they were raised more by the aunt than by Cézar. As a father, he was . . . distant. Michael manages the store—it's really two stores. Tía Miranda runs one featuring folk arts and crafts. Michael handles the other. It sells rare coins, stamps, estate jewelry, small objets d'art. He travels a lot, bringing in stuff from all over the world. Carla works in both."

"But Cézar actually owns it all," said Philo. I heard something in his voice, a note of irony perhaps.

"I've heard the rumors," Jamie said. "He's never been indicted."

"Might you be a little prejudiced where Carla's concerned?" Philo asked.

"I keep an open mind." Jamie heaved himself to his feet, leaving his dinner half-eaten. "I'm going to bed." The kitchen door slammed behind him. It was only six-thirty.

"What were you trying to say, Philo?"

"I saw a file on Zorya this thick." He held his hand five inches above his plate. "His investments are recession-proof."

"Good business practices?"

"More like a ready influx of cash whenever he needs it. He always has investors. But some of them are dummy companies set up by foreigners."

"He launders money."

"Not that they've been able to prove."

The phone rang. It was Toni. She wanted to speak to Philo.

"I have to go," Philo said when he hung up.

"Philo," I said, walking out to the truck with him, "if you wanted to find a building and you only had a floor plan, where would you start?"

"You're talking about Hector's file."

I nodded. "The school's closed tomorrow. They've got an environmental cleanup crew coming in. I want to find Hector's killer. I thought I'd start with that."

"Leave it to Toni."

"I want to help, that's all. I won't get in her way."

"Famous last words," he said, and sighed. "Do you have an extra copy?"

"I didn't mean . . . It's not your war, Philo."

"Call it a favor."

I thought about it. "No," I said. "A contract." I went back into the kitchen for paper and pen. Two minutes later he produced a handwritten statement that said that in exchange for home-cooked meals, including beverages and gratuities, he'd undertake a confidential investigation.

"Gratuities? Restaurants *receive* gratuities; they don't pay them."

"Can't blame me for trying." He watched me cross out "and gratuities" before signing the quasilegal document. "Chicken," he said softly, as he tucked the contract in his breast pocket with one hand and scooped up a handful of Halloween candy with the other. "Dessert," he said.

I took the printout from my Jeep and handed it to him. "It might have nothing to do with this morning."

He brushed a mesquite leaf from my hair with a touch so soft I barely felt it. "Don't get your hopes up, Frankie. The building could be anywhere. I'll know more when I see you at dinner tomorrow."

I felt restless when he'd gone, so after I finished the dishes, I headed down to the bunkhouse to visit Charley. The evening breeze tumbled down Soldier Canyon and rustled the paloverde pods. I said hello to Alba as I strolled by her corral. The light was on in the next stable down where Teresa was mucking out the stalls. I stopped to rub the noses of the twins' horses, half-Arabian geldings that nuzzled my shoulder, asking for treats I'd forgotten to bring. They smelled of dust and sweat, alfalfa and mesquite beans, the reassuring basics of life.

"Looking for Dad?" Teresa asked, leaning on her shovel.

"If he's not busy."

"He was on the phone when I left. Should be finished soon."

"I'll wait on the porch then."

"I repaired the hammock last week. There's a quilt on

the chair just inside the door." The dirt track continued past the tack room, an empty stable and corral, and the large show ring, before crossing Soldier Wash. The floods of 1993 had eroded the banks so quickly that my parents had had to pave this stretch of road the following spring. I'd contributed a Jeepload of riprap for the border and helped cement the rocks in place.

I hadn't brought my flashlight, but a sliver of moon lit my way, reflecting eerily from the feldspar eyes of augen gneiss in the border wall. I felt as if they watched me as I dipped down into the cooler air of the wash. On the Zorya property, a man and a woman argued, the sounds, but not the words, carrying easily on the night air. A door slammed. A garage door grumbled. A powerful engine roared toward their entrance gate, slowed for a moment, then tore away down Old Soldier Trail. I thought I heard a woman crying.

The porch light was off at the bunkhouse, but lamps shone behind the curtains of both bedrooms. I announced myself, grabbed the quilt and a cushion for a pillow, and settled into the hammock. It was like being rocked in a large cradle, comforting and familiar. City lights shone to the south and west, dimming the southern sky. But here the stars burned cold and bright. Scorpio's tail curled up, as if about to strike.

Teresa came, sharing the companionable silence until Charley sat down beside her on the front steps.

"Was it better today?" he asked.

So he hadn't heard of Hector's death. "No," I said, and related the day's events. "I'd like to stay here tonight. Outside. Do you mind?" They both just looked at me. "Okay, stupid question."

Taking a flute from his vest pocket, Charley played a melody that seemed to merge with the whisper of the wind in the paloverdes. Teresa picked up the threads and wove them into a night chant, her voice soft and rhythmic as water lapping the shore of a White Mountains lake:

The raven spreads his wings
His feathers are the night sky
Flowering clouds bloom coral-red
The mountainsides turn indigo
The mountaintops hold alpenglow
And now above us darkness
Folds raven wings around the beautiful mountains.
And now above us darkness
Enfolds the beautiful mountains.

A peaceful wind combs through my hair
And sets my hammock rocking
Tranquility before me
Tranquility behind me
Tranquility beneath me
Tranquility above me
Tranquility surrounds me . . .

PART IV

Friday, October 31
Halloween

Multiple working hypotheses: There are two fundamental modes of study. The one is an attempt to follow by close imitation the processes of previous thinkers and to acquire the results of their investigations by memorizing. It is study of a merely secondary, imitative, or acquisitive nature. In the other mode the effort is to think independently, or at least individually. It is primary or creative study. The endeavor is to discover new truth or to make a new combination of truth or at least to develop by one's own effort an individualized assemblage of truth. The endeavor is to think for one's self, whether the thinking lies wholly in the fields of previous thought or not. It is not necessary to this mode of study that the subject-matter should be new. Old material may be reworked. But it is essential that the process of thought and its results be individual and independent, not the mere following of previous lines of thought ending in predetermined results.

—THOMAS C. CHAMBERLIN
"THE METHOD OF MULTIPLE WORKING HYPOTHESES," 1897

CHAPTER 14

I AWOKE AT FIRST LIGHT, HAVING SLEPT MORE soundly than I had in months, perhaps more soundly than I should have. Tracks showed in the dust beside the front porch—human footprints made by short, wide feet that toed in. They didn't belong to Charley, Teresa, or me.

I backtracked them to Agua Caliente Wash, losing them in the heavy sand of the streambed. I wasn't fearful. It was probably a Mexican national, a border crosser, moving silently north in search of a job. If he'd wanted to harm me, he'd had plenty of opportunity.

I climbed up the bank to the house, sat on a bench among mesquite beans and prickly pear, staples of Hohokam and Tohono O'odham, Pima and Apache life. The original owners had framed the kitchen door with a footwide recessed mosaic of potsherds—Mogollon brownware, plain Hohokam redware and red-on-buff geometric, Mimbres black-on-white, Salado polychrome, and Sinagua incised—angular fragments of unknown provenance, a hodgepodge of different cultures, different ages. Most sherds, no doubt, had been collected on this spot during construction of the house.

How quickly civilizations rise and fall in one geographic area, leaving only fragments of their lives behind, clues to what they once thought and felt. Somewhere along the line, I'd stopped seeing the art, stopped wondering about the ancient artisans. But I'd always thought of it as a portal: No matter what happened in the world outside, behind this door lay safety and harmony.

I ran my fingers over a triangular sherd with a red zigzag pattern on buff background. A thousand years old, or older, its colors were still vibrant. I'd always thought of it as my touchstone, formed of earth and fire and imagination. As I touched it, I wondered if 9/11 and the violence I'd experienced of late represented the beginning of the end of our civilization. What clues to our lives and hopes and dreams would future civilizations find here in the Southwest? Echoing human-carved caverns and pits where we extracted ore, empty Titan missile silos, and perhaps the remnants of a highway system crumbled and half-buried by the desert sands. For by then, the iron would have oxidized to rust, concrete would have been reduced to sand and gravel, adobe would have returned to dust. Only rocks, and the spaces above and within them, would remain. Perhaps that's how it should be.

I touched the potsherds one last time, shook off the morbid thoughts, and went in to make breakfast.

Jamie was gone. He'd left me a note saying he had to work late. But the coffee was hot, bless him. I spent the next hour drinking coffee and thinking while I hung the damp aerial photographs of my field area on the clothesline to dry. The phone rang as I finished.

"*Buenos días,* Francisca. Rise and shine." Toni sounded as if she'd just won the lottery.

"I've been up for hours. My halo's glowing."

"Not as brightly as mine. I took Mom to Mass."

"Does she still go every morning?"

"No, but tomorrow's All Saints' Day," Toni said. "Mom's going a day early. Says somebody has to pray for my salvation."

"Your mother should have been canonized long ago for the trials you put her through."

"Ditto for yours."

"I polish her halo along with the silver . . . Tell me you didn't call just to chastise me for missing Mass."

"No, to tell you we still haven't recovered Angie's purse. The motive may have been robbery—though no one's used her credit cards. So be careful when you're on campus, okay?" Someone spoke in the background. "Philo wants a word."

"Slugabed," was Philo's greeting.

"Paragon. I suppose you've run five miles and done fifty pushups already."

"Seven miles, a hundred pushups and crunches."

"You're disgusting. What did you find?"

"Toni let me see Hector's disk. Unfortunately it had no more information than your printout. I asked an architect to look at it. All he could tell me is that it's a commercial complex."

"I could have told you that."

"I also did a background check on Michael Zorya. It was a curiously thin file, considering his family connections. No criminal record. Keeps a low profile. Resided in Spain for the last three years, flying here for business. Moved back this summer, along with his sister."

"This summer? That means he came back at the same time Hector moved to Tucson, the same time the Zoryas bought the property next door . . . Do you believe in coincidences?"

"I believe in patterns," Philo said. "I've come up short so far. I know that Michael likes sports cars . . . has two, right now. And he collects knives. Those seem to be his only vices."

"Owning knives and sports cars are vices?" I asked.

"When you prefer guns and trucks . . . Where was I? Oh, his store's clients include blue bloods, the nouveau riche, and legitimate corporations who want decorations for their offices or gifts for departing trustees. And he's considered an eligible bachelor by one of my sources, who ought to know. She says a family would tie him down."

"How'd you find out that last part?"

"I'm very good at what I do. Why, are you interested?"

"Tempting, but I'm not in the market."

"Truthfully, I asked Toni. They'd already done a background check because of Carla."

"I could have done that—asked Toni, I mean."

"But you didn't."

"Okay, so I still owe you dinner," I conceded, and changed the subject. "Any luck reaching your contact at Averry Pharmaceutical?"

"She couldn't tell me what he was working on—company policy—but he pulled his weight until his wife died. Then he went to pieces and his work went to hell. He showed up late, or not at all. They sent him to a shrink, but Hector walked out of the first session and wouldn't go back. Thought it was pointless. They had to let him go, finally. Rumor mill had it that he sold company secrets to a competitor, which is why my friend was brought in."

That explained why no letter of recommendation was attached to Hector's file. "Thanks, Philo. I mean it. Dinner's at seven—owl's-head stew. Bring Toni, if she's hungry."

"As a buffer, or so you can pump her for information?"

I hung up without answering.

Yesterday's clothes reeked of smoke. When I tossed them in the washing machine, I heard a clunk. The skirt pocket held a set of three keys, the ones I'd found after the blast. I'd forgotten to give them to Toni. What locks did

they fit? And did Hector leave them in my office accidentally or on purpose?

I picked up my purse and headed to the local Home De-
pot to compare the keys to locks they had in stock. It would
have been easier to go to a locksmith, but then I'd have had
to explain why I didn't know what my keys opened. The
two larger keys seemed to match front door locks used on
houses and apartments. The third key, much smaller and
unworn, was to a locker of some kind—maybe a gun
locker or storage cabinet.

I purchased a box of latex gloves and a bundle of red
cotton cloths, and drove up the street to Wal-Mart where I
picked up a box of diskettes. Thus armed for detecting, I
pointed the Jeep in the direction of Hector's apartment.

I didn't tell anyone where I was going.

CHAPTER 15

HECTOR'S APARTMENT WAS ON THE FIRST FLOOR AT
the rear of a quiet complex on North Swan. The two-story
fourplex had edgings of red tile at the roofline to suggest
this was the Southwest and not Virginia. A six-foot wall enclosed a small courtyard patio with a wrought-iron gate,
unlocked. No yellow tape barred the entrance. This wasn't
a crime scene—yet.

I locked the gate behind me. The patio contained a
glass-topped table, a couple of chairs, a few desiccated
potted cacti, and one bedraggled ficus in the shade cast by
the second story. Morning newspapers had collected like
windblown leaves on the simple welcome mat.

The second key fit the deadbolt lock. I couldn't tell
whether the buzz in my stomach was nerves or excitement
as I pulled on the latex gloves.

The floor plan was a simple square. The front door gave
onto the living room. To the right was a small bedroom
Hector had used as an office. The kitchen was at the back

right. A decent-sized bath and the main bedroom, entered through a short hallway off the kitchen, were in the southwest corner. The place didn't appear to have been searched. Something or someone must have held up Toni and Scott Munger.

The living room was tidy and well ordered. A bookshelf that served as an end table contained a few science fiction and fantasy novels from a used-book store in Tucson— Heinlein, Bradbury, Le Guin, Asimov. The coffee table held a remote control for the TV and a pile of scientific journals. No knickknacks. No CD player with a collection of favorites stacked beside it. The place looked like a residency hotel, minus generic prints on the walls. Even the pastel furniture matched. I turned on the television. He'd been watching *CNN Headline News* before he left for work yesterday.

I moved on to the kitchen. The dishwasher was empty. He was a wash-as-you-go kind of guy. The cupboards held sets of new cutlery, plain white stoneware, and generic glassware (service for four), salt, pepper, and a box of Product 19 cereal. The refrigerator contained apples and oranges, a quart of whole milk (gone sour), an open bottle of Chablis (one glass down), peanut butter, jelly, a half-used loaf of whole grain bread, and an unopened bottle of orange juice. In the freezer were two ice cube trays (five cubes missing) and a half-empty pint of Ben and Jerry's Phish Food ice cream. Hector must have been eating out.

The sterile environment lacked signs of domesticity. Hector wasn't in a committed relationship, unless they used her place. The white-on-white bedroom seemed almost virginal. The queen-size bed was made, though I couldn't bounce a quarter off it. The blinds were closed. The closet and chest of drawers contained a few clothes— clean, wrinkle free, and hanging neatly or folded . . . Unlike what he was wearing the last time I'd seen him, I thought. I pictured him, holding his mail and coffee mug.

He'd been wearing a rumpled green shirt and off-white pants, the same clothes he'd worn on Wednesday . . . What was missing from his room? Tattered college T-shirts, run-down shoes, family pictures on the dresser. It was as if he'd started life over recently, severing all ties with the past. Now there would be no future, either.

The bathroom had received a light cleaning, but probably hadn't been scoured since he'd moved in. Nothing odd or out of place, except a diaphragm in its plastic case. It was tucked at the back of a drawer.

From the wastebasket I pulled a crumpled yellow paper with a penciled note. *A—SU 11:45*. It was the only trash I found. He must have emptied the bins the previous morning. The dash between the first two letters meant it wasn't Arizona State University. Was Hector meeting a colleague named "A" at the student union for lunch? Was it a first initial or last, faculty or student? Sean Archer, who taught physics? Annette Liang, chair of the Chemistry Department? Did Hector know Angie?

I moved on to the office, looking for an address or memo book. Found only a Palm Pilot manual. If the device had been with Hector, it was either destroyed in the blast or Toni had it.

Who knew Hector better than I did? The head of his department. I took out my cell phone and dialed Annette Liang's office number. She answered on the first ring. I segued into the real reason for my call by asking her how the cleanup was going.

"Slowly. The bomb did a number on the chemistry storage room. They'll be at it all weekend."

"Will you be able to tell if there are any chemicals missing?"

"You're wondering if the bombing covered up a theft?"

"Something like that."

"I don't think we'll be able to tell," she said. "Too much damage."

"Have you seen Hector eating lunch with anyone recently? The detectives asked me, but I wasn't able to come up with anything. My mind was rather frazzled yesterday."

"I'm still in shock . . . Let's see . . ." I heard the sound of pages turning, as if Annette were searching for an answer in her desk calendar. Maybe she was. "I saw him sitting with Angelisa Corday a few times. It looked like they were writing a paper together."

"You're sure it was Angie?" I asked.

"I recognized her picture in the paper. When I offered my condolences to Hector yesterday, he just picked up his mail and bolted for the door."

"Was she in one of his classes?"

"No."

"Did it look like a chemistry paper?"

"Probably not. There weren't any formulae."

"A newspaper article?"

"Could have been. But they covered it up and began talking about the weather when I sat down."

I heard voices outside, followed by the sound of a key in the gate. Whoever it was seemed to be having trouble with the lock.

"Thanks, Annette," I whispered. "Gotta go. I'll see you Monday."

My first instinct was to hide. But curiosity won out. I peeked through the dusty window blinds and saw three heads above the gate.

"I am sure the police will not mind if I show you his apartment," said a man's voice. He spoke with a musical Indian accent. "The movers come tomorrow to box up his things. He rented by the month, you see, and tomorrow is the first. We prefer a lease, of course. We offer a ten percent discount on leases." More sounds of fiddling with the lock. His master key must not work. I hoped he was too dignified to climb over the wall. "I will have to call the locksmith. Could you come back this evening?" Two

voices, both male, said yes, they'd wait for him to call their
cell phone. I started breathing again.

Hector's desk contained the only photograph in the
apartment. I slipped the wedding picture from its pewter
frame and looked at the back. The photo of Hector and a
smiling dark-haired woman had been taken in New York
three years earlier. I replaced the photo and found Hector's
insurance and tax folders in the filing cabinet. Her name
was Consuela. She'd worked for a bank in the World Trade
Center.

Hector's résumé file contained a guarded letter of recommendation, dated December 2001, from Averry Pharmaceutical in New Jersey. Reading between the lines, I
surmised they were glad to get rid of him. It explained
why his personnel file at school didn't contain a copy of
the letter.

I turned on his computer. If I needed a password to
reach his desktop . . . I didn't, bless him. But I didn't want
to reset the modification dates or tamper with the files . . . I
had two choices: I could download them to diskettes, or attach the files to e-mails and send them to my home computer. But Hector used AOL, and I didn't have an AOL
account. So I could only send e-mail on Hector's machine
if he'd set up the automatic mail function, complete with
password . . .

I got lucky. Hector had regularly swept his e-mails into
his AOL file cabinet. I didn't need his password to access
those or to run the automatic mail. Angie's name and address were in his address book. There were dozens of
e-mails from her in his electronic file cabinet. Surprise,
surprise.

I found Philo's card with his e-mail address and forwarded all the e-mails to him—and to me. I attached relevant files from Hector's desktop to the letters. Then I
deleted the electronic trail from the sent mail cache in Hector's mailbox. Any expert who checked the hard drive or

the server would find what I'd done, but I'd deal with that when the time came. I shut off the computer and went back to the paper files.

I was looking for anything with "A" in its title, just in case Hector hadn't been meeting Angie. A Bank of America interest-earning checking account for Hector Torrejon Ortiz had a balance of nearly twenty thousand dollars. A passbook savings account showed . . . Jesus H. Christ—eighty-one thousand and change. Hector must not have trusted the stock market . . . His insurance records included a life insurance payout of two hundred and fifty thousand for Consuela Ortiz-Vega. A thick untitled folder held cashier's checks from various Nevada banks and a Mexican bank with a branch in Nogales. They were made out to HTO Chemical. Hector's initials. Apparently, he had a little business on the side. Each check was for just under ten thousand dollars. I did a rough count. Holy shit . . . nearly half a million dollars sitting in a drawer. Why hadn't he cashed them? And what was he selling?

Just in case Hector had hidden other valuables, I checked under drawers, lamps, and furniture. Nothing. But in the top drawer of the desk I found two tickets. One-way. Hector and Angie were flying to the Grand Caymans at the end of the term. The islands were probably just a way station. From there they could hop on a plane or a boat for anywhere. Perhaps Hector wasn't so nice after all.

But had Angie known about the tickets? Had Hector bought them in the hopes she'd say yes, only to have her turn him down? Had he killed her Wednesday night and taken her purse? It wasn't in the apartment. Could he have stashed the purse in his Lexus? If so, then whoever stripped the car had it now.

Next to the tickets was a key marked "storage locker." I slipped it into my pocket. I'd check the garage on the way out. In the second drawer I found a long, narrow cardboard box. Hector's business cards had a generic logo, the name

HTO Chemical, a box number at a local postal center. No fax number, and a phone number I didn't recognize. I pulled the file that said "PHONE" in his neat printing. It contained the manual for an untraceable cell phone, one with prepaid minutes. I copied down the phone and ID numbers. I knew they used local carriers. Toni might be able to recover his phone records.

I took a last look through the folders and found one lying on the bottom of the file drawer. It contained two newspaper clippings of stories by Angelisa Corday, and drafts of three more. They were from a series connecting the proliferation of Indian casinos and gaming halls with increased attendance at Gamblers Anonymous, Alcoholics Anonymous, and Al-Anon meetings. In the margins, Hector had scribbled comments and suggestions about references and sources. When I pulled out the file, I found another yellow sticky note on the inside. *A—4 p.*, was printed on the top, followed by a hastily written address on Fort Lowell Road. It matched Angie's address in the computer.

I used Hector's little copier to duplicate some of his account information, cashier's checks, insurance forms, and other paperwork. I copied the draft articles, too, all the while wondering who had killed Hector, and why?

Time to call Philo. "I sent you a bunch of files from Hector's computer," I said when he answered. "I didn't have Toni's e-mail address. Tell her I didn't open them or tamper with the originals."

"Breaking and entering's a punishable offense, Frankie."

"I'm street-legal. Hector left me his key." I thought I heard a snort. I ignored it. "Hector's paper files are pretty interesting, too." I told him about the checks and the business cards. "Tell Toni, if she doesn't hurry, they might disappear. The manager wants to rent the place ASAP, and if anyone wanted to cash those checks . . . well . . . it only takes a day to get new cards printed up with a different contact name, address, and phone number for HTO Chemicals."

"Then I suggest you get going before she gets there. She's en route as we speak. Dare I ask where you're off to next?"

"Ignorance is bliss, Philo." I hung up before he could reply.

I put everything back in order, even the crumpled note, and left the apartment door ajar. Might as well make it easy for Toni. As I softly closed the gate behind me, I heard the squawk of a police radio on the road. I hurried to Hector's garage locker. Empty. Not even a packrat's nest. Perhaps his stuff was in storage. Perhaps, like me, he hadn't had the time or energy to deal with it . . . I added the key to the three Hector'd left me. Toni wouldn't know they hadn't been there originally.

Stripping off the latex gloves, I lifted up the lid on a dumpster.

"Excuse me, miss," said a voice just behind me.

I froze. The dumpster lid slipped down on my fingers. I shook my hand and swore.

"Sorry to startle you, miss," said the middle-aged deputy with the dancing brown eyes. He had a heavy Spanish accent and looked vaguely familiar, as if I'd seen him on the evening news. "Could you tell me where apartment 35 is?"

His car, I saw, was blocking mine in the visitor's parking area. "It is a maze, isn't it? 35's around the corner at the back." I pointed with my injured finger. "Would you like my parking space?" I pointed again, this time to the Jeep.

He appreciated that very much, he said, and went off to move his car. With a sigh of relief, I picked up the glove I'd dropped in the dirt, deposited it in the dumpster, and retrieved my Jeep.

CHAPTER 16

MY NEXT STOP WAS ANGIE'S APARTMENT. BUT FIRST
I needed food. As I drove to the nearest shopping center,
A-10s in groups of two and three passed overhead, circling
toward Davis-Monthan Air Force Base. It was a subtle reminder that this quiet valley was also the training ground
for war.

I grabbed a turkey sandwich at Wild Oats Market. I
needed a quiet place to think about what I'd learned at
Hector's apartment. So I ate in the car, jotting down notes
on whatever came to mind.

Hector's personal belongings had to be somewhere . . .
I kept a phone book under the front seat. The closest storage facility wasn't far from miles away. But I found one listed that
wasn't far from school. I'd stop by on my way home.

Hector had a cashier's checks from money stashed away, much of it in
showed he'd been living Nevada bank. His personnel file
current job. What had his Vegas when he applied for his
Hector's company, H doing there? Setting up HTO?
nicals . . . What had Hec-

tor been buying? Chemicals for drugmaking? Too obvious, though not necessarily wrong. But he hadn't manufactured or sold drugs in that apartment—I hadn't found any paraphernalia or stored drugs. Was his company just the middleman, buying ingredients for crystal meth or Ecstasy or whatever designer drug was in fashion? Was that the source of the cashier's checks?

The cashier's checks were for amounts under ten thousand dollars, which meant that he didn't want to trigger an automatic report to the government. Therefore, his enterprise must have been quasilegal at best.

He lived in a sterile apartment. He could have moved at a moment's notice, leaving nothing of value behind . . . Was he scared? Was someone after him?

He was running away. He had two tickets to the Cayman Islands . . . But was Angie willing to run with him? And just where did Angie's death fit in? Had Hector, in some twisted mental state, killed her and then himself?

The e-mails proved that Hector and Angie knew each other well. His comments on the draft articles proved they had collaborated. Had that collaboration caused someone to kill them, or had their deaths been unrelated incidents that happened to occur on the same campus within twenty-four hours of each other? What had Philo said? He didn't believe in coincidence. He looked for patterns. So did I.

I pulled out the newspaper clippings and draft articles. Apparently, after meeting Hector, Angie turned from writing human interest and travel pieces to investigative journalism. These were from a series Angie had done for a Tucson paper. The articles told the stories of one man and one woman, Troy and Charlotte, whose lives had been derailed by addiction. Two of the three draft articles delved into cross-border money laundering schemes, including property, arms, banking, and the import-export business. The third draft article dealt with the lucrative business of moving undocumented people across the Arizona border.

Hector's scribbled notes—not the neat printing I'd seen on his files—were in the margins of all three. It was as if he'd been in a hurry. I deciphered "CZ-Storage" and "Arte Folklorico," but I'd have to work on the rest.

According to the first article, Troy and Charlotte had met at a compulsive gamblers support group. Charlotte's addictions had begun in college. She'd taken a summer job dealing cards in Reno, then lost her earnings in Tucson casinos during her senior year. After graduation, her job as a journalist couldn't support her habit. She took a second job with an insurance company and married a coworker. But gambling pulled them so deeply into debt that her husband gave up and left her. When she attempted suicide, her parents intervened and sent her to a treatment center. That was two years ago.

While Charlotte was rebuilding her life, Troy was at the bottom of the hill. His story was a tale of post-9/11 trauma. After his wife died in the World Trade Center, he stopped caring about work—about living. He took frequent sick leave and spent his weekends in Atlantic City, where the noise, flashing lights, and milling people helped distract him and fill the empty hours. He gambled away the insurance money and all their savings, maxed out his credit cards, resorted to selling his company's pharmaceutical secrets to competitors for cash. The company could have jailed him, but survivor's guilt affected the whole country. So they settled with their competitors and let Troy go. A pariah in the industry, he started over as a teacher. His first job was in Las Vegas, which was like giving a kleptomaniac the keys to a department store. This time he was rescued by a disguised voice on the phone asking for a favor. Troy would be given almost unlimited cash to lose at a Nevada casino. That was the point: to lose it to the house. Troy received a cut off the top. He could use it to pay off his debts or gamble with it—the voice on the phone didn't care. Troy set up a dummy company to mask his earnings. It was easy . . . too easy. It took the pleasure out of gambling.

Troy quit his job and moved to Tucson, which was desperate for science teachers. But the anonymous voice found him and threatened to report him for laundering money. They had him by the short hairs. This time he'd go to jail. But, the voice said, they'd call it even if he'd do one more favor. All Troy had to do was purchase the material for a few pipe bombs and deliver it to a storage facility. A simple matter for a chemist. Unfortunately, the last technician hadn't been careful enough, said the voice.

The material and directions for assembly were available on the Internet. Anyone could access it—including children, Troy rationalized. He was a pro, now, at rationalization. He bought the chemicals through his dummy company and delivered enough material for a half-dozen bombs. Immediately afterward he moved again, began using only an untraceable cell phone, and paid cash for everything. But he slipped up a few times at the racetracks and Indian casinos, spiraling down until a colleague at school asked him if he thought he had a problem. That night he called the compulsive gambling hotline.

Troy thought he'd left the past behind. But when a pipe bomb took out a lunch truck in Tucson two weeks ago, reality hit home. He and Charlotte gave Angie their stories, hoping to stop someone else from walking in their shoes.

A sonic boom rattled the windows, making me jump. I saw two stealth bombers, like huge hawks, in the southern sky.

The first article had been published Tuesday morning, three days ago. That night financier Mark Giovanni's car was bombed in the parking lot of the Tucson Convention Center. Troy didn't know Giovanni, but he'd built the bomb that killed him—he said as much in the second article, published Wednesday morning. Angie had died late that afternoon.

Troy's story was Hector's story. The pseudonym, I surmised, alluded to Hector, the greatest Trojan warrior. Was

"Charlotte" just as significant? I searched my memory banks . . . Charlotte, North Carolina . . . Charlotte Perkins Gilman, Charlotte Brontë, Charlotte Church . . . Charlotte Corday . . . That was it. Angie was telling her own story. In a one-woman crusade against evil, Charlotte Corday had stabbed Jean Marat, the French revolutionary. Hector and Angie had tried to strike back at what had ruined their lives and the lives of so many others.

Fire trucks, squad cars, and ambulances converged from three directions on the intersection next to my lunch spot. They all headed north on Swan. It brought back memories of yesterday, when I stood in the parking lot outside Hector's office . . .

I was the colleague who'd asked Hector if he had problems with alcohol and gambling. Without waiting for an answer, I'd left him at the casino. My challenge had triggered his search for help, his meeting Angie. It was the catalyst that had brought them together and led, indirectly, to their deaths. It was the reason he gave me the disk and keys. What tragic, ironic justice that one of the bombs Hector bought materials for was used against him . . .

My cell phone rang as I started the motor.

"You're okay?" Philo asked.

"I'm fine. What's up?"

"Just checking. I'll meet you at Angie's," he said, and hung up.

CHAPTER 17

ANGELISA CORDAY'S APARTMENT BUILDING WAS AN older, nondescript two-story box. Nearby thoroughfares provided a constant background hum. The place was perfect for big-city refugees who couldn't sleep without noise and for college students on a budget who commuted to campus. The sign advertised studio, one-bedroom, and two-bedroom apartments, utilities included.

I found Philo in the parking lot, lying on the tailgate of his truck, basking in the warmth of the autumn afternoon.

"I don't need rescuing, Philo."

He opened eyes that caught the metallic teal shade of his truck. "The thought never crossed my mind."

"And I don't need you to keep me out of trouble, either."

He smiled. "An exercise in frustration. Pointless, to boot." He stretched and climbed down, looking disgustingly refreshed.

"So why are you here?"

"I missed you?"

"Try again."

"I printed out the e-mails you forwarded." He handed me a manila envelope. "Toni said they didn't find anything on Angie's computer, which got me wondering. I figured you'd head here next. I wanted to compare notes and look around."

"And?"

"And I wanted to safeguard whatever you copied at Hector's apartment."

"But Toni's got the originals by now. I only copied samples."

"Toni's got zip. The bomber got there first."

So that sonic boom wasn't a sonic boom, after all. It was my turn on the tailgate. "Was anyone hurt?"

"Not this time, thank God. Everyone was at work."

"But I don't see how the bomber had time to set it up. A deputy arrived as I left. I spoke to him."

Philo gave me a sharp look. "Toni and Scott were on their way. There shouldn't have been another deputy at the scene."

"He was wearing a uniform and driving an official vehicle. He had to move it so I could leave. I gave him directions to Hector's apartment . . . gave him my parking slot, too."

"Ten to one that was the bomber. Which means he can track you down by your license plate number." He hit the speed dial on his cell phone and handed it to me. I gave Toni a description of the "deputy" and handed the phone back to Philo. "She'll call back in a minute," I said.

"In the meantime, could I see what you brought Toni?"

I told him about my conversation with Annette Liang as I handed over the folder of clippings, draft articles, and notes I'd just made. "I think the drafts with Hector's scribbles in the margin might be the articles they were working on during lunch meetings. I want to see if Angie left copies."

While he looked at my files, I scanned Angie's e-mails

to Hector. Their relationship had begun with Angie checking in daily as Hector's sponsor in the support group. By chance, they'd met on campus. They tossed each other verbal life preservers at first, physical ones later as mutual support deepened to love. Once they'd established trust, Hector had e-mailed her his story.

Angie's last e-mail had been Tuesday night. She thought someone had followed her home. I suspected she was right.

I looked up. Philo was watching me. "E-mail is a curiously intimate form of communication," I said, slipping the printouts back in the envelope and handing it to him. He locked everything in a fireproof safe behind the front seat. "What did you think of the articles?"

"I think we should be counting pipe bombs," he said. "Hector made a half dozen. The lunch truck bombing two weeks ago was the first. Mark Giovanni was the second. The odds are that the morning after Angie was killed, before he could talk to you, Hector received another anonymous call . . . at school. The third bomb took out his office; the fourth, his apartment."

"So there are still two bombs out there."

"Unless the anonymous voice has found a new supplier."

"Optimists of the world unite," I said. "We know that the voice chooses his suppliers with care. He wants to keep his hands clean—doesn't want any purchases traced back to him . . . or her. I suppose the disguised voice could have been female."

"Welcome to the twenty-first century, Frankie."

"Which will not, if I have any say in the matter, be dominated by condescending males."

Philo smiled. "As you said—optimists of the world unite . . . But the question's moot, anyway—the 'deputy' you saw at the apartment wasn't female."

His phone rang. Toni did all the talking. "Like Velcro," he said, and punched the power button.

"It's not good," I said.

"Worse than that. 911 got a call about a break-in at a house down the street from Hector's apartment. A deputy responded. He didn't report back in after he entered the premises. They were sending someone to follow up when the bomb went off. Toni just checked it out and found the deputy's body and that of an elderly woman. She'd been dead a couple of days."

"A couple of days?" I thought of the man I'd met at the dumpster. Was it the joy of killing, the prospect of destruction, that made his brown eyes dance? "What kind of animal is he?"

"The sociopathic kind. The kind that plans carefully and executes skillfully. He used the victim's house as a base of operations. He assembled bombs in the garage . . . which suggests he isn't local."

"I don't suppose there's any chance he's left town?"

"Only if he thinks you won't connect him to the bombing. I wouldn't count on it."

"If this guy was close enough to watch Hector's apartment Wednesday night and early Thursday morning," I said, "why did he wait until this morning to bomb it? And why, if he already knew where it was, did he ask me for directions?"

"Maybe he wanted you to see him. Maybe he saw you come out of Hector's apartment and wanted to get a good look at you."

"That isn't very comforting, Philo."

"You don't want to feel comfortable . . . or complacent. You want to stay alive."

I felt disconnected from reality. Killers don't smile and make small talk and call me "miss." Killers don't have eyes the warm color of brown zircon. "If he'd wanted to kill me, he could have bombed the place while I was still inside."

"Unless the bomb wasn't in place. Did you check under the desk?"

I shook my head. "So just how long are we going to be joined at the hip, so to speak?"

"I'm not sure." He smiled. "I've had worse assignments."

"I'll bet. Well, if it takes very long, you may learn more about geology than you ever wanted to know."

"Beats baby-sitting delinquents . . . A long story," he said, when I lifted an eyebrow. "I presume you have a key to Angie's apartment?"

"We'll know in a minute."

"And if it doesn't fit?"

"Maybe the manager will let her teacher in."

"Not her sister?"

"I don't lie that well."

"Lying's an art. It takes practice," he said, shutting the tailgate with a bang.

"And it's in your job description?" I asked as we walked toward the gate.

"Something like that."

Reality hit. "Shit," I said.

"What did you forget?" Philo asked.

"I tried to do something nice for Toni and it backfired—big time."

"Meaning?"

"I left the apartment gate unlocked and the front door open. I handed him the place on a platter."

"Trick or treat," Philo said.

CHAPTER 18

I OPENED ANGIE'S COURTYARD GATE. RUSTING PATIO furniture, thirsty palms, and oleander surrounded a rectangular swimming pool. A small child played alone in the wading pool, no parents in sight. I watched her as Philo knocked on the manager's door. No answer.

"Apartment 23-B's on the second floor, in the corner," I said, keeping one eye on the child.

We started up the stairs. Five steps up, I couldn't stand it anymore. I turned around and walked purposefully over to the wading pool. No caretaker came running out to see if I were abducting the child. I hunkered down at the edge of the cracked concrete deck.

"Hi," I said to the girl. She had light brown curls, sun-browned skin, and looked to be about three. "I'm Frankie. What's your name?"

"Jody."

"Hi, Jody. Is your mother around?"

"She's at work."

"How about your father? Is he here?"

"No."

"Who takes care of you while they're at work?"

"Miss Jill."

"Where's Miss Jill right now?"

"Laney pooped."

Okay . . . I tried a different tack. "Is Jill changing Laney's clothes?"

"Diaper. Laney doesn't wear big-girl clothes."

"Does Jill let you play out here by yourself?"

"Uh-huh. I'm a big girl. I can swim. Wanna watch me?"

"Not right now, Jody. Could you show me where you live?"

"Okay." She got out and took my hand, tugging me toward an apartment on the ground floor. I knocked on the door, which wasn't quite closed. A teenager, baby in one arm and phone tucked between ear and shoulder, opened the door. Her body stiffened as she correctly interpreted the look on my face.

"Hang up," I said.

She threw the phone on the couch. "I was only gone a minute."

"I've been here five. She could have drowned or been abducted in that time."

Her mouth turned down. "She can swim a little—"

"Not in the big pool. And kids drown in bathtubs every day, let alone wading pools. If it happens again, I'll report you to child protective services. Bye, Jody." And with that I turned on my righteous heel and marched back to where Philo leaned against the stair railing.

"Feeling better?" he asked

"Most definitely," I replied, leading the way up the steps.

Like the apartment below, the door to 23-B wasn't quite closed. I slid the key in the lock, just to see if it fit . . . smooth as butter. I pocketed the key and knocked. A thin, white-haired man answered. There were dark circles under his eyes and he moved stiffly, as if holding his emotions in check.

"Yes?" he said. Behind him, in the kitchen, separated from the living room by a counter, a woman wrapped glassware. "Who is it now, Joe?" she called in a weary voice.

I let Philo take the lead. He'd said he was good at lying. "Sorry to disturb you," he said. "We were looking for Angie."

A frown marred Joe's forehead. "You don't know?"

"Know what?" Philo asked.

"Angie died two days ago."

"Died? Two days ago? But I saw her on Wednesday. Was it a car accident?"

"No. She was . . . she was killed. The apartment manager asked us to pack up her things." He looked down at the CD in his hand, the soundtrack to *Sleepless in Seattle*. "She liked movies," he said, his voice cracking on the last syllable. "She could watch a movie once and know every line."

"I'm so sorry for your loss," I said, meaning every syllable. "Angie was a special person."

"You must be her father," Philo said.

"Joe Corday. This is my wife, Rebecca."

She had left her glassware to join him at the door, slipping her arm through his and patting his hand.

Philo introduced us as Fred and Diana. "We stopped by to see if Angie wanted to join us for dinner tonight," he said. "We met a few weeks ago through a story she was working on."

"The one about searching for your birth parents?"

"That's the one," Philo said.

"She was so proud of that piece, wasn't she, Joe? She'd hoped to be able to meet her own birth mother—with our blessing, of course."

"Of course. Was she successful?"

"Not really. She learned that her birth mother died many years ago. That was so hard on Angie. But she was able to talk to her aunt last week. It helped . . . Were you able to find your birth parents, Fred?"

"They also died," said Philo.

That, at least, was the truth. Philo's parents had died in an automobile accident when he was twelve. He'd moved to Tucson to live with his aunt and uncle. That's when my brother Kit met him. They'd played Little League together. Though I was only seven at the time, I remembered how lost Philo looked, how much he seemed to relish being on the fringes of our large family. His aunt and uncle were childless by choice, formal by nature.

"You never get over it," Philo said, in a tone that echoed the shock and grief we both felt—past and present.

"We have a little time on our hands," I said, moving the conversation into a safer channel. "Could we help you box up Angie's things and load them into your car?"

Joe didn't even hesitate. "Would you? That would be wonderful. We're giving her clothes and furniture to the Goodwill. The police already took her computer and some of her files, but the desk and filing cabinet need to be emptied." Joe pointed to the bedroom. "If you really wouldn't mind . . . ?"

"We'll have it done in no time," Philo said. He took my hand and led me sedately into the bedroom. Empty liquor boxes were piled just inside the door. There were dark smudges all over the bedroom where the police had dusted for fingerprints. The bedding was gone. They'd taken the computer hard drive, but left the peripherals. I knelt down to reach under the desk and unplug the monitor. On a high, narrow shelf at the back of the kneehole was a nylon carrying case. I pulled it out, unzipped it, and saw the slim profile of a laptop computer. Somehow the police had missed it. Maybe they'd been short on time, maybe they'd figured it had been in Angie's suitcase of a purse.

"Fred, honey, let me do the filing cabinet," I said. "You're better with computer things than I am."

Philo looked at me as if I'd lost my senses. I held up the blue nylon computer case and the floppy disks from my purse. "No problem, sweet pea," he said, dodging my elbow and taking the bag into the dimness of the walk-in closet.

I emptied the filing cabinet quickly, pausing only to look through her work folders for any more information that might link her to Hector. She had a file of tear sheets, samples of her recent work to accompany future proposals and queries. She wouldn't need them now. I folded a set and slipped it into my purse. To guarantee Philo a few more minutes of privacy, I went into the kitchen. Joe was nowhere about. I assumed he'd taken a load down to the car. "Do you have mailing tape and a felt pen, Rebecca? I'll mark these boxes for you so you'll know what's in them."

"Oh yes, dear. There, on the counter. You're good to help out like this."

"It's nothing, really. The least we could do . . . This must be so hard on you and Joe."

"She was our only child, you see. We adopted her when she was two. It seems like yesterday."

I could think of nothing to say except platitudes. I picked up the tape and marking pen. "Is there a water glass I could use? I'm parched."

Rebecca handed me one of the pottery mugs lined up on the counter, ready for wrapping. This one had an eggshell-white glaze and a prayer in indigo calligraphy: "God grant me the serenity to accept the things I cannot change, the courage to change the things I can, and the wisdom to know the difference. —Reinhold Niebuhr."

"That's my mother's favorite prayer," I said.

"Is she in AA?" When I looked blank, she continued, "They learn that in AA. In gambling support groups, too. Angie started attending meetings just a year ago. It changed her life . . . brought her back to us." She was holding on to the counter as if she'd never let go.

I put my arm around her and patted her shoulder, looking beyond her at the refrigerator. Angie had formed three poems among the magnetic words scattered across the door:

> *Bare winter gardens*
> *incubate delicate peach leaves*
> *and rose petals*
>
> *Mother tell me a lie but let me shine*
> *have drive behind arms, aching music*
> *under my tongue and power beneath fingers*
> *as I scream a thousand words*
> *of repulsive language to the storm*
> *but whisper essential secrets of life*
> *beating in the blood*
> *for I am bitter yet true.*
>
> *I fall, staring*
> *after soaring*
> *I am gone*
> *into an enormous sky*

"I'm sorry," said Rebecca, drawing away to fill the pottery mug with water from the tap. "I didn't mean to upset you."

"It's the poetry," I said, wiping my cheek with one hand and accepting the mug with the other. "I can't believe she's gone. Where did they find her?"

"At the community college. She was taking a couple of classes—poetry and science. When we talked the last time, she told me how much she loved her geology class."

I almost choked on the water. "Do they have any idea who killed her?"

"Not that they've told us. But it's early days yet."

I rinsed the mug and set it upside down on the counter. "You may keep it if you'd like, Diana."

It took me a moment to respond. I'd forgotten my pseudonym. "I'd like that," I said. "Thank you. I'd like that very much." And picking up the felt pen and tape again, I retreated into the bedroom. Philo'd finished boxing up everything that was going with the Cordays. I pointed again to the computer, raised an eyebrow. He nodded.

Joe appeared at the door. "How's it going?"

"Fred found this laptop computer under the desk. Did you want to give it to the police?"

"Guess so. I sure as hell wouldn't know what to do with it."

"Want us to drop it by for you? It's on our way," Philo said.

"Would you, Fred? It's more than we can handle at the moment. Ask for Detective Munger. Scott Munger."

All that scurrying about, when we only had to ask. While Philo carried the boxes down to their rented van, I gave the bedroom a once-over. There were condoms in the bedroom drawer. I threw them in the black plastic trash bag along with the other debris from her brief life. On the bedside table was the geology text from my class. Underneath it were Mary Oliver's *New and Selected Poems* and a dog-eared copy of *Romeo and Juliet*. Both had notes in the margins. Rebecca came in as I was leafing through them.

"We forgot to box these," I said, holding them out to her.

"If you want them, take them," she said. "I know she would have wanted a friend to have them."

I hugged her, such a small gesture in the face of their loss. "We . . . they'll find whoever hurt her, I promise you, Rebecca. Just be patient for a little while longer."

She looked up at me through tear-filled blue eyes. "Patience and time are all we have left, Diana dear."

And loneliness, I thought, as I said good-bye and carried my gifts down to the Jeep.

CHAPTER 19

PHILO STOWED ANGIE'S LAPTOP IN THE TRUCK SAFE and called Toni. I set the books and mug on the front seat of the Jeep and leaned against the door, thinking about star-crossed lovers . . . Hector and Angie. At some conscious or unconscious level, had Angie anticipated her death and Hector's? I thought of Angie, sprawled in her red skirt and white blouse, and of Carla . . . and Jamie. Weren't they star-crossed lovers, too? A shudder crept up my spine.

"Nice job in there," Philo said, interrupting my morbid thoughts. "You're really getting into this."

"You should talk . . . How'd you come up with 'Diana'?"

"You'd just done your Wonder Woman thing with the toddler. It was the best I could do on short notice," he answered from under the Jeep.

I realized he was checking for bombs. I opened the hood and acted as if I knew what I was looking for. He was behind me a moment later, brushing off his khaki pants. He peered over my shoulder. "It's clean," he said.

I felt my shoulders relax. "Where to next?"

"We need to hide the Jeep. The bomber might be looking for it. You can use my garage." He correctly interpreted the look on my face. "You won't be without wheels. You still have your parents' car."

"Okay, but we have to stop at a grocery store, so I can pick up what we need for dinner."

"Rincon Market? It's near my house. Toni said a sketch artist will meet us there. And I can transfer these files."

"You work at home?"

"An aversion to commuting . . . If we're lucky, Lena will be trying out a new recipe and we can beg for a sample. I missed lunch."

"Lena . . . Navarro? Toni's mother?"

"She manages my office. When things are slow, she experiments with recipes for her next cookbook. Which is why Toni and I remodeled the office and kitchen as soon as we finished the guesthouse."

We took Tucson Boulevard south to the Sam Hughes neighborhood, a historic district on the east side of the University of Arizona campus. Most homes there are small—rentals for college students and visiting professors. Some are fixer-uppers, others lovingly restored and occupied by couples or small families. "Centrally located" are the key words for Realtors whose ads tout, "Walk/bike to UA! Close to Himmel Park." Tucson has no freeway system other than I-10. The greater the congestion grows on Tucson streets, the greater the value of these properties.

My family had lived in Sam Hughes in a two-bedroom, one-bath house built in the twenties. I dimly remembered it—the old army bunk beds, the hardwood floors, the built-in cabinets and bookcases. I was two when we moved out of the city into the northeastern corner of the valley. I thought the new house was my birthday present. My eldest brother, Kit, and the twins were given the guesthouse, with an intercom so my parents could respond to donnybrooks.

Jamie and I shared the second bedroom in the main house. Three years later, when the bunkhouse had been remodeled, Jamie joined his brothers in their new petty kingdom. When I demanded equal rights, my parents informed me that the MacFarlane family wasn't a democracy. But at least I'd had a room of my own . . .

The Rincon Market, on the corner of Tucson Boulevard and Sixth Street, hadn't changed much since my childhood. Half the store was a deli, which attracted the lunch and dinner crowd. I reminded Philo I was cooking chili. He detoured down the antacid aisle on the way to the meat counter. I grabbed the beans and jack cheese and headed for the produce section where a shaggy-haired man was mulling over the melons.

"Hello, Gavin," I said.

Gavin dropped a cantaloupe, which rolled to a stop at my feet. "Ah . . . oh . . . yes. I say, Francesca Mac . . . Mac . . . ?" He pronounced my first name the Italian way.

"Francisca MacFarlane." I held out my hand. "Call me Frankie."

Gavin had no choice but to put down the cucumber tucked under his arm. He barely touched my hand, as if I'd developed a bad case of cooties. But I noticed he checked my left ring finger. "Awful business, that," he said. "Angelisa, I mean."

"You knew her, then."

"Oh no . . . not really." He changed the subject. "Shopping for supper?" he said, looking in my cart.

"Owl's-head stew," I said. "An old family recipe for chili."

"Ah, it sounds, um, delectable." He started to back away. Bumped into a white-haired woman with the body of a thirty-year-old.

"Have you rescheduled the auditions?" I asked.

"Oh, uh, yes . . . But you needn't audition again. You'll do."

I didn't know whether to feel praised or pummeled. "When can I pick up the music?"

"Same as Wednesday—five o'clock. Well, must be off." He almost ran for the door.

"What was that all about?" asked Philo. He'd collected the tomatoes, onions, tortilla chips, and chilies.

"He's the music director of the college chorus. Name's Gavin Plinkscale, can you believe it? I was auditioning for him when Angie's body was found. He knew her."

"Angie?" he said, as we got into the checkout line.

"Yes. He called her by her first name. And he got the rehearsal time wrong. Wednesday's rehearsal was at five-thirty. He just said that I could pick up my music on Monday at the same time as that rehearsal—but he put it at five."

"And that's grounds for hanging?"

"It's enough to make me suspicious. We know that the bomber killed Hector, but we don't know if he killed Angie. The two murders might be unrelated. Don't murderers usually stick to the same MO?"

"In general. But there's always the one that breaks the rule."

"Gavin was at the amphitheater yesterday morning, sitting in the top row, eating a doughnut." I paid for the groceries and handed one of the bags to Philo.

"That definitely makes him guilty," he said.

"Well, I'm keeping Gavin on the list. He's creepy."

Philo just smiled and put the groceries into his truck. I followed him the few blocks to his house and parked in a paved portion of the front yard. Parking was at a premium in Sam Hughes. Only a certain number of permits were issued to each house. Fine, if you wanted to bike everywhere. Not good if you had seven prospective drivers in the family. That's another reason my parents had moved.

The property was two lots originally, Philo told me as I locked the Jeep. A former owner joined them together and built a wall around the entire place. A dancing mutt, part golden retriever, part German shepherd, welcomed us into the small *zaguán*, the covered vestibule that connected the smaller house on the left with the slightly larger house on the right.

"Down, Pen," said Philo.

"You named your dog after a writing implement?"

"No, after Penelope, who waited patiently for Odysseus to come home from his travels."

"Loyal Penelope, who resisted the advances of a multitude of suitors while her husband dallied with Circe."

"Maybe Odysseus was a tough act to follow."

"Maybe she preferred the single state," I said, scratching Penelope's head. "His dog Argos, as I recall, gave him a more enthusiastic reception."

"True, but the name wouldn't fit. Argos was male." He opened the sliding glass door on the left.

The living and dining rooms of the smaller house had been remodeled into an office. A formal entrance led to the street. Three of the office walls were painted eggshell, the fourth a pale coral. The east wall held an intricate Navajo sandpainting of the rainbow goddess arching over whirling logs. A Diana Maderas watercolor of Mission San Xavier del Bac hung on the south wall. A potted rubber plant grew in a corner, behind two comfortable-looking leather chairs. On one side of the street entrance were framed photographs of Monument Valley and Shiprock; on the other was a John Dohrenwend digital physiographic map of the western United States. Philo dropped the disks, computer, and copies on one of the oak desks. Quite a haul for one day's work. Smells of baking bread wafted through the breezeway doors and drew us into the kitchen.

Marielena Navarro was stirring a pot on the stove and singing along with Linda Ronstadt's *Canciones de Mi Padre*. Lena hadn't changed—a little shorter and heavier, perhaps, but her dark hair was caught back with the silver clasp I remembered.

Toni's father had died in Vietnam when she was a baby. Lena had never remarried. She'd worked as a cook for a Mexican restaurant while taking business courses. When her mother died and Lena inherited the old family recipes, she put together a cookbook for her family and friends, adapting the recipes for ingredients found in contemporary markets. A publisher found her, and that book was followed by others containing Lena's original recipes. My mother had coauthored one volume on frontier ranch recipes, incorporating some of the MacFarlane standards. It was a far cry from my mother's scholarly research on British and American poets, but she'd had so much fun they planned another collaboration, this time with recipes utilizing native Sonoran Desert plants.

"Whatcha cooking?" I asked Lena. "It smells wonderful."

"Frankie, welcome home," she said, giving me a hug. "I'm baking mesquite cornbread and muffins. I used the mesquite pods I harvested at your house last summer—thank you very much. I'm substituting various percentages of mesquite flour for cornmeal, and you, Philo, and Toni are my guinea pigs. There's prickly pear jelly to go with it, and tortilla soup on the back burner."

"This doesn't get you off the hook for dinner, Frankie," Philo said. "I'll just take a rain check."

"Are Amy and Mac back from England?" Lena asked, stirring the soup.

I told her my parents weren't due home till spring. My hand hovered over a muffin shaped like an ear of corn. She'd baked others in cast-iron saguaro molds. "May we eat? I'm starved."

"Give me thirty minutes to finish up here," Lena said. "Toni should be home by then."

"Home for dinner? That's a first," Philo said.

"She said you were bringing her something."

"And so I am. Frankie, why don't you look around the house while I feed Pen and transfer the files from Angie's laptop? I'd like to have them done before Toni gets home."

I brought the perishables in from the truck, then wandered through their remodeling project. The larger house had been gutted down to the hardwood floor. The ceiling had been raised and pitched so they could harvest rainwater into huge cisterns for use in the garden. Walls had been torn out and space reconfigured. The floor plan now included a living room, open kitchen with cooking island and workspace, and an eating area large enough to accommodate twelve comfortably. Beyond the kitchen were a large bathroom, a utility room, and a walk-in pantry.

The smaller house had also been gutted. The roof had been raised and the interior space divided into the office and three bedrooms, only one of them finished. There were skylights in every room. The bedroom doors opened onto the passageway that used to lie between the two properties. The original dirt of this breezeway was now floored with cement inlaid with pebble, tile, and glass mosaics of animal designs copied from Mimbres and Hohokam pottery and baskets. A twelve-foot-high carved double door closed off the north end. The mesh canopy above the breezeway and a multitude of potted plants gave the effect of a greenhouse. The other end was open to the rear of the property, which contained the one-bedroom, one-bath guesthouse with tiny kitchen and sitting room. All three structures had doors opening toward the rear garden, the former backyard of the smaller house. To one side was an in-ground spa. In the shade of a grapefruit tree stood a round table with an umbrella, folded now. Looking back at the main house, I saw a circular stairway leading to a notch in the parapet. Curious, I climbed up.

The back part of the roof had been reinforced as a second story, open to the sky. Benches wide enough to sleep on had been built around the sides. More petroglyph designs—spirals and rayed suns, rippling water, desert bighorn sheep, lizards and snakes—decorated the earth-tone walls and benches. Planters contained cacti and succulents. In the center, a telescope was mounted on a base secured to the floor. A ramada of ocotillo vigas cast stripes of light and shadow over the benches. It was a place to be alone with one's thoughts amid the bustle of the city. To the north, angular black shadows slashed between the salmon-colored ridges of the Catalinas; to the south, I saw a matching aerie on the roof of the guesthouse.

"We built that one first," Philo said from the top step.

"You could sleep here most of the year."

"That's the idea. I . . ." It was the first time I'd seen him at a loss for words. He shrugged. "I sleep better outdoors."

"Except during the monsoon season," I said.

"Even then." He reached out and lightly traced my cheekbone with his finger. "Skin's the ultimate wash-and-wear fabric."

"Maybe. But I have a healthy respect for lightning storms," I said.

He smiled. "So do I. There used to be a huge eucalyptus where the spa is now."

"And you're hoping that lightning doesn't strike twice in the same place?"

"On the contrary. I'm hoping it does."

He flicked a switch on the wall. Water slipped softly from the center of an inlaid spiral to fill and fall from a graduated series of bronze basins. The street noise faded away. There was only light and shadow, the waning heat of the day, the sound of falling water. I looked down at the garden. The paths, edged with plants, resembled a petroglyph pecked through the desert varnish of a cliff. In the center was the spa—a clear aquamarine eye tiled with the Tohono O'odham man-in-the-maze design.

"Sometimes," Philo said, following my gaze, "you need distance to gain perspective." He could have been referring either to the recent murders or his own narrow escape from death . . . or to the fact that I'd had a crush on him when he left thirteen years ago.

"And to see the pattern," I said, changing the subject to avoid that shaky ground. "I'm doing my damnedest to find the pattern behind these murders, Philo, but things are happening so fast."

"You're too close to connect the dots," Philo said, reaching behind me to switch off the waterfall. The traffic hum returned, a white noise, like the muted roar in a seashell held to the ear.

CHAPTER 20

WHEN WE REENTERED THE KITCHEN, LENA HANDED me a stack of handwoven place mats and pointed to a round table set into a recessed area of the breezeway. Philo plugged in the tiny Christmas lights stretched over the arched doorway and along the roofline. It looked like a cantina. I set the table while Lena served up four bowls of soup and plates of bite-size pieces of cornbread. Colored toothpicks marked the different cornbread recipes so we could vote on our favorite. Toni arrived just as I carried the last plate to the table.

"Eat, eat," Lena said. "You're skin and bones, Francisca."

"If you'd been camp cook for me last summer, I'd be twenty pounds heavier."

"And you'd have cursed her as you hauled that extra weight up the mountain every day," Toni said.

"It would have been worth it." I savored a bite of cornbread before slathering another piece with the wine-colored jelly. "I've died and gone to heaven, Lena."

Philo and I talked as we ate, sharing with Toni what we'd learned. She had developments of her own to report.

"Corday was killed between four-thirty and five-thirty. The weapon was a stiletto-like knife. But she wasn't stabbed. It was thrown. Caught her at the base of the skull—killed her almost instantly. And if she screamed, no one heard her. At least no one who's come forward."

"How many people are that good with a knife?" I asked.

"Few." Toni ate in silence for a minute. There were circles under her blue eyes. "About Ortiz . . . The pipe bomb was taped under his computer desk. No signs of forced entry to the office. They probably came in through the patio door. The room wasn't locked until the janitors finished the night before, and that door had been propped open part of the morning. They think the bomb was detonated by a phone call. Same as the Giovanni murder and the lunch truck bombing."

I felt as if I hadn't been paying attention in class. "Hector alluded to Giovanni's murder in Wednesday's article." I tapped the stack of photocopies. "Who was he?"

"An international financial advisor," Toni said. "Or so he claimed. He worked out of his home. Specialized in tax shelters, offshore accounts, moving money around. Had an exclusive client list that included businesses from Central and South America. He also owned several mobile-catering trucks."

"It was one of his trucks that was bombed?"

"Yes, though Tucson Police didn't make the connection until after Giovanni was killed. His ownership was deliberately obscured, and the situation was complicated by a vendor dispute going on at the time—a lunch-truck war, so to speak. We attributed the bombing to a rival vendor."

"Was anyone killed in the first bombing?"

"No. We think it was a warning."

"I read of a case a couple of years ago in California . . . the vendor was selling more than hot dogs and burritos from a lunch truck," I said. "At office buildings and schools, mostly. The parents caught on when one of their future Olympians tested positive after a swim meet."

"What happened to him—the vendor, I mean?" Toni asked, taking out her notebook. It was nearly full. I wondered how many she went through in a year.

"She committed suicide," I said. "While she was out on bail."

"They're sure it was suicide?" The doorbell rang. "That'll be Keith Bernstein," Toni said. "The sketch artist."

For the next half hour, while Philo did the dishes, Keith attempted to capture on paper the man I'd seen outside Hector's apartment. Toni sat with us at the kitchen table, reading through the material Philo and I had collected. But her eyes kept straying to Keith's hands and face as he worked. He produced a credible likeness, right down to the dancing brown eyes . . . Had the bomber been laughing with anticipation, I wondered, or had he been laughing *at* me? I shivered.

"What's wrong?" Philo asked. Wiping his hands on a towel, he came to peer over my shoulder. The dishtowel dropped to the floor.

"Philo?" Toni came around the table to join us. "You know him?"

"He looks like a man named Morocho, a member of Los Pepes, a vigilante group in Colombia."

"The group that took out Escobar?"

Philo nodded. "They were partial to bombs, remember? And they had a love-hate relationship with the U.S. They brought down my helicopter. Morocho was my host for a couple of days . . . His hair was longer, then, and he had a mustache and beard, but Keith's caught his eyes."

"What the hell is he doing here?" Toni asked.

"I wish I knew." Philo turned to me. "Was anyone with him in the squad car?"

"Not that I saw."

"Morocho was a loner, but he didn't work alone . . . Maybe I'm wrong."

The doorbell rang again, and I heard a chorus of "Trick or treat" when Lena opened the door. I'd forgotten it was Halloween, All Hallows Eve . . . two days before el Día de los Muertos, the Day of the Dead . . .

"I need to go," I said, pushing back my chair so abruptly it tipped over. "Lena, the food was wonderful. Thank you." I righted the chair and handed her the blue toothpick. "That's my choice."

Of course it wasn't that easy. Life's never that easy—at least, my life isn't.

Toni wanted to discuss the murders, to put everything on the table and see what we had. So much for taking the night off. She'd already cleared the information-sharing with her superiors. She was willing to talk at my house; she granted me that much. But the sketch had its effect— she insisted on attaching someone to my side, like a chiton on a surf-battered rock. Just for the next few days, she said. She wanted to keep her only witness in one piece.

I suggested what she could do with her proposed guardian. Toni countered with the offer of a jail cell. It's hard to teach from a jail cell.

Philo volunteered for the assignment. He'd just finished a major job and was due a weekend off. I responded that the assignment was comparable to baby-sitting a juvenile delinquent. He countered that I wasn't a juvenile any-more—though I was behaving like one. So, somewhat less than graciously, I listened to the terms of surrender.

My Jeep would be hidden away in the garage behind Toni's bungalow. Philo would drive me home. Toni'd al-ready requested a uniformed officer for the grounds and a bomb-sniffing dog to check the house. She called Jamie and Teresa to let them know what was happening. Jamie said he'd wait at the bunkhouse with Teresa and Charley until Toni told him the house was safe.

I accepted the plan with the caveat that I be allowed to stop by my office. I'd left books drying outdoors overnight and needed to bring them back in.

Philo packed an overnight bag while I moved the Jeep and transferred my belongings to the truck. Lena added a doggie bag of goodies, and Toni handed me a copy of the sketch.

"Just a reminder, Frankie. This guy doesn't mess around. Don't underestimate him."

CHAPTER 21

AT THE CAMPUS, LIGHTS WERE ON IN ALL THE CLASS-rooms and offices, including mine. Glaziers were working overtime to replace broken windows. In Hector's classroom I could see figures cleaning up shattered beakers and graduated cylinders. The gaping hole in his office wall was covered with plywood. I refused to contemplate what hazardous mixtures had been formed inadvertently in the chemical storage room when the bomb had detonated.

The patio door to my classroom was locked. The workers inside wore headphones—they'd be no help. When I pulled my keys from my pocket, something fell on the ground with a clink of metal. Hector's key ring. Light reflected off the smallest key.

"What is it?" Philo asked.

"I just remembered something. At the beginning of the semester, Angie asked if she could use an empty microscope cabinet." I held up the key. "Or this might fit one in Hector's lab."

"I'll bring in the books while you check," he said.

"*Buenas noches,*" I said to the janitor, who was buffing the concrete floor. "*¿Qué tal?*" Victor assured me things were fine before replacing his headphones.

The key turned smoothly in the steel lock of the matching cabinet. Inside was a black-leather purse with enough pockets that it could serve as a briefcase. On top was a note, torn from a yellow legal pad and folded in thirds. "Dr. MacFarlane" was scrawled on the outside, as if she'd been in a hurry. I could hear Angie's voice saying my name, asking a question. I hesitated, then reached for the note. My fingers trembled.

"Wait," Philo said. "Don't touch it. Does your stock run to latex gloves?"

My brain was fragmented. I had to open five drawers before I remembered the box of disposable gloves I'd transferred to his truck. Philo brought us each a pair and watched me struggle into mine. The janitor turned off his buffer. The glazier paused in the middle of replacing an upper window.

Philo handed me the note.

> *Dr. MacFarlane—I'm meeting Dante Montoya in a minute. There are tapes and notes in my purse that will explain. I won't be alone. Hector said he'd keep an eye on me—from a distance, of course. I want my first conversation with my birth father to be private. When Dante called to set up this meeting, he knew all the right information . . . but I have this niggling little doubt. The reporter in me, I guess. So I'm leaving the tapes where you'll find them and giving Hector the locker key. —Angie*

Philo picked up the purse and took a cursory look through the pockets. "Her phone and tape recorder are here. Do you have a plastic bag?" he asked.

The janitor and glazier went back to work. I found a roll

of plastic wrap and helped him wind a cocoon around the purse and note.

"I'll ask Toni for copies of the tapes, since Angie gave them to you. Lena can transcribe them tomorrow," he said as we climbed into the truck. He started the motor and headed for Sabino Canyon Road.

"If Hector was there, why didn't he protect her?" I was thinking aloud.

"It might have gone down too quickly."

"Then why didn't he say anything to the police? He could have called anonymously. Why did he wait to speak to me, instead?"

"Maybe he was too scared. It happens."

"I don't buy it. He had the presence of mind to drag the janitor's cart to the middle of the walkway so that whoever came to get it *had* to see Angie's body."

"Just because Hector was there, it doesn't mean he moved the cart, Frankie. We don't yet know what happened. Finding the purse rules out robbery as a motive, but we don't have a substitute. We don't know who actually killed Angie, or if she died before, during, or after her father showed up . . . if he showed up. We do know, however, that at least three people were supposed to be in the vicinity of the amphitheater—Hector, Angie, and Dante Montoya—"

"Who may or may not have been Angie's biological father. He could even be the bomber."

"It's all speculation at this point, Frankie. Other people could have been there, too . . . Gavin Plinkscale, for instance."

"Granted there are too many unknowns," I said, "but it doesn't hurt to speculate. So let's get back to Hector. If he was close enough to see what happened to Angie, then he was close enough to overhear their discussion. That center mark is an acoustical marvel. What if he heard them talking about him?"

"You mean his whereabouts?"

"Exactly. That might scare anyone shitless."

"And cause him to steer clear of his apartment that night."

"He wouldn't have stayed in his office, either. Not with the killer on campus," I added.

"If—and it's a big if—the killer got the information he needed from Angie, he wouldn't have any reason to go to her apartment. So Hector might have stayed there. He had a key," Philo said. "And it's something Toni can check easily enough. The person in the apartment below will know if someone was moving around."

"He wore the same clothes to school on Thursday that he wore the day before."

Philo smiled. "You pay attention to what your colleagues wear?"

"Don't you?"

"Yes, but I was trained to remember details. Just for the record, what was Keith wearing?"

Philo reminded me of Gallegos-Martínez, interrogating me in Mexico. "A pale blue denim shirt, button-down collar, rolled-up sleeves; no tie or coat; new jeans."

"What color was his belt?"

"Other than noting the color of his pants, I kept my eyes above his waist."

"He'll be disappointed to hear that," he said.

We turned onto Tanque Verde Road. "Woven dark olive with a sliding brass buckle," I said softly when Philo stopped at a red light.

I could hear gears clicking in his head. The light turned green. The car behind us honked. Philo ignored it. It took an eternity for him to respond. "Say again?"

"Your belt. Looks like military issue. Seems to be in good condition."

"So's everything else," he said, with a smile that crossed the space between us like sheet lightning on a summer night.

CHAPTER 22

WE PASSED GHOSTS AND GOBLINS IN SMALL GROUPS on the road, all carrying flashlights. A squad car was parked off to the side of our gravel drive. The deputy stopped us, checked our IDs, and radioed ahead for permission to let us through. He said that the bomb-sniffing dog wasn't here yet, but that Toni was at the bunkhouse.

Toni met us outside. While Philo handed over the purse, I carried in the doggie bag Lena had made up for Jamie.

The bunkhouse was a two-bedroom, two-bath, adobe and brick building with a loft, kitchen, and family room. It slept six, but had accommodated three times that number at family reunions. The previous owners had built it for the hired help sixty years ago when the stables were full of horses. My twin brothers paid rent and lived there when they were in town, which wasn't often these days. They preferred to live simply, own little, travel light. But their horses required a home base. Trading free housing to Teresa in return for caring for their stock was a no-brainer.

The family room had changed little over the years.

Wrought-iron floor lamps shed soft light on the built-in bookcases. A computer occupied a desk to the left of the door. Two brown-leather sofas, draped with brightly striped Mexican blankets, flanked a mission-style coffee table. Facing the fireplace of river cobbles were a frequently refurbished armchair, my parents' first purchase after their marriage, and an oversize rocking chair with the old MacFarlane brand burned into the hide. It had belonged to my great-grandparents. In it I'd listened to poems and stories, learned to read curled up against my mother's side, been rocked to sleep countless times.

Charley was in the armchair, reading a psychology journal. Teresa was curled up in the rocking chair, watching Jamie. My brother sprawled on a sofa, one leg on the floor, staring at the logs in the fireplace as if they would spontaneously ignite. The bowl of Halloween candy sat on the coffee table. In the background, Trisha Yearwood sang "How Do I Live."

Charley and Teresa greeted me with smiles. Jamie didn't seem to notice I was there.

"Lena sent tortilla soup and mesquite cornbread. Anybody hungry?"

"Dad and I ate already. Jamie says he isn't hungry," Teresa said.

I put the soup in the refrigerator and joined them in the sitting room. Trisha moved on to "The Song Remembers When," guaranteed to deepen Jamie's depression. I flicked off the CD player, and he stirred enough to sit up.

"Waiting is the pits," he said. "I feel helpless and inept and stupid. I keep thinking there must be *something* I can do . . . It's like being in a windowless building when the power goes out." He combed his hair with his fingers, trying to restore order. It didn't help.

"You need comfort food." I reheated the soup in the microwave, added tortilla chips, avocado, and jack cheese, handed him two squares of cornbread, and watched everything disappear. So much for voting on the best sample.

Philo came in alone. Toni, he informed us, had driven to the closest sheriff's station to secure the purse, and the dog had arrived at the house. He set a plastic grocery bag on the tile counter. It didn't contain food. "The printouts of some of Angie's files," he said. "It's a first cut—whatever I thought was relevant."

I held out my hand. "Sorry," Philo said. He left the bag on the counter and sat next to me on the second sofa. "Toni asked us to wait until she got back."

We sat around for a few minutes, looking at each other. We were all in the waiting mode, but I was no better at it than Jamie was. We both needed exercise and distraction.

"Teresa," I said, "is the volleyball still in the closet?"

The sand court was just behind the bunkhouse. While Jamie and Teresa tightened the net, Philo and I raked the feral cat poop out of the sand. Charley rustled up water bottles.

I was eight or nine when I recognized the therapeutic value of volleyball. It wasn't just that physical exertion kicked endorphins up into the brain; it was the intellectual challenge of setting up a play and responding to the backset, the floating serve, the mishit ball; it was the fluid grace of executing a dink, a fake . . . or a kill. Even the language of the game resonated. It was chess with live pieces on a constantly shifting board. It was war, but with inviolate rules and a code of ethics: if you hit the net, stepped over the centerline, threw, slapped, lifted, or palmed the ball, you called your own foul.

We were in the middle of a game when Toni returned. Our blood was pumping. The files could wait. Toni joined Jamie and Teresa's team, making it three against three. We played by floodlight and groundlight. It was a night of shadows and cursing and laughter. We'd all been working so hard that our skills were rusty. It didn't matter. After splitting the first two games, Jamie's team won the match on a dink, a soft little return that dribbled down our side of the net and left us sprawled in a tangle of limbs, listening to their whoops and high fives.

"Is this the way the world ends?" I said, shaking my hair free of grit.

"That was definitely a wimpy shot," Jamie admitted, his blue-gray eyes alight with laughter as he ducked under the net and pulled me to my feet. This was the old Jamie, not the shade I'd been sharing the house with the last three weeks. "But we'll take it." He extended his hand to Philo, who was brushing sand from his sweaty skin. "Need a boost, old man?"

Philo looked at me and grinned. "Why not?" Taking Jamie's hand, he leaned back, planted a foot in Jamie's midsection and tossed him over his head. Jamie landed with a thud that knocked the air from his lungs.

"Cool," he said when he could breathe. "Go again?" And an impromptu jujitsu match ensued on the court, Jamie with Philo, Toni with Teresa. It was as if volleyball had been just the warm-up.

"Look at them. They're having so damned much fun," I said to Charley. "Next semester, after my dissertation defense, I'm going to take lessons."

"Bet your boyfriend would teach you for nothing," he said with a straight face. He was looking at Philo.

"He's not my boyfriend."

"If you say so."

Protesting would only confirm his statement, so I gave up. The temperature dropped rapidly and air blew cold against our faces. R. Carlos Nakai's flute music came softly over the outside speakers as Orion, Taurus, and the Pleiades rose over the Rincons. Since I'd first taken biology, I'd envisioned Orion not as an archer but as a giant mitosis spindle in the sky. I looked at the pattern of stars, familiar, eternal—Betelgeuse and Rigel at either end, a belt of stars across the middle . . . Did a similar pattern link all the deaths of the last three weeks, or were there several constellations existing side by side? Jorge, Mark Giovanni, Hector, Angie, a sheriff's deputy, and an elderly woman . . . If Jorge was red Betelgeuse, and the Tucson murders the belt and sword, where was Rigel? Was there a murder still to come?

A great horned owl hooted near the stable. Instinctively, Charley's head turned toward the sound. I remembered he had no more love of darkness than he had of graveyards. Spirits walk at night, and owls carry men's souls to the afterworld. A pack of coyotes yelped and barked as they cornered some whimpering, squeaking creature in the wash. We cannot, I thought, keep death at bay through sheer willpower . . .

Jamie cried uncle first. "I'm too out of shape for this, Philo."

"Even against a gimpy old man?"

"I take that back. But I want a rematch soon."

"Anytime you think you're ready."

Teresa was five inches shorter than Toni, but they seemed to be well matched. Ten minutes passed, fifteen, twenty. "Call it a draw?" I suggested.

"You don't know Toni," Philo murmured, low enough the combatants couldn't hear. But when they bowed to each other a moment later, he whistled softly. "Well I'll be damned."

"I've had more fun tonight than I've had in a long time," Toni said. She looked around. "There's something special about this place."

"A thousand years ago the Hohokam gathered here," Jamie said. "It was a happy place, I think."

"Maybe they're still around," Teresa said.

A squad car pulled up and a deputy got out. "All clear," he told Toni. "Want us to check this place too?"

That silenced all of us. "Good idea," Toni said. "Just let us get a few things and we'll wait at the main house."

In the bunkhouse I grabbed my purse. Philo picked up the bag of printouts.

"Damn," said Toni. She was staring at the counter. "I dubbed copies of Corday's tapes while I was at the station. They're gone."

CHAPTER 23

"ANYTHING ELSE MISSING?" I ASKED.

We did a quick survey of the bunkhouse. The purses, wallets, and fanny packs hadn't been touched.

"Did you listen to the tapes?" I asked Toni.

"I dubbed them at high speed, so I couldn't tell what was on them, except that it was conversation. I copied the info on the outside—dates, followed by Angie's initials and a combination of letters and numbers. At least the originals are safe. I'll dub you another set on the way home."

Charley shook his head. "Whoever did this is good. He didn't even set off the motion detector lights out front."

"Or we were having too much fun to notice," I said.

We moved the vehicles down to the main house. Jamie dumped the last of the Halloween candy in the middle of the scarred oak table in the kitchen. I brewed a pot of coffee and heated water for tea. While Toni made a couple of calls, we rounded up paper and pencils. Energy was high. It was time to brainstorm.

Philo had unloaded the truck. On the sink was Angie's

mug, the one her mother had given me. The second line struck me, then, as it hadn't before: "Courage to change the things I can." Angie and Hector had taken that challenge literally. They'd set out to effect change by exposing corruption and bringing a shadowy figure into the light.

Toni summarized for the group what we knew so far, and added several updates. Hector's fingerprints were found on the janitor's cart, which confirmed he was at the amphitheater when Angie Corday was killed. They were running Dante Montoya's name through the database. No hits so far. The name might be someone unrelated to the murder, or an alias for the bomber. But they were no closer to figuring out who'd killed Angie. Or why.

"Have you checked out Gavin Plinkscale?" I asked her.

Toni didn't have to look at her notes. "Educated in England—Bristol and Durham. He's a resident alien. Married, no kids. No alibi for the time of Corday's murder. He was alone in the music hall."

"He doesn't act married," I said, relating my encounter with Gavin at the grocery store. "He checked out my left hand, Toni. And the way he spoke of Angie . . . He called her by her first name, as if he knew her. It made me wonder if he'd been hitting on her before the audition."

"I'll check it out," she said, then continued her summary. A joint task force was working round the clock on the bomber case. Toni showed Morocho's sketch to Jamie, Charley, and Teresa, in case they saw someone hanging around. It had been circulated to the media, and 88-CRIME had been inundated with calls after the late-night news. They'd found the stolen squad car, wiped clean, abandoned in a coffee shop parking lot off I-10. If the bomber was still in the area, it was only a matter of time until they caught him.

"How did he kill her—the elderly woman?" I asked, wondering if her death was similar to Angie's.

"You don't want to know," Toni said. "It took a long time."

I heard Philo's pencil lead snap. "That's one of Morocho's trademarks," he said, getting up to pour another cup of coffee.

"Which makes Angie's murder an anomaly," I said. "Her killer threw a knife, and death was almost instantaneous."

"Your visitor this morning carried a knife," Charley said to me.

"What visitor?" asked Jamie, Toni, and Philo in unison. Teresa just shook her head.

"You followed his tracks from the bunkhouse down to the wash," Charley said to me. "I waited around until he came out of the wash—after everyone left for work. But he'd snooped around the buildings before that. Saw his footprints under a window. He took off up the wash when he saw me."

"A little detail you forgot to mention, Frankie?" Philo asked.

I shrugged. "If he'd wanted to hurt me, he could have done it while I slept in the hammock. Was he wearing shoes when you saw him, Charley?"

"Nope. He was carrying them, laces tied together and looped around his neck. The knife was in a sheath at the back of his belt."

"A border crosser?" Teresa asked.

"He was Indian, I think. Could be local. Probably someone looking for work. He didn't seem nervous, just careful."

"He could still be hanging around," I said. "And he could have taken the tapes . . . but why would a stranger be interested in them?"

"I haven't a clue," Toni said. "But nothing makes sense in these murders, and we're due for some kind of break in this case. So would you work with the sketch artist tomorrow, Charley?"

"Not sure it'll help much. He was wearing a hat. His face was in shadow."

"Then why do you think he was Indian?" Philo asked.

"The way he carried himself, the way he reacted . . . the way he moved. I can't explain it."

"Anything else?" Toni asked us.

Philo set the printouts of Angie's files on the table, which reminded me that I'd stuffed her tear sheets in my purse. I pulled them out. They included the first of a three-part series, published six weeks ago, on the emotional cost of tracing and reuniting with birth parents. She hadn't used a pseudonym. She also hadn't found her parents. The adoption papers had been sealed. But Angie's adoptive mother had overheard the name Juanita, and that she had no fixed address.

"Rebecca Corday said that Angie talked to her aunt last week," I said. "Could she have had anything to do with Angie's death?"

"Maybe the tapes will tell us," Philo said. "Her other files appear to be background for future articles—heavier stuff like money laundering, *coyotes* abandoning border crossers in the desert, the import-export business, and lighter stuff like tarot. But take a look at this." He pushed a thick file to the middle of the table. "She was doing research on Los Pepes."

"Morocho's vigilante group in Colombia?" I asked.

"That's right. They created the campaign of terror that flushed out Escobar. Angie also gathered information on the Castaño brothers. They led Los Pepes and built up the AUC, the right-wing paramilitary machine that's turning Colombia into a fascist country." Philo massaged the muscles on his thigh as if they hurt. But this time a front wasn't moving through.

"Morocho was a point man . . . a torturer, a butcher, a bomber," Philo continued. "And he stayed involved with the Castaños until they formed the AUC. Then he disappeared. I thought he was dead."

Philo's words echoed those I'd said to him that first night . . . was it only two nights ago?

"How the hell did Hector and Angie find the connection between Los Pepes and a Tucson bomber—who I assume was the anonymous voice on the phone?" Toni asked.

"Who knows?" Philo scratched his head. "Morocho might have let something slip on the phone . . . or perhaps Giovanni did. Angie's got a file on him as well. Anyway, it explains why Morocho's here and why he bombed Hector's office and apartment. When he disappeared, he must have started a new life somewhere else—a life he didn't want connected with the mess in Colombia . . . a life he'd do anything to protect."

Philo helped me load the dishwasher when the others had gone. "What's on tap for tomorrow?"

I looked at the calendar on the wall. "Lunch with Cézar, 1 P.M." was circled. Damn, I'd forgotten.

Philo was standing so close behind me that his breath moved the hair on my neck. "You're not going alone. But I'll sit at another table."

"You'll do no such thing. I'll call Cézar in the morning and cancel."

"Too bad. I'd have enjoyed seeing him." I didn't say anything. I wasn't thinking clearly. "I'll just get my sleeping bag," he said, but he didn't move.

An emotional undertow tugged at me, and I tried to find my footing. "You can use my parents' room."

"I sleep better outdoors, remember?" His limp was pronounced as he walked to the door. "But I will borrow their shower."

"Want company?" It slipped out.

He turned and smiled. "Yes . . . but no, thank you. Until this is over, I need to keep my wits about me."

I couldn't sleep, couldn't turn off my mind. Someone had been in the bunkhouse, someone who didn't trigger the motion-sensitive floodlights outside. I tried counting desert bighorn sheep—more entertaining than the domestic variety. Gave up at one thousand seven hundred and seventy-five, the year, coincidentally, that the Irish mercenary Colonel Hugo O'Conor and Padre Francisco Garcés chose the site for the Tucson presidio . . .

I continued to toss and turn. At two in the morning, frustrated, I padded into the kitchen to make hot cocoa. Old Bû, the great horned owl, was back, calling from the rooftop, but no sounds came from wherever Philo was sleeping.

The silence, broken sporadically by the owl's call, reminded me that tomorrow was el Día de los Muertos. I pulled out my mother's recipe box and found the recipe for *pan de muerto,* bread for the dead. It was comforting to putter, to think of nothing but measuring ingredients, dissolving yeast, scalding milk, melting butter, beating eggs, sifting flour, kneading dough. While I waited for the dough to rise the first time, I checked my personal and school e-mail from the computer in my bedroom.

I found the usual spam, a note from my parents, departmental memos, announcements . . . and an e-mail from Hector, sent moments before he died. The message, in all caps, was terse: "I'M SORRY." No signature, but he'd attached a file. Did I want to download now? the server asked. Shit yes, I wanted to download now.

The attachment had two pages. The first page held a website address and what looked like a shopping list for pipe bombs. I scrolled down to the second page. It held the same building plan that was on the disk Hector had left in my office, but this time he'd penciled in dashed lines to square off the southeast corner of the complex. And he'd added a cryptic drawing at the top: x- and y-axes, with the letters "GSR" in the northeast quadrant and the numbers "24/27" in the southeast quadrant.

I grabbed the e-mail address Toni had scrawled for me before she left.

"What's up?"

I jumped. Philo stood in the doorway.

"Couldn't sleep," I said. "I'm forwarding Toni an e-mail Hector sent on Wednesday just before the bombing." I printed out the files and handed the pages to him.

He sat down on the edge of the bed to study the drawing. "Nothing rings a bell," he said after a few minutes. He handed it back to me. "If you work on that, I'll check out the website."

Back in the kitchen, I pondered the problem while I separated the dough into three parts, rolled each into a foot-long snake, braided them, and then brought the ends together to form a circle. I moved the wreath onto a greased cookie sheet and covered it with a towel. Then I climbed into bed and let my mind free-associate. It was like doing a jigsaw puzzle blindfolded.

What came at last was the image of a topographic map. I threw back the covers and pulled the U.S. Geological Survey index of topographic quadrangles from the file cabinet. Thank you, Thomas Jefferson, for insisting on the grid system. Township 24 south, range 27 east, Gila and Salt River meridian . . . It was like an address. And the address narrowed the search down to thirty-six square miles in and around Douglas, Arizona.

Philo finished printing out some pages and shut down the computer. "Besides his shopping list, I have instructions for assembling and detonating the pipe bombs." He looked at what I'd found. "Township and range. Of course. Nice work, Frankie."

"Thanks to Hector. Shall we call Toni?"

"Let her sleep. You, too," he said, as I climbed back into bed. He dropped a kiss on my hair and turned out the light. "Sweet dreams."

But my dreams weren't sweet. This time the cat had Carla's eyes and a collar of precious stones that changed from deep green to purple-red when she moved. She met me at the entrance to a house. In the center was an octagonal glass-enclosed two-story conservatory, a jungle of orchids, *Monstera,* bromeliads, and cycads, reaching for the sun. At one side, sea-green water rippled over angular boulders of pale pink welded tuff to collect in a pool bordered by black-onyx slabs. I saw our reflections—the cat's and mine—in the still water. She looked at a coin tossed into the depths, one like the jewelry Carla was wearing the last time I saw her. The sun reached its zenith and shone directly down, reflecting off the coin until a great golden carp swam up and swallowed it. The cat jumped up on a small table in the center of the twelve-by-twelve octagon. She swatted at a pink lady, a sphinx moth trapped in this glass cage. A second cat, with matching collar but blue-jade eyes, joined her from some dark, hidden place under a climbing philodendron. They looked like twins. I felt the humid air press down until I couldn't breathe. I fought my way to the glass door. When the handle refused to budge, I picked up a chair and threw it with all my might at the door, shattering the dream . . .

PART V

Saturday, November 1
All Saints' Day

Jadeite: Cleavage and optical characters like pyroxene. Usually massive, with crystalline structure, sometimes granular, also obscurely columnar, fibrous foliated to closely compact. . . . Extremely tough. . . . Color apple-green to nearly emerald-green, bluish green. . . . Essentially a metasilicate of sodium and aluminium corresponding to [the mineral] spodumene. . . . Jadeite has long been prized in the East, especially in China, where it is worked into ornaments and utensils of great variety and beauty. It is also found with the relics of early man, thus in the remains of the lake-dwellers of Switzerland, at various points in France, in Mexico, Greece, Egypt, and Asia Minor.

—EDWARD SALISBURY DANA
A TEXT-BOOK OF MINERALOGY, THIRD EDITION

CHAPTER 24

PHILO OPENED THE KITCHEN DOOR AS I SLID THE
pan de muerto into the oven at six-thirty the next morning.
"Just like the old days," he said. "Your mother used to
make bread."

"I remember that when you were in high school, you
used to find excuses to visit Kit on the Day of the Dead.
Mom knew you'd drop by. She always made extra." I set
the timer on the stove. "I was going for a short walk while
this bakes—want to come along?"

"Isn't that why I'm here?"

Outside, Cézar's horse was gone from the corral. We
waved to the deputy on duty at the entrance, walked down
the road a bit, and turned off toward Agua Caliente Park.
The sky above Mica Mountain was the color of ripe pump-
kins. A flock of mourning doves flew low and fast, heading
for the spring-fed pools of the park. Most of the white-
winged doves and vultures had migrated back to Mexico in
the last few months, leaving the airways to ravens and
hawks. A phainopepla, feeding on mistletoe, chirruped

softly from atop a mesquite. Under our feet, streams of cut leaves and flowers, harvested and ported by ants, flowed like a green and violet river into the throat of a miniature sand volcano. Winter was coming.

Behind us, a shoe scuffed gravel. I turned just in time to see a man in a straw hat disappear among the creosote, cactus, and paloverde. Philo jogged off to check it out while I walked on, gripping my walking stick more firmly. He caught up a couple of minutes later.

"Not Morocho," he said. "But it might have been the guy Charley saw yesterday."

"Or just another walker, enjoying the morning. You've got me jumping at shadows."

"Good."

The path led past three ponds to a cluster of park buildings undergoing renovation. My senses were on high alert, as if someone were watching me. But I saw no one except a gardener, busy raking leaves. A curve-billed thrasher whistled from a palm at the edge of the pond. Last summer's leaves littered the depths where carp swam lazily. A large gold one surfaced, reminding me of my nightmare. I wouldn't let my mind go there.

"Tell me something?" I asked Philo.

"Depends," he said, leading the way onto a short bridge. Mallards and wood ducks swam toward us, turning away when we didn't toss bread.

"I feel as if I know you," I said. "But I don't. When I was little, you seemed so much older . . . and your hurt was so new—losing your parents, I mean. I didn't want to ask prying questions."

"None of you did. That's one of the reasons I was drawn to your family. You accepted me as I was. I could talk, or not talk—it made no difference . . . So what do you want to know?"

"Is Philo a family name?"

He ran his index finger along the rough wood of a post.

"You mean, why would any parents in their right minds saddle their son with a name that means 'love'?"

"Something like that." I watched a red-winged dragon-fly describe figure eights above the dark water.

He smiled. "My parents were hippies—peace, love, flower power. You know the drill. I lived in a commune in Oregon until I was five."

"Couldn't you use your middle name?"

"Can you see the other kids calling me Graevling? Grave, for short? It's my mother's family name."

"It has a lugubrious ring." An Anna's hummingbird paused for a moment on a twig, her iridescent green feathers catching the first rays of the rising sun. "I suppose it could have been worse—your last name could have been Valentine."

"Thank heavens for small favors."

"How is it that you've reached the venerable age of thirty-five without following in Kit's footsteps?"

"You mean, why don't I have a wife and 2.6 kids by now?" When I nodded, he went on: "I broke up with a woman last December. We'd been together seven years . . . We met after I got out of the service, when we were both in grad school. She's an engineer. After we graduated, we were concentrating on our careers." He paused, watching koi swim lazily under the bridge. "It never seemed the right time to make it permanent. She wanted the flexibility to take a transfer if it was offered. She got her wish. She's with a defense contractor in D.C. Distance didn't make her heart grow fonder. She hasn't had second thoughts about splitting up." He led the way off the bridge and onto a path that circled the ponds. "My turn?"

"I guess," I said warily.

"Why did you stay away so long?"

"You were there, Philo. You remember what it was like."

"I remember being happy to be included in the activities

of a normal family. My aunt and uncle never planned on being saddled with a child."

"You saw my brothers as friends and teammates. But there's a different chemistry when you live with them . . . Your best friend, Kit, was a typical older brother—responsible, to the point of being a control freak; always sure he was right; part defender of his siblings, part torturer of the unwary. With the twins, it was always two against one—unless Jamie was there. He and I were so close in age that we had a special bond from the start. I was the peacemaker, the bridge-builder, the lone female, the odd one out in their squabbles. It was survival of the fittest. I learned to fend for myself." I picked up a piece of palm bark and shredded it as we walked. "When I started dating, they went to the opposite extreme. Let me tell you, being surrounded by four overprotective brothers, not to mention a host of overprotective friends, would smother anyone. So I took the volleyball scholarship in California, played long enough to establish residency, and then threw myself into geology. It was an all-consuming passion that provided a different kind of family—brilliant oddballs and eccentrics, some of them, but tolerant of my foibles."

"I suspect that your father found much the same thing when he went into archaeology. And your mother among her poets."

"I suppose so. I hadn't thought about it. Anyway, I needed those twelve years to find out who I was apart from the MacFarlanes. But what allowed me to take risks and fail on my own was that, wherever I was and whatever I got myself into, I knew my family had my back. I only had to pick up the phone. With that foundation and confidence, I could face anything."

"And when you'd learned that, you came home." He glanced down at his watch.

"The bread!" I said. "I'll race you back."

* * *

The dapple gray was in the corral, but Cézar was nowhere about. Jamie was taking the bread from the oven when we opened the kitchen door. He seemed happier this morning, as if last night had broken a spell . . . or cast one. He whistled a song from *The King and I* as he dusted the bread with powdered sugar, then devoured two pieces on the way to his car.

I called the Zorya house, but no one picked up. A few minutes later, as Philo and I finished breakfast, the phone rang. Toni'd gotten Hector's forwarded e-mail and had asked Douglas PD to check it out. She and Keith were bringing over the dubbed copies of Angie's tape. While Philo gave her an update, I took down the aerial photographs from the clothesline. They were too warped to use with a stereoscope, but my geologic contacts, attitudes, and sample localities were intact.

"Do I smell baking bread?" Charley said behind me.

"Why don't you wear a bell so I can hear you coming?"

"And spoil the fun?"

"Pan de muerto," I said.

"Jumping the gun, aren't you? That's tomorrow."

"I couldn't sleep."

He grinned. "Now I wonder why that would be."

"You can have bread if you carry my photos into the house. Toni and the sketch artist will be here in a few minutes."

"And where will you be?"

"I'm going next door for a minute."

I took the back way in, walking up Soldier Wash and then crossing between the outbuildings. It was quiet as a chapel at four in the morning, which was odd. Construction workers in Tucson normally worked on Saturday. Thinking that Cézar or Miranda might be out on the patio, I circled around to the side garden. But this, too, was empty. The kitchen door was slightly ajar. I knocked and called, but there was no answer.

The guards were absent from their gatehouse, and the front door was open—just like the kitchen. What the hell was going on? Worried about Cézar, I went in, calling his name as I wandered through the kitchen, dining room, and living room.

They'd done a good job matching the new wings with the old adobe ranch house. Simple, dark, mission-style furniture from Mexico dominated the white-painted rooms. Woven wall hangings from Peru, pillows from Guatemala, carved and painted gourds and crosses, and beaded animal figures added touches of color. Votive candles flickered in niches, lighting *retablos* and the statues of saints. It was like being in a church.

I called again as I entered the bedroom wings, three rooms on each side, with doors opening on the central courtyard. Even the bedrooms were stark white, with splashes of red in Carla's room, sky blue in Miranda's, gold in Cézar's, and charcoal in Michael's. The guest rooms, in the middle of each wing, were beige on white.

Miranda's room was crowded with keepsakes, many of them religious, all carefully dusted. School pictures of Michael and Carla adorned one wall; a formal portrait of Cézar was on the bureau. No photos of her own family, not even her sister. It was as if Miranda's world had revolved forever around Cézar and his offspring.

Michael's quarters were simple, almost Spartan, as if he were rarely there. The only decoration was a black Madonna above the bed. A few clothes hung neatly in the spacious closet. He was partial to white shirts, black suits, and bolo ties.

On Cézar's dresser were photos of him with a couple of former governors, senators, and congressmen, a wedding picture, and a family portrait taken just after Carla was born. Carla's mother was not smiling . . . she looked as if her mind was elsewhere. Pushed to the back of the grouping was a black-and-white photo of a flamenco dancer. I thought at first it was Carla, but the yellowed clipping pasted to the back proved that it was taken in Spain forty years ago.

Carla's room had two posters on the wall—one of herself, dancing in Seville, and the other of the guitarist Alessandro. In this poster his hair was longer. He reminded me of the man who played at La Roca that night. On her dresser was a photo of herself with a blonde man. They looked young, and luminously happy. Curled up on Carla's bed was a black cat with white feet and amber eyes.

A deep walk-in closet stood open. I stepped inside. From the door at the back, a stairway led down into darkness . . . I'll just take a peek, I thought. Cézar might be down there having a heart attack. I flicked on the light and called Cézar's name as I went down the stairs. At the bottom was a large room that ran under the entire wing, like a bunker. But it wasn't cold. The long walls were mirrored; the dance floor was of wood. It was newly finished—a present, I guessed, for Carla.

At the near end was a bar with a sink, a small refrigerator, and cabinets full of glassware. A Tabriz-patterned Persian rug covered this part of the dance floor. Colorful floor pillows were stacked in the corner near a state-of-the-art music system. At the far end, built-in glass-fronted cabinets ran from floor to ceiling, and another stairway led, presumably, to Michael's room.

My shoes squeaked as I walked the length of the room . . . I pressed a switch on the wall. Soft light flooded the cabinets.

Carved pieces of jadeite and nephrite jade, from every corner of the world and in every color from white and lavender through the range of greens, surrounded the crown jewels of the collection: a heavy-lipped Olmec blue-jadeite mask; seven celts incised with the panther god; a necklace of beads carved into flowers; and a number of small carved figurines of weremen—half-panther, half-human. I wanted to touch the jade. I could have stood there for hours.

On either side, as if guarding the treasure trove, were cabinets of throwing knives, stilettos. Some were plain, some of Damascene inlay, others enameled or bejeweled. But all had long, narrow blades, efficient and deadly.

I heard a sound in the room above, Michael's room. I flicked off the lights, wrenched off my shoes, and ran silently back across the dance floor. I was at the top of Carla's stairs when the light came on below. I stepped into her closet and left the door as I'd found it. As quietly as I could, I let myself out into the courtyard, where the black cat swatted at something in the fountain. I sprinted for the safety of the wash. By the time I reached it, I was limping from the burrs and spines my socks had collected.

"Serves you right," said Philo, behind me.

I dropped my shoes. "That was you in the house?"

"Um-hmm. I thought we had an agreement."

"Call it a minor mutiny." I sat down on the bank, stripped off my socks, and put on my shoes.

"What stone was that mask carved from?" he asked me, as we started walking again.

"A form of translucent jadeite called Olmec Blue by gemstone dealers. The Olmecs were a mother civilization that lived along the Gulf Coast in ancient Mexico. But they had extensive trade routes all over Mesoamerica, and they handed down many of their beliefs and traditions to the civilizations that followed. We don't know that much about the Olmecs, but we know they treasured the blue jade, saving it for their finest carvings. It supposedly represented the sky, water, the breath of life—many things. For years, archaeologists couldn't identify the source area . . . until Hurricane Mitch swept through Guatemala in 1998, exposing jade outcrops around the Motagua River valley. What a find."

Philo was lost in thought. We didn't speak again until we reached home.

"No Cézar," said Philo, opening the front door. "And a house full of treasure left wide open. It doesn't look good. Any ideas?"

"We go to plan B."

"Refresh my memory."

"We show up at the restaurant and play it by ear . . . Do you suppose Michael's any good with those knives?"

"They might not be his, Frankie. They could belong to Cézar or Miranda."

"And I suspect any number of them might match the wound that killed Angie."

"Now there's a scary thought," he said.

Toni, Charley, and Keith were at the kitchen table. I poured a cup of coffee and took it out to the front patio. Philo joined me with the microcassette recorder. Toni brought the tapes.

"Ready?" Toni asked. It took me a minute to pull my mind back from Planet Mongo. I was still dazed by what I'd seen at the Zoryas. "Angie's tapes," she said, and started the recorder.

The first interview took place a week ago. A tag line at the beginning of the tape gave last Saturday's date, time, place (the Zorya shops), and subject of the article. Angie was researching the art of tarot. Miranda Xeres de la Frontera had been recommended by a friend.

"That's Carla's aunt," I said.

"The one who doctored your coffee," said Philo.

"The world's getting smaller all the time," I said.

It was disconcerting, at first, to listen to Angie's voice, a voice from the grave. I recognized Miranda's odd, sibilant tones, more pronounced on the tape. The information she gave Angie was interesting, but one could hear a similar spiel any night down on Fourth Avenue. Miranda, however, moved on to offer Angie a free reading. But it wasn't from any deck I'd seen used. Miranda called her deck "healing" cards, and talked about animals—lizard, owl, buffalo, and others. Angie asked if the deck had a death card.

"No," said Miranda. "Only rebirth . . . renewal."

I heard Angie shuffle the cards, and then the sounds of three cards being dealt. A long interval of silence followed. "Quail, weasel, ant," Angie said. "But the cards are inverted. Does that mean anything?"

"Everything has meaning—a cloud covering the sun, the track of a coyote, a buzzard circling . . . everything. The first card, the past, suggests that you were in an unhealthy, downward spiral . . . from substance abuse perhaps? Things were out of control."

"Go on."

"The second card, the present, suggests that you are involved in some matter that involves intrigue, stealth. The third card, the future . . . advises you to be careful. There are those who would take advantage of you. Do not be too trusting, young Angelisa. The world is filled with those who would trick you."

Another long pause, as if Angie were disconcerted by Miranda's familiarity and the warnings. "Thank you," Angie said at last. "I'll be careful."

"One last thing, child. Your ring . . . the craftsmanship is lovely. Can you tell me where you purchased it?"

"It belonged to my mother—my birth mother. It was on a chain around my neck when I was abandoned. It has a name inscribed inside . . . Juanita. But I haven't been able to find her."

"How sad for you." I heard bells tinkle in the background. "A customer. I must excuse myself . . . But I have enjoyed our talk very much. Would you like to continue it over tea at my home? Tomorrow afternoon, perhaps?"

"I'd like that very much," Angie said, and switched off the tape recorder.

"That reading was why she left the tapes and the note for me to find," I said, rewinding the tape. "Miranda warned her to be careful, and she took the words to heart."

"Not careful enough or she wouldn't have gone alone to meet a stranger who claimed to be her father," Toni said.

"But she wasn't alone. She'd asked Hector to keep an eye on her." I put in the second tape. It was recorded at the Zorya house last Sunday afternoon. How odd to think she'd been next door while I was making lamb curry.

Angie and Miranda had tea outside with Cézar. I could hear a cactus wren's chatter in the background, the chirping of a cardinal, and, once, the throaty whir of a roadrunner. They talked about Angie's search for her birth mother. She knew only that she'd been left at a hospital by a beautiful woman with long black hair. Angie presumed her first name was Juanita, the name engraved in her ring.

This was followed by the clatter of a teacup against a saucer. "What?" Angie asked. "What did I say?"

"Nothing, my dear," said Cézar. "Now, if you'll excuse me, I'm very tired." This was followed by the scraping of a metal chair against flagstone.

"I didn't mean to offend him," Angie said.

"You brought back memories, that is all . . . memories of my sister, also called Juanita. She was more restless than her husband. Roots and tethers made her unhappy. She left us, for a while, but she was no happier when she returned. She died less than a year later, after her daughter was born . . . You bear a strong resemblance to them both."

Angie was silent.

"Yes, my dear. And when Juanita returned to us, the ring Cézar had given her was gone . . . the ring you wear."

"Cézar is not my father?"

"No. Your father was Kalé—a Spanish gypsy, as restless as your mother. They met here in Tucson, when he hired on as day labor for Cézar. Juanita went with him, leaving a son behind. He was only three."

"Did you look for me?" Angie asked.

"No. I did not wish to hurt Cézar even more than he had been hurt. You would have reminded him of what he'd lost—and to whom."

The tape captured footsteps approaching through the house. A man's voice, a baritone—not Cézar's soft tenor. "Do not count on me for supper, Tía. I have an—"

"Michael, may I introduce Angelisa Corday?"

Silence. He must have noticed how much she looked like Carla. But he recovered quickly. "A pleasure, Ms. Corday. Tía, I have to go. We will talk later, hmm?"

The taped clicked off. How frustrating. Whatever else the three might have said or done would remain a mystery.

"Well, that explains why I was confused when I saw Angie's body," I said. "The ring was identical to the one Carla wears . . . and they're half sisters . . . or whole. I wonder how many months after Juanita returned Carla was born?"

"I don't know," said Philo. "But lunch should be interesting."

CHAPTER 25

TERESA RODE UP ON HER BICYCLE, HELMET DANG-ling from the handlebars, just as Keith and Charley came out with the sketch. She stripped off her gloves and unstrapped a hunting knife from her calf. The rash of murders had made her as careful as the rest of us.

"Ready for the race?" I asked her.

"I will be." She looked at the sketch. The straw cowboy hat threw shadow over the subject's face. "That looks like the hat that's hanging in the tack room. Same bite out of the brim."

I was no help. I hadn't been in the tack room since I returned to Tucson. But when we checked, the hat was gone, along with some of the windfall apples Teresa had left in a basket on the table.

"Anything else missing?" Toni asked.

"A blue long-sleeved canvas shirt," Teresa said.

"He was wearing it," said Charley. "Might explain why he ran off."

"Well," Toni said, "I'll keep this in the file anyway. Let me know if he shows again."

The group dispersed, Charley and Teresa to spend the day with Rosa's clan, Toni and Keith back to work. It was only nine.

"Is there anything you need to be doing right now?" I asked Philo.

"Your wish is my command—within reason."

"Will you take me down to your target range?" Though there were guns at the house, I hadn't practiced since I was twelve, when the family sold the old MacFarlane ranch.

"Getting spooked?"

"After last night and this morning, yes."

"Just name your weapon."

"Pistols." A gun wouldn't protect me from a bomber, but it might even the odds a bit with a knife thrower.

A gusty wind was blowing as we drove down Houghton Road. Dust devils appeared and disappeared like smoke signals on the valley floor. The golden air obscured the Santa Ritas to the south. It tasted gritty.

We turned left on Valencia and drove a short distance to Desert Trails. The facility had separate ranges for pistols, rifles, and archery. Philo was a member, but I was an outsider, and treated as such. I paid the guest fee, signed the waiver, bought ammunition at the store, and put on my plastic badge. At the pistol range, in the shade of an awning, I helped Philo load the two weapons he'd brought—a Smith and Wesson .38 Special Combat Masterpiece and a Model 100 Beretta. Shell casings littered the dirt and concrete pad. I put in my earplugs. After half an hour with each gun, I decided I preferred the Beretta. It fit my hand and had less recoil. More importantly, it put more bullets in the center of the target. I took out the clip, checked the chamber, set down the gun, and became aware of a small knot of men behind us.

"Not bad," said one.

"I'd treat her nice if I were you," said a second.

Philo grinned. "I'll keep that in mind."

"Come back anytime," said the owner, when I turned in my badge.

At twelve-forty-five, after showering off the gunpowder residue, I locked the front door and joined Philo at the pickup. He wore pale gray slacks with a forest-green knit shirt. I'd changed into a turquoise silk blouse, black linen pants, and sandals. I'd even used a little makeup—mascara and lipstick, nothing fancy. He reacted as if it were the first time he'd ever seen me in anything but field clothes. "You look nice," he said.

I ignored the surprise in his voice. "You clean up pretty well yourself."

Sensing that I was not looking forward to this meeting, he hustled me into the truck.

The Eclectic Cafe's tucked away at the eastern edge of a refurbished strip mall on Tanque Verde Road. It was one of the few establishments that hadn't changed hands or locations while I'd been away. Best of all, the menu still carried my favorites. The place was so popular they'd put tables outside, with an overhead mist system for hot days and blinds that could be lowered for shade.

Having found that Cézar's house was deserted, the doors standing open, I'd half-expected him to stand me up. But the smaller of his two guards sat at the table closest to the Eclectic's front door. The gatekeeper, I presumed. Cézar was inside, looking unperturbed, seated with a younger man at a circular booth in the back.

"I tried to call and reschedule this morning, Mr. Zorya," I said. "I have a . . . houseguest this weekend." I introduced Philo.

"But Mr. Dain is most welcome to join us, Ms. MacFarlane." Cézar apologized for not standing, an impossibility in that booth. "This is my son, Michael. And I think you have already met my driver, Bruno."

Bruno was the gate guard who'd been cloned from a water tower. He was sitting at a nearby table with a good view of the front door.

I shook Michael's hand. His nails were carefully kept, if slightly long. But his fingers were calloused, which surprised me. I didn't take him for a man who worked with his hands. "It's Francisca," I said. "Call me Frankie."

I sat across from Michael. He looked familiar, somehow . . . but then I remembered I'd seen his photograph in Miranda's room. His face was striking, rather than handsome, framed by short, wavy black hair with the faintest hint of silver at the sides. When he turned to talk to his father, I noticed his neck was a lighter shade than the bronze of his face, as if he'd recently cut his hair. The pleasantries and smiles of greeting didn't reach his eyes. He was here under duress, I guessed. He would hold his personality in check, presenting nothing but this smiling mask.

The men took a few minutes to read the menu. I already knew what I wanted, so I studied father and son. The family resemblance was strongest in their eyes—eyes that reminded me of chatoyant minerals, with bands of light that shifted as they moved so that they seemed ever watchful, yet revealed nothing. Cézar's were the golden brown of tiger's-eye; Michael's, the dark blue-gray of hawk's-eye. Carla's, I remembered, were the deep red-brown of ox-eye . . . and Tía Miranda's? Pale green cat's-eye. I wondered what color Juanita's eyes had been.

"What do you do?" I asked Michael, after we ordered our food.

He smiled. "I search the world for precious objects. My clients have money and a love of rare things, but lack time to search for themselves."

"For example?"

"Flawless emeralds, old coins, Fabergé eggs and dinosaur eggs, Stradivarius violins, rare books and stamps, carved ivory, jade."

"What was the oddest object you were hired to find?"

He thought for a moment, twiddling his teaspoon between thumb and forefinger. "An Egyptian sarcophagus carved from rose-colored granite. My client, a small man with a large ego and an even larger bank balance, wanted to be buried in it. I sold the prior occupant to a museum—one that asked few questions."

"And what was the oldest?"

"My father tells me you are a geologist, yes? It was something you would treasure—a piece of moon rock."

"But they're kept under lock and key."

"Haven't you discovered yet, Francisca, that everything's for sale? You just have to negotiate a price."

"Everything?"

"Animal, vegetable, and mineral."

I shook my head. I wasn't that jaded, and never wanted to be. My lunch arrived, Leo's Special Chicken Burro, enchilada style, with tomatillo sauce. I was glad I'd eaten a light breakfast.

"So is it the search, the negotiation, or the cat-and-mouse game with Customs that you enjoy most?" I asked Michael.

"None of the above."

What else was there? I wondered.

"For me," Philo said, entering the conversation for the first time, "it would be touching and holding, even for a short time, something unique and exquisite. I wouldn't want the burden of owning it, the responsibility of protecting such an object. But to hold it? To connect with the craftsman who created it, the history of its journey? Now *that* could be addictive."

Michael nodded. "True. Things, however beautiful and rare, can come to own you if you are not careful. As for being addictive . . . also true, but blessedly without the physical repercussions." Michael took three small folded squares of paper from his pocket and tossed them down in front of me. "Go ahead, open them."

I set down my fork and carefully unfolded the first square of heavy ivory stock. Inside, the cabochon-cut star ruby was the size of a mourning dove's egg, split lengthwise. I silently passed the paper to Philo. He raised his left eyebrow as he saw the play of light across the surface. The second square held the largest star sapphire I'd ever seen. Michael watched me closely. This was some kind of test. I wondered what Philo was thinking as I opened the third. The deep green oval-cut faceted stone was perhaps two centimeters long. It was carved with a coat of arms surrounded by Cyrillic letters. I lifted it out of its paper nest and held it up to the light of the window. The color deepened. I picked up the candle from the center of the table: the color shifted to fiery red, rich and pure.

"An alexandrite," I said, handing it to Philo. "One of the rarest gemstones in the world. Named for Tsar Alexander II because it was discovered in Russia on the day he ascended the throne."

"He wore this in a signet ring. It was one of the first rough stones to be cut and polished. That is his crest," Michael said.

"Carla has a lovely alexandrite ring," I said, as Philo passed the gem to Cézar.

Cézar nodded. "There were two. I gave the first one to Michael's mother when he was born. They had been handed down in my mother's family for generations." He paused, as if the memory was not a happy one. "An ancestor was a slave in the original mine. He escaped with a few rough stones. I come from a family of metalworkers. The stones were set in silver and gold."

"Where was your family from?"

"Until the fall of 1941, we roamed the Volga Republic. Then the Germans came. I was only six years old. They killed my father and his brothers, herded the others into a boxcar. My older brother, Mikail, and I were down at the river when they came. When the train was loaded, we climbed on top of the boxcar. I remember it was very cold, very dark. My mother handed coats to us through the vent. We planned to let everyone out when it stopped, but it pulled off on a siding in the middle of the night. They unloaded the car and shot everyone, even my sister. They didn't want to be bothered transporting them. What were a few gypsies, more or less?"

Cézar stared into the alexandrite as if it held the past. "There was nothing Mikail and I could do. We rode on the car until it slowed for a steep grade. We jumped off and ran into the woods, traveling south, stealing food from gardens, sleeping in the forest and fields. We found another Rom camp. They took us in . . . until they, too, were rounded up and deported to Kazakhstan, my brother with them. I had been out collecting firewood. Then I was alone . . . But mother had the sight. She knew what would happen. In the lining of the coat I found gold coins and gems . . . and the two rings. I made my way to a port, stowed away on a boat, and ended up in Spain. The Kalé took me in. That was where, much later, I met my wife." Tears glinted in Cézar's eyes as he looked at his son. "For years Michael has searched for my brother. He found no trace . . . My people lost everything, Francisca," he said, as the server refilled our drinks. "Over and over again. 'And when we lost, we wept . . .'"

" 'And when we wept, we sang,' " Michael continued, adding, "and when we sang, we danced."

We all were silent, reminded, I think, of Carla who danced the flamenco.

"We often speak in proverbs, a habit my father learned as a boy in the Soviet Union," Michael said. "Do you know why oppressed peoples so often resort to proverbs, Francisca?"

I shook my head. I'd never thought about it.

"I read a theory that it's safer. There are so many layers of meaning that can be conveyed with subtle changes of

voice tone and body language—just as in dance or music.
The words of a proverb are simple and true on the surface,
but they hold infinite possibilities of meaning and social
commentary for people who live where freedom is re-
stricted. And for people like the Rom, or the Jews, who
have been oppressed and on the move for more than a mil-
lennium, the need for proverbs is great."

We were silent for a time, digesting this. Around us, in
contrast, people laughed and talked.

"What led you into the antiquities business, Michael?"
Philo asked, breaking the silence.

"I had a flair for languages, a love of travel and research, degrees in art history and archaeology, a knack for
dealing with people, and a photographic memory. During
school breaks, I worked for museums. After graduation,
Sotheby's Paris. At an auction of jade and ivory, one bidder
seemed so distraught at losing a particular netsuke that I
offered to find her a similar piece. I already knew where
the piece was. It was simply a matter of agreeing on a
price. That was ten years ago . . . And you, Mr. Dain? What
is your line of work?"

"Please call me Philo, Michael. I recover what people
have lost."

This was news to me, but I tried not to let it show.

"Mostly white-collar crime," Philo continued, "fraud,
money laundering, industrial espionage. But I also handle
personal losses—jewels, boats, money, securities, stolen
identities . . . and occasionally, children and spouses."

"So, Philo," Michael said, spooning sugar into his coffee, "what is the . . . sexiest thing you ever recovered?"

"Literally?"

"Or figuratively."

"Literally speaking, the trophy wife of an aging CEO.
She'd signed a stiff prenuptial agreement, and when the
trophy tarnished in less than a year, she faked her own kid-
napping. My fee was a lot less than the ransom demand."

"I'll bet," I said, under my breath. Cézar's eyes crinkled at the corners. His hearing was fine.

"And figuratively?" Michael asked.

Philo thought for a few seconds. "Depends on your definition of sexy."

"It is, I admit, an individual response. But let us say, for argument's sake, that the object evokes a desire that tugs at you, deep inside . . . and the memory of it lingers long after you part company."

"Then I'd have to say an Arabic enameled dagger reputed to have belonged to T. E. Lawrence. There was something about it . . . I can't explain."

"And you returned it to its owner?" Michael's fork made little furrows in an extra napkin.

"I'm not at liberty to say."

"I would like to hire you, Mr. Dain," Cézar said.

I set my glass down so quickly the water sloshed onto the Formica. Philo stopped the flood with his napkin. Michael's hands stilled.

"I want you to find someone—" Cézar began.

"Be patient, Papa. My contacts—"

Cézar's look stopped Michael midsentence. "Finding rare objects is different than finding people, Michael. It uses different skills, different resources."

I watched the shutters come down on Michael's face. It's Carla, I thought, as Cézar turned back to Philo and handed him a business card. "It is important, Mr. Dain. My condition worsens, the doctors tell me. You will do this thing for me?"

Philo hesitated. "It depends on who it is and if I have to travel."

"I will give you the details so you may decide. Agreed?"

"I'll listen."

To give them privacy, Michael and I waited outside the glass doors of the restaurant. Grackles squawked and strutted across the parking lot. A red-tailed hawk circled above the recreation center across the street.

"You look somber, Francisca. Did my father's story upset you?"

"Yes."

"Save your feelings for someone who deserves them."

I was taken aback by the harshness in his tone, the edge and intensity. Tension vibrated in the atmosphere around him, triggering my fight-or-flight instinct. But I refused to run. Instead, I held his eyes, searching them for answers, finding none. I looked away first.

A heavy silence lay between us until the door opened and Cézar broke the spell. "Devils live in quiet pools," he said.

"As you say, Papa."

"And now, if you have time, Michael will show you our shops," said Cézar.

I saw the muscles tighten around Michael's mouth. "We'd be delighted," I said. "Shall we meet you there?"

"Certainly. I will join you in a few minutes," said Cézar. "I must make a few phone calls first."

Michael excused himself, strode rapidly to a white Miata, and roared off. I recognized the license number. It was the same car that had run me off the road two days before.

CHAPTER 26

THE ZORYA SHOPS WERE SET BACK FROM TANQUE Verde Road in a strip mall with a Santa Fe–style facade. Michael's car was there, but he hadn't waited outside for us.

Brass bells jangled when we opened the door of Tía Miranda's Arte Folklorico, but no one appeared to greet us. Glass cases of Native American jewelry and carved-stone fetishes vied for floor space with furniture, clothing, fabrics, pottery, and carvings from Central and South America. Through the connecting door to the rare-arts shop, I could see Michael talking on the phone.

"Let's split up," I suggested. "I'll take Miranda."

While Philo checked out Michael's domain, I pushed open the batwing doors into a back room. At the same moment, a horn honked outside, and Miranda opened the top half of a door to the alley behind the mall. A small, dark-haired woman got out of a battered truck. Miranda gave me a less than welcoming nod before turning to greet her in a language I didn't recognize. Miranda checked her eyes, her palms and fingernails, rubbed a lock of her hair between thumb and forefinger. Meanwhile, no one watched the high-priced goods in the front part of the store. Someone could have stolen her blind, and I didn't think she'd have cared. That was Carla's and Michael's business. This was hers.

Miranda took her time at the door. I suspected she wanted to keep me waiting—a power trip. I refused to play, entertaining myself instead by browsing among the merchandise. Pottery bowls, plastic bins, and baskets of every size and weave cluttered the shelves that lined Miranda's inner sanctum. They contained amulets of pewter and "genuine" stainless steel, colored glass markers for games, heaps of beaded bracelets, copper rings, and crystals, spheres, obelisks, and pyramids. The effect was a rainbow of color: amethyst, rose, and citrine quartz, turquoise and chrysocolla, malachite and azurite, rhodonite and rhodochrosite, hematite, amazonite and moonstone, jasper, agate, and bloodstone. One corner contained boxed sets of tarot cards, and books on astrology, tarot, palmistry, numerology, and herbology. In another, bins held small cellophane packages of dried chili peppers for cooking and various herbs and spices labeled "For potpourri or soapmaking. DO NOT INGEST." I wondered what the lower cabinets contained—eye of Gila monster and hair of javelina?

I sat at a small round table covered by a black wool shawl embroidered in shades of rose and gold. While I thought about the discussion at lunch, I idly shuffled the oversize tarot deck on display. Not a classical deck, but one with animal symbols . . . perhaps the same deck Miranda had used for Angie's reading just one week ago. I could hear Angie's voice asking if inverted cards meant anything. "Everything has meaning," Miranda had replied, "a cloud covering the sun, the track of a coyote, a buzzard circling . . . everything."

I watched Miranda take a basket from a stack in the

corner. In it she placed a couple of small cellophane packets, an amethyst crystal, and a holy card. The woman exchanged a cloth-covered basket for Miranda's. With a bob of the head and a spate of words, she turned away. No money changed hands. There would be no bookkeeping.

"Double-yolk eggs," Miranda exclaimed, lifting the cloth from the basket. "And fresh *mole* sauce." She saw the cards I was studying. "You are curious, eh?" She set the basket aside and took up the deck, shuffling efficiently. Handing them back, she said, "Choose five."

I shuffled them again, spread them facedown on the table, and chose five at random. I set them down in a line, right to left. She reorganized them into a cross, the last card in the center, then turned them over: coyote, opossum, antelope, lizard . . . The lizard and coyote were upside down. She turned over the center card, badger, and drew back with a start.

"What?" I said, as she abruptly got up from the table.

She ignored the question. From a basket, she took a chunk of turquoise, used by Native American healers to ward off evil. I watched her slip it into the pocket of her apron. I asked more questions, but received only baffling, disjointed replies about 'possums and lizards. Then she selected a clear quartz crystal and took two cellophane packets from a low cupboard. She handed these to me. I fumbled for my wallet.

"No," she said. "Take them. They are gifts." And she hustled me into Michael's store.

Michael was showing Philo and Cézar old Roman coins. Bruno lounged by the door. My eyes were drawn to the lighted display case that ran the length of the wall behind him. It held jade—intricately carved scenes and statues, necklaces, pendants, and rings—Asian, primarily, with a few pre-Columbian pieces. But no Olmec blue jade.

"You like jade?" Michael unlocked the cabinet and took out an exquisite hexagonal box, roughly ten centimeters in diameter, with a bas-relief scene carved on the lid. He handed me a loupe. The expressions on the faces at the Chinese court had been captured to perfection—greed, furtiveness, lust, anger, pride, gluttony. And in one corner sat a scribe, recording the scene.

"It's stunning," I said.

"T'ang dynasty. Seventh century."

"I've never seen one like it."

"I prefer one-of-a-kind pieces."

I decided to prod him a little. "You have no blue jade in the case."

"You know of it? It is very rare indeed. The Olmec treasured blue jade above all other materials, believing it represented the life force. Or so I am told. There's a wonderful collection in D.C., perhaps the best outside of Mexico. Have you seen it?"

"Just photos, unfortunately." I thought of the photos in Carla's purse, the bracelet she gave to the vendor on the beach, the mask and celts in the Zorya house. "But someone recently mentioned a blue-jade bracelet and a mask. I thought you might know something about them or have similar pieces, large or small."

He knew I was testing him, but not why. He chose his words carefully. "I do not know of any pieces that are currently on the market, but I will let you know if I hear of something. Now, you will excuse me?"

Miranda seemed relieved when Philo and I approached the front door. Cézar and Bruno followed us out to where the smaller bodyguard waited. I stopped for a moment to let my eyes adjust to the brilliant sunlight, fumbling in my purse for my dark glasses. Rubber squealed on asphalt as an SUV tore at us from the far end of the parking lot. I glanced toward the sound, took a step, and halted abruptly as the vehicle drew abreast of us. It was a dark green Range Rover. The man in the front passenger seat had a phone to his ear. He looked at me and smiled.

And then the world exploded.

CHAPTER 27

AMBER GLASS FROM WALL LAMPS AND PIECES OF Michael's Miata rained down on us. I heard the SUV make a squealing U-turn and speed west on Tanque Verde. Police sirens blared in the distance.

We were the only ones in the parking lot. Miraculously, the metal shards had missed me, but both bodyguards were bleeding from small cuts on their heads and hands. Philo was lying six feet away, shielding Cézar. Philo lifted his head and looked at me. Tiny slivers of glass made dancing prisms in his hair. "You okay?" he asked. I nodded.

"Papa?" Michael ran down the steps.

"I am in better shape than your car," Cézar said, as Michael helped him to his feet.

Philo got up, then . . . gracefully, too, damn him. My dignity and my silk blouse were in shreds from skidding across the pavement. Two squad cars closed off the parking lot, leaving only enough room for the ambulances and fire trucks to get through. It was a three-ring circus and we were the main attraction.

"That makes five bombs," I said to Philo. Though I tried to be nonchalant, my voice shook. "Did you see the license number of that Range Rover?"

"Arizona plate. I didn't catch the number."

"Well, I could swear Morocho was riding shotgun. And there were three in the backseat," I said.

Cézar sighed and rubbed his left arm. "My daughter and your brother. A man sat between them. I believe he held a gun."

A knot of tension grew in my stomach as I waited for the police to sort things out. It took awhile. They weren't about to be rushed. After seeing the bodyguards into ambulances, they drove the rest of us to the sheriff's office a block away. Deputies separated us for interviews. I sat at a wood-grained Formica table in a small cream-colored room. A tape recorder whispered as I gave my statement to Deputy Schwartz. I explained that I didn't know why anyone would want to blow up Michael Zorya's car. I gave him descriptions of Jamie, Carla, and the man in the right front seat. But while I answered Schwartz's questions with the logical part of my mind, I kept my emotions locked away in a separate compartment. There would be time to let them out later, when I was alone.

Afterward, I joined Michael in the lobby as we waited for Philo and Cézar to finish. Michael didn't acknowledge me as I sat down next to him. His eyes remained closed, and he alternately rubbed his forehead and his neck. He had to be as sick about the situation as I was. If Cézar was right, my brother and Carla were being held by the man who had killed Hector. I didn't know why the man wanted Jamie and Carla, but I was sure their danger increased with every passing second. Yet I couldn't think of any way to help them. I had never felt quite so helpless.

"If that was Carla in the car, I'm sorry," I said at last.

Michael opened his eyes. "Thank you. And if it was

your brother with her, I also am sorry . . . Are you
hurt?"

"Just scraped a little. It could be worse."

"You could be dead, Francisca."

I didn't want to enter that place where I'd stowed my
emotions. I stared out the glass doors toward the parking lot,
trying not to think about Jamie and Carla. It didn't work. To
distract myself, I said the first thing that came to mind. "Tell
me how it works, this trade in priceless objects."

Thrown off-kilter by the change of subject, Michael
searched for an answer.

"Isn't that amount of money a bit bulky to carry
around," I prompted, "not to mention, a dead giveaway?"

"It is deposited with a *hawala*."

"What's that?"

"A money-transfer system. It began in Southeast Asia
and was adopted by the Arabs."

"Do you have to be Muslim to use the service?"

He gave one of those European little shrugs that says it
all. "The Arabs have always been traders, and the Rom net-
work is extensive. Some are Christian, some are Muslim. I
speak their languages, know their customs, have studied
their religions. I use the appropriate contacts. I never touch
the money."

"Never?"

"Never. Money is delivered to a local *hawala* who contacts an agent where I'm going. At that end, the agent de-
livers cash to the seller. I authenticate the purchase and
depart with it. They receive a percentage. Everyone is
happy."

"No awkward questions. No paperwork."

"An old-fashioned handshake still works, or a cup of
coffee or tea . . . though, if I'm actually transporting the
object, I usually insist on a bill of sale—net cost, of
course—made out to whomever has possession of the object. My name never appears. It is only a formality—for

the journey. The seller does not declare the sale. Nor do I, unless it is for my father's store. I'm simply a courier."

"A courier who stops off in Switzerland or the Cayman Islands on the way home and makes a deposit."

"On the next trip, actually. I cannot accept my payment in good faith until I deliver the object."

"Honor among thieves."

"I am not a thief, Francisca. I pay fair market value for the object and have it transported."

"Across the border."

"Across many borders, sometimes."

"For a fee."

"A finder's fee and expenses, yes. They increase with the number of borders I need to cross and the difficulty of transporting the object. The smaller the object, the easier it is."

"Naturally. Aren't you ever stopped?"

"Of course. Then I show them my business license and the bill of sale."

Silence. "Some of the most precious things in the world are crudely made or carved or faceted, Francisca, and so old that the refined techniques of machines and assembly lines haven't been applied. Only art experts and perhaps archaeologists wouldn't dismiss them out of hand. And honest archaeologists know nothing of an object's monetary value. They are lost in the mists of history."

Or prehistory. I thought of the crudely carved basalt head among the onyx baubles that Jorge had given Carla. Tiny. Easily dismissed, even by one trained to notice the different, rare object amid the dross . . . And then there was the blue-jade bracelet. "How did Jorge fit in?" I asked bluntly.

"Who?"

"Jorge García Desierto. We found his body in Mexico."

"Ah. They did not tell me his name, only that he was the brother of the fishing boat's captain."

"He gave trinkets, postcards, and a small basalt carving to Carla in exchange for a blue-jade bracelet."

"Did he? Then perhaps he was a courier."

"Like you?"

"As you say."

"Did you kill him?"

"No. I have killed in self-defense, but never for sport or pleasure. A sadist killed that man and left him for the sharks. I have been called many names, Francisca. Sadist is not one of them."

"But you know who did kill him?"

"I suspect. And he is untouchable, for the moment."

"What about Angelisa Corday?"

"I could not kill my sister—my half sister," he amended.

"Miranda told you."

"I guessed. She and Carla were very much alike."

"Do you mind?"

"My mother," he said, with a bitter twist of the lips, "the lovely Juanita, missed the freedom she'd known before my father settled here in Tucson. One day when I was three, they tell me, a group of Kalé stopped by to trade with Tía Miranda. My father hired one man as day labor. My mother left with him that night. She was away for more than two years . . . until her lover tired of her." He studied his hands as if they belonged to a stranger. "My father took her back. He did not know she'd had a daughter, had put her up for adoption . . . And Cézar believes to this day that Carla is his, though my aunt suggested otherwise, later . . . after my mother died. He never forgave Tía for that . . . I found her, you know—my mother—in the swimming pool . . . I was five." He rubbed his forehead as if he could banish the pain. "Postpartum depression, they called it. But I think her heart was broken."

"I'm sorry," I said. But he was too lost in memory to hear me.

"When Carla was a child, my father gave all his energy

and attention to building his business. Carla had Tía Miranda, but Tía was part of the problem . . . She didn't want Carla to turn out like our mother. Juanita was a dancer in Spain before my father brought her to America. I have memories of my mother, dancing just for me, flamenco music playing in the background. But Carla had no memories, only a sense of abandonment . . . My mother lacked the mothering instinct, Francisca. My father should have married Tía Miranda. She raised us. And she always loved him."

I now understood Michael's resentment toward his father. Cézar had created a vacuum around him, withholding his attention and affection from Michael, as well. "Did Miranda tell Carla that Cézar wasn't her birth father?" I asked him.

"Yes, when she was fifteen—though I am still not convinced it is the truth. But Carla believed her. She became moody, angry—more so than normal for a teenager. She went to college, but dropped out after three years. She spent all her time and energy on dance . . . until she fell in love. He was . . . inappropriate. A drug dealer. Scum. He was killed by a hit-and-run driver as they walked along the edge of the freeway. His car had run out of gas. Carla was convinced my father arranged it."

"Did he?"

"I don't know. He's capable of it." Michael stared at a tiny jumping spider that was crawling down the front window. "Isn't that a terrible thing to say about your father?"

"Yes," I said. "Did Carla leave?"

"Not then. She stayed, but withdrew from us emotionally. She had bouts of anger, and spells where she lost touch with reality. The doctors called them fugues. We put her in treatment. The psychiatrist diagnosed a detachment disorder, brought on by trauma." Michael stopped, as if his mind were drifting back to that scene. "Carla became even more dependent on me. When I was traveling, her condition worsened. Dancing was the only thing that seemed to help. The doctor recommended taking her away from Tucson, so we went to Spain, back to our mother's people, where Carla could focus on her dance. I could work just as easily from there ... She immersed herself in training, working with the masters. The talent was in her blood, our mother's only gift to her. Through flamenco, my sister rediscovered a sense of self-worth, a reason to live. And she finally gained the attention and approval she craved—from audiences, yes, but from my father, most of all."

Philo and Cézar arrived, interrupting Michael's reminiscences. I saw Toni approach the front door with my inquisitor from Mexico, *agente de policía* Gallegos-Martínez. He nodded at me without speaking and sized up my companions.

"Sorry I couldn't get here sooner," Toni said.

"Have you found them?" I asked, getting right to the point.

"No, but we've put out an alert for a green Range Rover with Arizona plates, heading west, with hostages inside," Toni said. "I'll be notified if anyone spots it."

"My father is not well. I'd like to take him home to rest, if you don't mind. You can reach us there," Michael said. And without waiting for a reply, he turned and escorted his father outside.

Gallegos-Martínez watched them leave. Michael hadn't even acknowledged his presence.

CHAPTER 28

TONI USHERED US INTO THE LARGEST INTERROGA-
tion room. "Officer Gallegos-Martínez is investigating
Carla Zorya's disappearance," she said, making the intro-
ductions.

"Señorita MacFarlane and I have already met," said
Gallegos-Martínez, extending his hand. His grip was firm,
his palms calloused, as if he'd been digging ditches recently.
Or graves. "It was the night Carla Zorya disappeared."

"I remember," I said. It seemed we'd found Carla today,
only to lose her again—and this time, my brother as well. I
turned to Toni. "So what do we do now?"

"First, we need to cross-check what Cézar Zorya saw."
Toni pushed a phone across the table to me. "You can help
by calling the hospital to see if Jamie's at work. And check
your messages at home, while you're at it. I'm going to
have the Zoryas do the same, in case there's been a ransom
demand. I'll be back in a minute."

With a brief nod, Gallegos-Martínez followed Toni out,
leaving Philo and me alone.

Philo pondered a squashed fly on the wall while I called. No messages at home. Jamie wasn't there, or at the hospital. He'd left the hospital in a hurry, just before noon. No, he hadn't said where he was going. I hung up, feeling depressed, and tried my brother Kit's home number. I had to leave a message on the answering machine. Ditto at Kit's law office. Ditto for Charley and Teresa at the bunkhouse. No one stayed home on a beautiful Saturday afternoon.

Toni and Gallegos-Martínez were back in ten minutes. "No luck?" she asked. I shook my head. "The Zoryas haven't heard anything either," she said. "But Douglas PD called. They matched Hector's building plan to a Zorya facility, CZ-Storage. They checked out the southeast corner, units 12 and 13. They were empty."

"Nonetheless, it's an odd coincidence."

"Don't worry, Frankie, I'll ask them about it."

We all watched Toni scribble in her notebook. Philo spoke up for the first time—but it wasn't to me or Toni. "When did Carla cross the border?" he asked Gallegos-Martínez.

"Yesterday afternoon. I was told last night," Gallegos-Martínez said.

"Michael Zorya said he'd stashed Carla in a motel on Tanque Verde and Sabino Canyon Roads," Toni added.

"But that's almost next door to where we ate lunch!" I said.

"Ironic, isn't it," Toni said. "Michael was going to take Cézar there after you finished lunch. But then Cézar asked him to show you and Philo the stores." She consulted her notes. "We checked out the motel. Jamie's car was parked around back, hidden from the street."

He must have arrived while we were nearby, having lunch. What would have happened if Michael and Cézar had gone there instead of the shops? Would it have made any difference? Would they be prisoners of Morocho right now . . . or dead?

"Do you know where Carla's been for three weeks?" I asked Gallegos-Martínez.

"*Sí*. Let me go back for a moment . . . We began questioning people that same night. They were reluctant to talk—more so than usual. But over time, rumors came to me. They all led back to a man named Reyerto. Ramon Reyerto."

"An independently wealthy businessman," Toni said, anticipating my question. "Works out of his home in Nogales, Sonora. Calls himself an investment advisor, but he doesn't deal with stocks, bonds, and securities—at least not directly. He's a middle-man, a broker of sorts. Say you're a corporation or business with a lot of money to invest. For a one-time fee, a percentage of the transaction, he puts you together with someone who wants to sell something or who needs an influx of cash in return for a partnership—a silent partnership, more often than not. Real estate, construction, casinos, bus companies, banks, lending institutions, catering trucks . . . He doesn't negotiate the deals, he leaves that to the lawyers and accountants. He's a kind of matchmaker. His name came up during the investigation of Mark Giovanni's murder. We think Giovanni reneged on paying his fee. Reyerto made an example of him."

"You said he's independently wealthy?" Philo asked. "Where'd the wealth come from?"

"A very rich lawyer in Colombia, who was targeted by Los Pepes during the hunt for Pablo Escobar. As far as we can tell, the lawyer had no ties to Escobar, yet he and his entire family were assassinated when a bomb took out their home." Gallegos-Martínez paused when he saw Toni and Philo exchange looks. "What is it?"

"A man named Morocho, with ties to Los Pepes, has set off several bombs recently in Tucson," Toni said, "including the one today."

Gallegos-Martínez nodded. "That is why I came to you . . . The lawyer's will left everything to one Ramon

Reyerto, of Mexico City. The will was certified by the family lawyer and upheld by the courts. It was signed and witnessed shortly—very shortly—before the family's death. No one knew this Señor Reyerto, but per his lawyer's instructions the estate was duly liquidated and the proceeds deposited in an offshore account . . . to which we have no access."

"And I'm betting this Reyerto has no record on file with Interpol, no fingerprints, no photo," Toni said.

"It is true. He is a shadow figure. He has no birth certificate that we can find. He employs a driver, so has no license. No Mexican passport. He uses a fleet of small planes for business trips, and lands at small airports. If he has other passports, they are not under that name."

"No family?" I asked.

"We thought not. But a woman who calls herself Señora Reyerto Carvahal has been in his Nogales residence for the past three weeks."

"So he is a Spanish-speaking man without a past, who set up shop in Sonora—how long ago?" I asked.

"It has been four years. We do not know where he was between 1993 and his arrival in Nogales, or before his time with Los Pepes."

"He keeps a low profile, entertains at home, has a trusted and loyal staff—" Toni began.

"Two only, whom he brought with him from elsewhere. The cook, the housekeeper, and the groundskeeper are from Nogales."

"Plenty of money, and no visible means of support," Philo said. "In other words, you suspect he advises the Sonoran cartels on how to launder money."

"*Sí*. And also the Colombian cartels and the Autodefesas, the AUC. They are the largest businesses in Central and South America.

"Busy guy," I said. "Besides rumors, what made you suspect he was connected with Carla?"

"This." Gallegos-Martínez took a photo from the inside pocket of his jacket and laid it down in front of me on the table. It was one of the photos he'd shown me in Sonoyta. Two men stood, like bookends, on either side of a hammerhead shark.

"It is the only picture we have of Reyerto, unfortunately. We found the photograph at the home of this man." Gallegos-Martínez pointed to Jorge García Desierto. "And as you suspected, Señorita MacFarlane, he ate dinner at La Roca the night Señor García Desierto disappeared."

"Jorge is the man we fished out of the Sea of Cortez," I said to Philo and Toni. The memories of that trip flooded back.

Philo pulled the photo toward him. I saw his jaw muscles tighten as he studied the blurred image. Philo had his own memories.

Toni tugged the photo from under Philo's forefinger, then swore softly in Spanish.

"He called himself Morocho when we met in Colombia," Philo told Gallegos-Martínez. "Ten to one, he killed the lawyer himself. I guarantee that he won't be satisfied by being a middleman who scopes out money laundering opportunities. He likes the hunt; he enjoys the kill . . . but he relishes inflicting fear and pain. Man, woman, child, it doesn't matter. I have never met anyone quite like him. And if our paths cross again, I'll save the state the expense of a trial."

"I think your paths have already crossed again, and you ended up on your butt, Philo," Toni said.

"That was only round one. The match isn't over yet," Philo countered, in a neutral tone.

So Ramon Reyerto, alias Morocho, was our bomber, the man with the dancing eyes . . . the same man who was eating at La Roca while Carla danced. But he had a beard and mustache then, as he had in the photo. "I have a question, señor—has anyone seen Reyerto's wife?"

"Only the people who work on his estate. Until yesterday. Señor Reyerto left on a business trip on Wednesday. On Friday the señora went shopping with the housekeeper. The señora made a phone call at a drugstore, then slipped away after lunch to rendezvous with someone. Cameras at the border caught them reentering the country."

"Carla Zorya," I said. "Rescued by her brother."

So Michael had known since yesterday that Carla was back in the country, yet he hadn't told his father. Otherwise, Cézar wouldn't have hired Philo to find her . . . But how had Reyerto tracked her down? It didn't matter now.

"Would Carla have gone back with Reyerto voluntarily?" Toni asked.

"No," said Gallegos-Martínez. "She was escaping. She will not go back."

He was intimating that if we didn't find Jamie and Carla quickly, Reyerto would kill them both. I looked down at my left hand. My fingernails had left deep impressions in the palm.

Toni noticed. "There's nothing more you can do here," she said. "Go home. I'll call you as soon as I learn anything."

Some silent communication passed between Toni and Philo. He nodded and pulled me to my feet, holding my hand firmly, as if he expected me to run off. I lacked the energy and inclination to run anywhere.

We walked back to our vehicles under soft Indian-summer skies. Late-afternoon shadows stretched bony fingers across the pavement.

"Remember what you said that first night, in the pool?" I asked Philo.

He thought for a moment. "I said I was lucky to be alive—that it could have gone either way."

"What did you mean?"

"Are you sure you want to know?"

"If I can understand Morocho, maybe I can guess his next move with Jamie and Carla."

"Nobody understands Morocho. He's unpredictable, secretive, and fanatically protective of his privacy."

"But he brought Carla into his home. That's a chink in his armor. Maybe there are others . . . I have to do *something,* Philo."

"Okay. Shoot."

"Morocho found you at the crash site?"

"I was the lone survivor . . . But I'd be in an unmarked grave in the jungle if it hadn't been for Gil—Toni's first husband—and a few others. It took a couple of days, but they tracked down Morocho . . . They cut it pretty close. I was half dead when they got there."

"But wasn't Morocho working for us? Weren't we funneling money to Los Pepes in order to flush out Escobar?"

"Indirectly. But apparently he had a bone to pick with the payment schedule . . . or maybe he'd just gotten out of bed on the wrong side that morning."

"Okay. He's unpredictable. But if Morocho wanted to kill Michael, why didn't he wait to detonate the bomb until Michael was in the car?" I asked.

"Perhaps he just wanted to frighten Michael or Cézar. That's Morocho's specialty. Or perhaps he wanted to torture the Zoryas by showing he had Carla. Who can say? The man's twisted." He stopped and faced me, putting his hands on my shoulders. "I love Jamie, too, Frankie. We can't kid ourselves about Morocho, but we have to trust that Jamie's trying to figure out how to stay alive—and how to get Carla out of there."

There were two squad cars guarding the entrance to our gravel drive. News crews were setting up on the road. At the house, I tried to punch in Kit's phone number, but there seemed to be a short between my brain and my fingers. I handed the phone to Philo and headed for the shower. After a cursory examination of my silk shirt, I tossed it into the waste basket. I wondered if my insurance covered accidents like this, or if they were classified as "acts of God." Undoubtedly, the latter, I decided, as I stood in the shower, trying to drown my worry. I wasn't successful.

Back in the kitchen, Philo told me he'd reached Kit at his office, given him a brief account of the day's events, and asked him to notify the rest of the family. We stood there, looking at each other. I opened the refrigerator and handed him a Negra Modelo. The knot in my stomach was saying no to food, but cooking would distract me.

"Frankie?" Philo asked a minute later, as I stood looking blankly into the freezer.

"I don't know whether to call my parents or not."

Philo closed the freezer door and looked at the old plastic clock on the kitchen wall. "It's almost one in the morning, London time. Why don't we wait a bit and see what Toni comes up with?"

"Fine by me." I didn't want to make that call anyway.

The phone rang, the first in a series of calls from uncles and aunts, cousins and friends . . . and the media. Word was spreading. It was decided, by that unknown force that decrees such things, that the local clan would gather here for dinner at seven. By then Toni might have something.

I took steaks from the freezer in the guesthouse and put them on the kitchen counter to thaw. While I checked the refrigerator for salad makings, I tried to think of where to look for Jamie. The SUV could be in Mexico by now.

Philo stared at the steaks with such intense concentration that I half expected them to levitate. He suddenly reached for the phone on the wall and dialed a number.

"Toni? Philo. Did you call the border stations to have them keep a lookout for the car? Okay . . . Good." He paused to listen. "Yeah, I'll tell her. Can Lena take Pen home with her? That works for me . . . My cell will be on. Good luck." He hung up.

He set the half-finished beer on the counter and folded his arms around me. He was four inches taller—my temple rested against his jawline. "Nothing so far," he said. "The car hasn't been sighted at the border, so they still may be in this area."

I pulled back a little and looked at him. "It's like watching shadow theater on a canvas wall . . . the Trojan War, maybe, full of lust and murder and deception. You see the action, backlit and bigger than life, but you can't touch the players or see their faces . . . and you can't affect the outcome. It's already written."

"Yes," said Philo, "it is a shadow war. But the ending isn't written, Frankie."

"I wish I could believe that."

"Believe it."

"Why?" I cried. "Give me one good reason why I should believe you?" I could feel tears of frustration welling up.

Philo could see I was losing it. He gripped my shoulders. "Listen to me, Frankie. I've been where Jamie is now. If I could survive two days with Morocho, in the middle of the goddamned jungle, how much better are the odds for Jamie and Carla right here, in the middle of civilization?"

It wasn't a great reason, but it'd have to do. I scrubbed the tears off my cheeks and took a deep breath. "I'm going to go wash my face," I said.

"Frankie," he said, stopping me as I reached the door. "When you said it wasn't my war, you were wrong. It was mine long before it was yours. And I guarantee I'll end it this time, once and for all."

Yes, I wanted to say—but would Jamie and Carla survive?

CHAPTER 29

CHARLEY'S TRUCK DROVE BY THE KITCHEN WINDOW on the way to the bunkhouse. But when I tried calling him a few minutes later, the line was busy. So I asked Philo to monitor the phone, and went to break the news to my godfather.

God almighty, what a mess, I thought, as I walked down to the bunkhouse. What had Jamie stumbled into when he hooked up with Carla?

When I knocked, Charley answered, a phone at his ear. He pointed to the sofa before continuing the call in the bedroom. I ran a hand down the smooth leather back of the rocking chair as I passed. On the pine end table next to it was a rough pottery bowl filled with polished white quartzite pebbles. I stirred them with my index finger, liking the smooth feel of the stones against my skin. There were pictographs on the pebbles, stylized drawings of animals done with a fine brush. I recognized a bear with a heartline, an antelope, a wild goose in flight. I wondered if they belonged to Charley or Teresa.

I sat in the center of the sofa. On the coffee table was a deck of the same type of tarot cards I'd seen in Miranda's shop . . . was it only four hours ago? It seemed like a life-time. The same text I'd seen at the store lay next to the cards. Charley came in as I was listlessly reading about the various layouts and their meanings.

I'd left only a brief message on Charley's machine. No details. I could tell by his face that he hadn't heard about Jamie and Carla and the bombing. Now that I was here, I didn't know how to tell him. I was afraid I'd start crying.

"Who paints these, Charley?" I asked instead, picking up a pebble with a badger symbol.

"My daughter," he said, avoiding the use of her name. He'd taught me long ago that names have their own power—and life span. Whenever possible, he used a generic term, or a term of endearment. "They come to her in dreams."

"They're lovely." I put the pebble back. "How was your day?"

"I spent the morning with your godmother's clan. Slipped away when they headed for the graveyard to picnic with ghosts." He studied me for a moment, then sat down in the rocking chair. "How was your lunch with the neighbors?"

I picked up the healing cards. "Lunch was fine. It was what happened afterward . . . You heard about the bomb?"

"Another one?" He looked at me sharply, trying to read my thoughts.

Everything tumbled out. I told him about the visit to the store and the aftermath, shuffling the tarot deck as I talked. Finally my voice ran down, like a tape recorder low on batteries.

"And you've had no word about your brother?"

"No. And I'm waiting to call Mom and Dad until I know something." I must have shuffled the deck again, because I saw him looking at my hands. Several cards were bent. "I'll buy you a new deck," I said.

"It doesn't matter."

"These same cards were on Miranda's table at the store. She asked me to choose five, but didn't tell me what they meant."

"Can you remember what they were?" Charley asked.

I found the cards and laid them out as Miranda had done, in the form of a cross—coyote, opossum, antelope, lizard, badger. "She turned the cards over one by one, in a clockwise direction," I said. "But starting at the three o'clock position. She didn't react until she turned over the center card."

"Did she say anything?"

"She just stood there for a moment, staring at them. Her face was pale and her hands trembled." I took the two cellophane packets and the quartz crystal from my pocket. "She handed me this packet—powdered herbs, I think— saying it was for my nightmares. I asked her how she knew about them and she pointed to the upside-down lizard card, saying something about my having known death. Then she gave me the quartz crystal and a packet of white powder."

"You said the center card startled her?"

"The badger? Yes. She didn't seem to know what to do or say. She collected the cards and hustled me from the room."

Charley tapped the card. "Badger medicine is connected with roots, the Earth, aggressive healing. Badger may symbolize her medicine. When it turned up as your center card, where she believes the physical and spiritual planes cross, she might view you, or someone close to you, as a person of healing power equal to her own . . . a threat, perhaps. The badger is stubbornly persistent, a fighter who doesn't panic. But when badgers are out of balance, they're quick to anger . . . which may be why she hurried you out the door. She would want to keep you at a distance. It's safer for her."

"But I'm rarely angry . . . except . . . well, one time I tossed a man for grabbing me."

Charley smiled. "Uh-huh."

"This is all mumbo jumbo, Charley."

"Maybe so. But while you were having lunch with the Zoryas and checking out their shops, I took the opportunity of visiting their gardens."

"Charley!"

He was no more repentant than I had been that morning. "I checked out the greenhouse and drying shed, too."

"And?"

"In the herb garden, the aunt's domain, I found yerba mansa, yerba buena, and fifty others. She's a traditional healer, though I suspect some might call her a witch."

"I'm tempted to paint the doors turquoise, just in case," I said. In Mexico and the Southwest, turquoise doors, like the stone Miranda had slipped into her pocket at the store, were said to ward off witches. "Did I tell you she tried to poison my coffee yesterday morning?"

"I doubt that she was trying to kill you, though her garden contains most of the traditional herbs that are native to the desert and canyons. Many of them are for topical use only. Taken orally, they can make you pretty sick."

"She told me one of them was pennyroyal. Do you know what it's used for?"

"To stimulate menstruation—or prevent pregnancy."

I wondered if it was for sale, or for Carla. I handed him the packets she'd given me. He took them into the kitchen, opened and examined the first, sniffing, tasting a granule or two of the white powder before spitting into the sink. "The white powder is ground-up aspirin. It will help you relax enough to fall asleep, but it won't hurt you . . . This, on the other hand," he sniffed the orange-brown powder, "is ground arrowroot balsam. If you mix it with water—or spit—and apply it as a poultice, it will draw the poison out of a wound." He handed the packets back.

"So what do I do with them?"

"That's up to you. They are gifts. You can either trust

that she has some power and is helping you, or you can throw them away. It's called free will."

"As in will they or won't they hurt me?"

"Remember, she doesn't know whether it's you that is the healing force to be reckoned with or someone around you—me, perhaps. So she'll be wary. And that's a good thing."

Pshaw, I thought as I slipped the packets into my pocket.

"What was that?"

"I didn't say anything."

"I heard something . . . sounded like 'pshaw.'"

Blow it out your ear, Charley, I thought.

He pinched his nose and blew, then tugged on his ear-lobes. "Much better," he said, smiling. "Don't deride what you don't understand or can't explain away with science."

The phone rang in the bedroom. "For you," he said, handing me the receiver. "Your detective friend."

They'd found a woman, shot in the head, just off the trail that led from the Sabino Canyon parking lot toward Bear Canyon. It was Carla.

CHAPTER 30

"FRANKIE? YOU THERE?" ASKED TONI.

"What about Jamie?" My voice sounded like a poorly tuned cello. It was hard to force air through the tight muscles of my throat.

"He wasn't at the scene."

"What do you mean? Did Morocho keep Jamie?"

"Not according to the witnesses. A trail runner saw two people sprinting toward the rocks. A man and a woman, he thought, though the light was almost gone. He heard shots and saw them both fall. Called it in on his cell phone."

So Jamie had been shot. But since they hadn't found him, he must have been mobile enough to run. "You said there was more than one witness?"

"A man was walking his dog near the boundary fence. Said he heard two or three guns. A minute later, he saw a dark late-model SUV drive by going west toward the parking lot. No headlights, and it was too dark to get the license number, but it had to be the Range Rover. No cars are allowed on that trail. The entrance is purposely narrow to discourage drivers."

"Except Morocho," I said. "Did the dog-walker see what happened to Jamie?"

"He went toward where he heard the shots. He and the dog got to Carla before the runner did. Jamie was already gone. He headed toward the creek."

"Will Carla be okay?"

"She was barely alive when they found her. Massive brain damage. She died on the operating table."

I couldn't believe that Jamie had abandoned Carla while she was still alive. It went against everything my brother stood for. "Does Cézar know?" I asked her.

"He collapsed in the waiting room. He's in surgery, now. They're seeing if he's a match for Carla's heart."

"Are they searching for Jamie?"

"Yeah, but by the time we'd cordoned off the crime scene, it was too dark. Forest Service personnel are keeping an eye out for him tonight. S and R will begin again at daybreak. I'm sorry, Frankie, but they'll need a piece of Jamie's clothing for the dogs."

I wouldn't wait till morning to start searching. But I wasn't going to tell Toni. She might try to stop me. "The clan's gathering here at seven," I said. "If you drop by with an update, I'll give you the clothing then."

"I'll bring my appetite," she said, as if I'd invited her to a family picnic.

I hoped I'd never become that inured to the emotional aftermath of violence.

Philo was waiting at the house. "Kit called your parents," he said.

I stabbed at the still-frozen steaks, trying to separate them. Philo gave me a wide berth. Taking a fortifying swig of beer, he picked up a steak knife and began to slice and dice red and yellow bell peppers and onion.

"There's too much happening, too quickly," I said. "Reyerto's manipulating events, and I hate it." The waving knife came a little too close to Philo's nose. He caught my wrist and gently pried the blade from my grasp. "It puts us on the defensive, Philo."

"So what do you want to do?"

"Find Jamie. He's the linchpin." I sought Philo's eyes. "And it won't wait till sunrise."

My parents called back while we were setting up outside. They were catching an 8 A.M. flight from Heathrow. They'd be home by noon tomorrow. In the meantime, two of my father's brothers, Mitch and Dave, and their wives, Annie and Justine, would serve as surrogates. As soon as they arrived, Philo would drive home to collect his gear.

My aunts and uncles, with four of my cousins, carried in chicken, a pot of refried beans, guacamole, chips, and six different Mexican beers for the impromptu potluck. Charley and Rosa were right behind them, with tortillas, salsa, and green-corn tamales—more comfort food to go along with the fajita makings already on the grill. Kit's wife, Lara, brought cornbread, green salad, and my two small nephews. A few minutes later, Kit drove up in Jamie's MG. He parked it in its usual spot in front of the guesthouse. It looked forlorn.

The old folding banquet tables were lit by flood lamps attached to the walls of the house and strings of multicolored Christmas lights that made me think of a fiesta. The festive lights, reflecting from the dark surface of the swimming pool, revealed the smallest family gathering in years. The twins were on an Andean mountainside; Jamie was in the foothills behind us; and my parents were in the air, somewhere over the Atlantic. I missed them. I missed sharing the burden of planning and decision making. I missed the reassuring presence of each one of them.

Normally the hubbub on the patio would have been

deafening, but a pall had settled over the group like smoke from a controlled burn. People spoke in hushed tones. This wasn't a wake with laughter and storytelling and tears. This was limbo, the waiting time, while we nibbled at the edges of our private fears and tried to bring order out of emotional chaos.

My godmother, Rosa, sat on my left, touching my hand reassuringly from time to time. This warm, outgoing, black-eyed nurse had fallen for Charley the first time she'd seen him at the VA hospital long ago. Now, she brought me up to date on their two sons, who were like brothers to me. I haven't a clue what I contributed to the conversation. I don't remember eating, either, though I cleaned my plate.

Toni and Gallegos-Martínez arrived with an update just after the food was cleared away, the cloths removed. Philo was right behind them. The family let Toni fill her plate and swallow one mouthful before they peppered her with questions. Gallegos-Martínez sat toward one end of the table, reserved, observing from under those hooded eyes. Philo maneuvered so that he took the seat across from him. They studied each other for a few minutes, until Philo asked a question in rapid, idiomatic Spanish. I saw a flash of surprise, quickly hidden, before Gallegos-Martínez replied. Rosa straightened and leaned ever so slightly toward that end of the table. Across from her, Charley pretended to be totally engrossed in watching me wipe down the table. I felt the tension around me, as if the air were stretching the thin membrane of a balloon. Any moment now, it would burst.

A car alarm sounded close by, and I lost control of the sponge. It skittered down the slick surface toward Philo. He slapped it with his hand. My breathing stopped, too.

I couldn't listen anymore. Inside, the dishwasher hummed. Teresa was wiping spills from the stove. "You shouldn't have cleaned up alone," I said.

"I needed to keep busy."

"Did you get some dinner?"

"Wasn't hungry." She flashed me a smile. "But I fixed a doggie bag for later—you never know."

I picked up a roll of U.S. Geological Survey topographic maps that stood in the corner, leafing through them till I found the Sabino Canyon 7.5-minute quadrangle. I unrolled it on the coffee table, using black-on-black Maria Martínez pots as paperweights. A sacrilege—they were collector's items. I didn't care.

"You're going tonight," she said. I didn't deny it. "I went to the canyon . . . right after Papa called. Couldn't get near the site where Carla was shot—it had already been secured."

"I'll find a way. Can you show me where it happened?"

She studied the map, pointing to a spot on a section of dirt trail that connected the parking lot with Bear Canyon. "The parking lot's always open, but the attendant left at five. The kidnappers squeezed their SUV between the rock wall and vegetation at the trailhead, crushing some plants and leaving a lot of paint on the wall. I think they were heading for the Sabino Canyon picnic area. The last shuttle pickup at the Bear Canyon loop was at 4:10, so the picnic area was deserted by dark. I talked with Waldo Sykes, the endurance runner who called 911. He's a friend of mine. Said he'd started at Marshall Gulch around eleven. Ran down the Wilderness and upper Sabino Trails, and then cut over to Bear. About twenty-five miles in seven hours, including a late lunch at Hutch's Pool. Not too bad."

"Sounds brutal."

"That's what he said, though it's easier at this time of year." Teresa draped the damp dishcloth over the faucet. "Did you know that during the summer they run the trails at night, when the rattlesnakes are out?"

"Which proves that trail runners are a separate subspecies."

"I suspect they'd think the same of geologists."

"But we don't check out the rocks in the dark . . . So what did wacky Waldo tell you?"

"He was at the top of this rise," she tapped the map, "when he saw the SUV stop. The driver got out. He was holding a gun. Three people got out of the back—one with a gun. Of the other two, one was very tall, one small and agile, he said."

"Jamie and Carla."

Teresa nodded. "Waldo saw Jamie throw dirt in their faces. Then Jamie and Carla sprinted uphill. They didn't get far. Carla was shot first. Waldo thought Jamie was hit, too . . . Jamie spun around and dropped, then picked Carla up and carried her the rest of the way. The men started to follow, but a guy was walking his dog nearby. When the dog raised a ruckus, the men got back in the SUV and drove away." Though Teresa's face was impassive, I saw worry behind her eyes. "Waldo called 911. He was running toward Carla and Jamie when he saw Jamie take off."

"Teresa, why do you think Jamie left Carla?"

"I don't know—but there had to be a damned good reason." Teresa picked up the topo map and rolled it tightly, as if her hands were around Morocho's throat. "I'll take this out to the others," she said.

"I'll be there in a minute." I stopped Teresa at the door. "Did Jamie talk to you before he left the hospital?"

"No. But I was told he left in a hurry—after receiving a phone call."

"From Carla?"

"Nobody seemed to know."

"Assuming it was, then Morocho must have had someone watching Jamie. That's how Morocho found where Carla was staying."

"Maybe that guy Papa saw in the wash."

I'd forgotten about yesterday's visitor. Grabbing a steak knife for protection, I went next door to get something of

Jamie's for the search dogs. His room was a mess, just as he'd left it—towels and clothes on the floor, loveseat, and chair. The bedsheets were twisted, untucked. He hadn't slept well . . . I picked up a T-shirt, the one Jamie'd worn when we played volleyball last night . . . Where was he? Was he unconscious and slowly bleeding to death in the canyon? Why hadn't he shown himself when the police arrived? Why had he still felt threatened after the SUV left?

The balmy air held no answers.

Toni was prepping the family on the shooting site when I returned to the patio. I handed her the plastic bag with Jamie's T-shirt.

"Thanks," she said. "Don't worry, Frankie—we'll find Jamie. And we'll find him alive." But she wouldn't have convinced a three-year-old who still believed in Santa.

Gallegos-Martínez took my hand. His eyes, less secretive than when we'd first met in Mexico, studied my face. He was smart enough not to offer platitudes. He'd seen too much death. "You are not afraid, Señorita MacFarlane?"

"Only of finding that Jamie didn't survive the night."

Gallegos-Martínez nodded, then gave me a little smile. "My prayers go with your family. Thank you for sharing your food with a stranger."

I felt Philo's hand on my shoulder. *"Por nada,"* I said. "And we have spent too many hours together to be called strangers. I suspect you know more about me than most of my friends do. Please call me Frankie—or Francisca."

"As you wish," he said, and opened the back door of the house. He flicked a glance at Philo, then back at me. "Good luck tomorrow. We will speak again soon. *Buenas noches,* Francisca."

The family would meet at the canyon at daybreak. We left the tables up, our way of throwing down the gauntlet to Fate . . . Tomorrow night, or the next, those bare tables declared, would witness a more festive gathering.

*   *   *

While Philo organized the gear, I tracked down Michael at the hospital to convey my condolences and ask after Cézar. His father was still in surgery, he said. There were no words of comfort I could offer, only prayers to whatever graces watched over Cézar that Michael would not lose his father the same day he lost his sister.

I went online and ordered flowers—lilies and orchids, showy purple and magenta ones for the living, white ones for the dead. I had them sent to the house next door. And while I was online, I e-mailed one of the part-time geology teachers, told him what was going on, and asked him to cover for me on Monday, if I didn't show up. He sent back an instant message, saying no problem.

I wrote a note for my parents who'd arrive home in the early afternoon. Hopefully, all would be resolved by then. We'd have found Jamie, he'd be in good condition, nothing more would go wrong, I hoped. But luck hadn't been running my way lately.

CHAPTER 31

IT WAS TEN O'CLOCK. THE THERMOMETER READ sixty-eight degrees. Jamie had been lucky—the first hard frost still lurked in the wings. But I feared he was in shock, losing body heat to the cold rocks. As a doctor, he'd know what to do to compensate, but only if he were conscious and thinking straight . . .

I dressed in layers—black turtleneck, khaki workshirt, hiking pants, windbreaker, and hiking boots. In the living room, Philo had laid out all of the paraphernalia he thought we'd need. I surveyed the scene with awe. Next to each daypack were three quarts of water, sports drink, trail mix, Luna bars, apples, dried fruit, sunflower seeds and jerky (for salt), flashlight, small plastic bags, poncho, first-aid kit, and matches. My torn and faded field vest carried compass, topographic map, multipurpose knife, driver's license, keys, a large bandana, money (I don't know why), and hat. Compared to Philo, I looked like I was going for a picnic in the backyard.

"What—no bedroll?" I asked, in an attempt at humor.

Philo grinned. "Is that a proposition?"

"Just an observation. You sure you want to tag along?" I asked. "I'll be okay by myself."

"Whither thou goest—at least until this is over. Besides, Jamie'd do the same for me."

Philo stowed the gear, adding rope, his .38 special, the Beretta, extra clips, and a hunting knife in a leather sheath to his pile. He caught my quizzical look. "If your brother is alive, he's a witness. Morocho doesn't leave witnesses."

I stopped loading my daypack. "That's what Gallegos-Martínez was hinting at? That we might have company on the mountain?"

"Uh-huh. And they won't be city slickers. Morocho and the men loyal to him cut their teeth in mountain wars . . . Is your cell phone charged?"

"Yes. But I'm not sure it'll do much good in the canyon."

"I'll give you one of my radios. It's only good if we're in line of sight, but better than nothing."

"Don't worry. I plan to keep you well within my line of sight. And I can use the radio to call for reinforcements if your back gives out under that load you've packed."

He rewarded me with a baleful glance. "Don't get your hopes up, *chica*. And by the way, nix the vest. In daylight, should this take that long, red makes a great target."

I quickly emptied the vest, redistributing the necessities into my backpack and pants pockets. I stuffed a well-worn Shetland sweater on top. After a last look around, I followed him out to his truck.

Sabino Canyon Recreation Area is a refuge just beyond the city limits. Even in May and June, when the temperature in Tucson can top 113, water flows from the top of the Santa Catalinas to pool among the boulders of granite and gneiss. Back in the thirties, New Deal make-work programs such as the Civilian Conservation Corps crafted roads, bridges, and restrooms, using local stream-rounded cobbles. My family picnicked here when I was a child. Back then, we could drive to the top of the 3.7-mile winding one-lane road. But when overuse threatened the fragile ecosystem, the Forest Service closed the road to cars, except the shuttle operated by the visitor center. Now, it's a place to walk, bicycle, muse, and wade; a place to listen to the music of falling water, and watch the cardinals, phainopeplas, black phoebes, and cactus wrens dart among the saguaros, ocotillo, willows, and cottonwoods. Best of all, it's accessible twenty-four hours a day.

Before the Tohono O'odham, Pima, Apache, Spanish, and Mexicans arrived in southern Arizona, Paleo-Indian hunters and the Hohokam used Sabino Canyon. They hunted, gathered, and played there; loved and laughed, told stories and slept there; built irrigation dams to water corn, squash, and beans; scraped away the desert varnish to leave petroglyphs in recesses that offered scant protection from the elements. This canyon had water, which made it a sacred place in this parched land.

Last summer, the Aspen fire had crept inexorably down the south flank of the Santa Catalina Mountains, threatening the recreation area. Blessedly, the fire line had held. The damage came later, when monsoon rains sent black ash-charged runoff barreling through the canyon, and when rockslides closed, for a time, the access road. Wildlife biologists, preparing for the worst, had evacuated endangered fish before the storms hit, but it would take a long time before the water ran clear enough to allow restocking of the habitats. And the authorities still hadn't found the idiot who started the fire.

When Philo and I turned into the parking lot, we found squad cars, a crime scene vehicle, media trucks, and a Lincoln Continental with tinted windows that reflected the starlight. We pulled into the slot next to it near the trailhead that leads to Bear Canyon.

On the drive over, I'd forced myself to confront the

facts. If Jamie had been in good shape, he'd have shown himself. Ergo, he was either dead or badly hurt. Waldo Sykes had said that Jamie had entered the brush at a run. At that point he was headed north. If he had continued in that direction, he could hit the water and follow the creek bed into the heart of the recreation area. If he'd doubled back in the darkness and followed the stream south, he'd pass close to my school. No one would notice if he walked through the grounds in the dead of night. If he weren't too badly hurt, he might have done just that. He might be sitting outside my classroom door right now . . .

"Wait a minute," I said to Philo, who was opening his door. I phoned Kit and asked if he'd check my office. His house was only ten minutes south of the school. No problem, he said.

We slipped on our gear in silence. A dog in the Lincoln woofed and scratched at the window, begging to go with us. Poor thing. I hated to see animals confined. Philo jotted down the license plate number in a small notebook.

"All set?" asked Philo.

"Let's go," I said.

We walked east toward the site where Carla had been shot. An area on the south-facing slope was cordoned off with official yellow plastic tape, that near-universal symbol of violent death. Under bright lights, crime scene investigators crawled over the earth like ants. What a stupid, cruel waste, I thought—one woman's unique grace, beauty, and promise lost for no reason . . .

"They tried to reach those rocks," said a voice behind me.

I whirled around. "You scared the hell out of me, Charley."

"That's because you weren't paying attention," he said. Perched on a rock near the trail, he blended in with the desert. He pointed to an outcrop thirty yards away. "Someone followed your brother—a man wearing city shoes with slick soles. He had a dog."

Maybe that was why Jamie ran for the water, I thought—so the dog would lose his scent. But why would he be afraid of a dog?

"Was city shoes the witness who was walking his dog by the fence?" Philo asked Charley.

"I expect so. I'll see what I can find."

We left Charley casting for sign by the pallid beam of a flashlight, and walked toward the creek. Following it north, a sudden coolness in the air told me we were near the small lake. The winter rainy season had not yet begun, and stagnant pools reflected stars. Saguaro, barrel cacti, prickly pear, and cholla grew among grasses, mesquite, paloverde, creosote, willow, and acacia. Most of them had thorns or spines. I hoped the rattlesnakes were hibernating.

We found our way along a narrow ancient path, our footsteps the only sound. My flashlight picked up a few fresh scuff marks. High above us, Saddleback Ridge hunched its black bulk against the sky. The moon showed through a notch in serrated cliffs and bleached Thimble Peak. The night wind blew down the canyon, rustling the cane grass and sycamore leaves, familiar, comforting sounds.

I'd always loved walking in the mountains at night. The rocks seem to breathe. Mountains aren't static. Weathering and erosion are continuous forces—wind, water, heat and cold, roots growing into cracks and wedging them open, animals making tracks that deepen with runoff. In the silence one can hear the occasional pebble, displaced by scurrying mammals, trickle down the mountain; hear water shifting sediment down the valley—reassuring evidence of change, the only constant in our world . . .

Somewhere ahead a branch snapped.

CHAPTER 32

I FLICKED OFF MY FLASHLIGHT. WE WAITED WITHOUT speaking, without moving. Minutes passed . . . I heard munching and tearing, and seconds later a pack of javelinas filed by across the stream. I started breathing again.

Philo moved as if it were broad daylight, a surefootedness I envied. We held a steady pace, pausing every few minutes to call Jamie's name softly. I turned on the flashlight in the patches of deeper darkness. Up the creek, I heard something plop in the water.

A great horned owl called. The echoes reverberated off the canyon walls and lost themselves in the black night. But I'd read somewhere that owl calls don't echo. My skin prickled. I looked at Philo. He nodded. We had company.

Ahead, the trail petered out against a wall of rock that glowed in the moonlight. We'd have to cross the creek, just as Jamie must have done. I turned my flashlight beam on the water, looking for a crossing . . . and stepped into nothingness.

The flashlight went out when I hit the ground, plunging

us into darkness. I was on my back, fighting for breath. Miraculously, I'd avoided landing on anything with thorns. Philo's body half-covered mine.

"You okay?" he whispered. He didn't seem to be in any hurry to move. The grains of our bodies fit together as if they'd been carved from the same chunk of wood. When I didn't answer, his teeth flashed white in the darkness and he lifted his torso onto his hands. "Better?" he asked.

I dragged in a deep breath and contemplated kneeing him in the groin. "If you had rocks digging into your back, I imagine you'd be more enthusiastic about moving."

I smelled the dampness of nearby water . . . and something burning. Heard a shoe grinding on gravel—a cigarette butt? My chest felt tight. I was breathing rapidly, as if I'd been running. I fought to slow it down. Philo warned me with a finger across my lips, and rolled to his right. Almost without a sound, he went into a crouch. His left hand was on my shoulder, keeping track of me. His right hand held a gun.

I hunkered down beside him, peeking out over the low ramparts of our gully. Footsteps approached a circle of boulders by the water. A voice spoke in Spanish, sounding harsh in the soft night. I heard a clicking sound. A lighter flared briefly across the creek, reflecting off the rocks. More talking, then laughter. I didn't recognize either man.

"Not Morocho," Philo whispered, his breath was warm on my ear. "But they work for him."

So Morocho was here, somewhere—with how many more men? "Do they know we're here?" I whispered back.

He nodded. "They know roughly where we are. They were talking about us—and Jamie. They found his footprints over there, but lost him a little further up." He picked up the flashlight. "We can't go back. They said Morocho's in position—which means he's covering the exits."

"The pistol?"

"A last resort. It would bring the authorities, but we

might be dead before they got here." Philo took out his cell phone. The mountain walls blocked the signal. No help there. He slipped the phone back into his pocket. "I know you hate waiting, Frankie, but that's what we're going to do . . . at least until we come up with a plan B."

"I hate waiting for other people to act," I corrected. "But I'll wait all night if it's the best way to get what I want."

Philo shifted to a more comfortable position. "When Jamie was able to run, Morocho must have moved to his own plan B," he said. "If he could drive Jamie up canyon, we'd follow. Looks like we played right into his hands."

I should have anticipated that Morocho and his men would want to finish the job here, tonight. Jamie wasn't the only one he wanted—he wanted us, the only other witnesses left . . . unless Cézar pulled through. Morocho must have wagered I'd be too anxious to wait until morning to search for Jamie. The departing SUV had served as a decoy. I felt stupid.

"We still have options," I said. "We can follow the creek down to the campus and call in the troops. Morocho wouldn't expect that. We'd have to trust that they wouldn't find Jamie in the meantime, and that he'd survive until we brought help."

"That's a lot of trust. Could you live with yourself if you were wrong?"

"No."

"Scratch one option. What else have you got?"

"We can turn the tables on them," I said. "We know they lost Jamie's trail. They know we're here, but they've made no move to close in and finish us off. I think they want us to find Jamie for them. If we pretend to play their game, they'll focus on us, not Jamie. And they won't kill us while we're searching."

"Right," Philo said. "But I don't think we can keep up the pretense very long. And what happens when we find Jamie? How do we help him without getting all of us killed?" He didn't wait for an answer. "I think we have to disappear after we've lulled them into complacency—maybe when we're hidden by a screen of brush or a curve in the trail. They'll rendezvous in order to regroup. We can see how many we're up against, where they are, and when it's safe to continue searching."

I leaned against the rock wall, tilting my head back and closing my eyes. I pictured the topographic map of the canyon and prowled the edges of the problem like a coyote on a scent. Philo, bless his heart, didn't interrupt.

"The Phoneline Trail," I said. The trail followed the contours of the canyon, about halfway up the eastern wall. It was rocky walking, even in daylight, but there were nests of boulders here and there, a myriad of hiding places. Best of all, once there, we could be seen from the ridge above, but not from below. But how to get there? If we climbed straight up the mountainside, we'd be exposed by moonlight . . . I considered and discarded approaches until I found one that satisfied all the criteria, safety being paramount. We couldn't help Jamie if we were dead.

"There's a ravine up ahead that intersects the main road at an angle. It's deep enough to have shadow and to screen us while we climb. What's better, the trail crosses a bench a short distance further along. Lots of boulders to screen us from below. Only a lunatic would climb the ridge above us at night. You could leave me hidden and follow the trail back out to call Toni," I said. "I'd be safe enough."

"Let's take one step at a time. Too many things could go wrong with just getting to the trail," he said as we stood up.

I was scared to leave the relative safety of the cut. Philo sensed it. "They want to kill us," he reminded me, "but not until we find Jamie."

"Well, that's reassuring. I was worried there for a moment."

He handed me the flashlight and clasped my other hand. We crossed the dam and turned onto the road. When we

passed a cluster of cottonwoods, I smelled cigarette
residue. They were there, hiding, waiting . . .

"Jamie," I called. My voice sounded breathless. I prayed
he was still alive. I wondered if he could hear me.

They fell in behind us, staying just far enough back to
avoid being seen. We followed the road for the next hour,
walking slowly, calling Jamie's name at intervals, stopping
once to use the restrooms. Gradually, we lulled them into
our routine.

The moon passed the serrated crest of the west wall.
The breeze died, the night was silent, except for the cricket
song in the damp undergrowth by the stream. We stepped
off the road and into the deeper shadow of a desert willow.
The men following us were approaching a bend in the road
that would hide our movements. Philo touched my shoulder. Staying in the shadow, I ran forward six steps, dropped
to the ground, and rolled to the right, coming to rest behind
a rock. Philo was right behind me.

I lay still, hugging the earth. My mouth was dry. The
smell of crushed creosote came on a puff of breeze. I lifted
my head just enough to fix their position, easy enough
from their chain smoking. I gathered a deep breath, drew
one knee up slowly, dug my toe into the sand, and
waited . . . Closer . . . closer . . .

"Go," Philo breathed in my ear.

I pushed up suddenly, put a hand on top of the boulder,
vaulted over, and took the stream in three giant steps. Philo
was right beside me. Another couple of steps and we were
hidden by the brush and shadow of the ravine. We climbed
quickly, hoping the men were close enough to the creek that
the sound of running water would cover any noise we made.

We stopped once, halfway to the Phoneline Trail, to
catch our breath. Peeking over the protective rampart of
the ravine wall, I saw the glow of cigarettes by the creek,
but further upstream than where we'd crossed. Morocho's
men had paused, as if they'd just realized we weren't on

the road. But they weren't looking for us two hundred feet up the mountainside. Even if they did, they couldn't see into our ravine. We started climbing again, moving as quietly as possible.

We missed the trail in the dark. Glancing back, I saw it forty feet below us, a pale snake in the starlight. We dropped back down and followed the trail north, leaving it where it crossed a bench maybe fifty feet wide and ringed by fallen rocks. We were roughly four hundred feet above the road.

Sand had collected among the boulders. I flopped down, feeling exhilarated. We'd accomplished the first stage of our mission.

"You sure know how to show a guy a good time," Philo muttered, raking rocks out of the way with his fingers.

"It's a litmus test I give all my dates," I whispered back.

"Is that so? You might have warned me." He took binoculars out of his pack and focused on the road below. He studied it for a few minutes in silence. "Has anyone ever passed the test?"

"On the first try? Only one."

"Travers?"

Few people in Tucson had met my ex-fiancé, or knew the story behind our breakup. I'd spent last summer alone, trying to deal with the aftermath of Geoff's betrayal. He'd plagiarized large portions of my dissertation research. He'd been given a second chance by the department, but I wasn't as forgiving. I'd asked him to leave my rented house. He'd threatened me, then disappeared. They'd found his body later—or thought they had.

"You know about Geoff?" I asked Philo. When he didn't answer, I turned over and used my pack for a pillow. The night sky was bright was stars. "Philo, do you run background checks?"

"That's our bread and butter—security clearances on government personnel and defense contractors."

"Something's been bothering me ever since Mexico. I'd like to hire you to check it out."

"Some*thing* or some*one*?"

"Geoff."

"What do you want to know?"

"You're saying you already checked him out?"

"Would you believe I was just curious?"

"No." I knew he couldn't tell me who hired him, so I'd puzzle it out for myself . . . Who would want information on Geoff? My parents, Kit, Toni . . . "When did you check?"

"Mid-August."

After Geoff's body was discovered in California, but before my trip to Puerto Peñasco. That eliminated Toni. But my parents were on sabbatical then in England.

"My parents conveyed their condolences to Geoff's parents, about the same time I sent them a letter," I said. "But something didn't smell right, something that convinced Geoff's parents he might be alive. I'm betting they said as much to my parents, who called you to find out the skinny." I looked at Philo. "You can jump in here any time and tell me I'm way off base."

He smiled. "No, I can't."

Which could have meant I was on target, or that he couldn't even give me a denial. But I knew I was right. My parents had asked him to look into it. "So what did you find out?"

"That the Travers case has been reopened."

I waited for the other boot to drop.

"The remains were found at the base of a cliff, as you know from the newspaper reports," Philo said. "They didn't find an ID with the body. It was identified as Travers based on dental charts supplied by his brother."

Ah, that was it. "But Geoff had no brother."

"Unfortunately, you weren't around to tell them that. The remains were cremated and released to the brother, to be taken back to England. No memorial service, no obit in the local paper. His parents were never informed. The number in Travers's school file wasn't theirs. It was, in fact, a cell phone number."

"So my letter and my parents' visit must have come as a shock. Let me guess what happened next. Geoff's parents contacted the school and authorities. They sent his real dental records, and the police haven't a clue whose ashes got away."

"That's about it."

I told him, then, of my interrogation in Mexico. "Gallegos-Martínez brought up Geoff's name and implied that I was somehow involved in his death—or disappearance. I didn't know what he meant. But if they've reopened the investigation, why haven't they contacted me?"

"The case was only reopened three weeks ago, just before Carla disappeared. I'm sure they have more pressing murder investigations, ones where the body's still present. But don't worry, they'll get to you."

"Did you find any evidence that Geoff's alive?"

"No. His trail went cold the day you kicked him out . . . unless it was Travers who claimed the body. I'll let the police figure that out."

The new information troubled me. Was the cell phone number substituted for Geoff's parents' number because he didn't want his parents to know where he was? We'd had such a short engagement that I'd never met them. Geoff had said they lived south of London, but I wondered, now, if that was true . . . And who had been cremated? If it wasn't Geoff, then he probably was alive . . . somewhere. Did *he* claim the body, as Philo suggested? Did Geoff know we'd thought he was dead? Had he planned it? Was he involved in something more clandestine than stealing my research—the reason the geology department had disciplined him and I'd thrown him out—or had he just disappeared for a while?

I was never convinced he'd committed suicide. Geoff was too much of a coward to take his own life. An accident, perhaps, but not suicide. I'd found out, almost too late, that his charming exterior masked a controlling, possessive personality.

Philo interrupted my musings. "I believe that when things are left unfinished, we're given a second chance—for better or worse. For me, Morocho's unfinished business, just as Travers is for you. You'll have your chance, Frankie."

"Even if I don't want it?"

"Especially if you don't want it."

PART VI

Sunday, November 2
El Día de los Muertos—
The Day of the Dead

Hollow: A low tract of land surrounded by hills or mountains; a small sheltered valley or basin, especially in a rugged area.

CHAPTER 33

IN THE CANYON BELOW US, THE MEN SEARCHED FRAN-
tically, but did not find where we'd crossed the stream. Finally they split up, one man staying behind to smoke endless cigarettes at shuttle stop 6, the other walking out. He
returned much later with radios. Reception would be poor
unless the radios were in a direct line of sight, but they'd
find that out soon enough.

From our vantage point, we searched the canyon bottom
and walls with Philo's night-vision binoculars. If Jamie
was still in the canyon, he wasn't moving about.

We took turns on watch during the next few hours,
catching sleep when we could. It was approaching four
when I heard a grunt and the click of metal on rock, followed by the sound of rocks tumbling down from the ridge
above. I felt Philo's hand on my arm. He'd heard it, too.

We grabbed our packs and ran back to the trail. We sat
with our backs against the cliff, hidden from above. But
when the sky grew light it would be a different story—the

search for us and for Jamie would be directed by someone with a bird's-eye view.

"It occurred to me that your truck's been in the parking lot all night," I said. "Plenty of time to attach the last pipe bomb." Philo was quiet, thinking. "We need to call Toni," I said. "I think we have to split up. It's still dark enough to cover you while you follow the trail back."

"Why don't we both go?"

"I've thought of one place where Jamie could hide—if he made it that far up the canyon." I wouldn't allow myself to think he hadn't. "There's a little hollow up on the hillside. We used to play there when we were kids." I could tell Philo didn't like the idea. "I can't leave him here alone, Philo. Trust me. I'll just move up the trail until I can find a safe place with a view of the hollow. I'll come down to the road when you bring help."

"Take this," he said, pulling the Beretta out of his pack and handing it to me along with an extra clip. "You remember how to load it?" I nodded. "Okay, then promise me you won't take stupid chances."

I promised, without asking him to define his terms, and put the gun in my pack.

"I'll be quick," he said, and disappeared into the night.

I told myself I was safe, but I wasn't convinced. I waited, listening, reassured by the normal night sounds. No gunshots, no screams. But as I started north on the trail, I felt fear shoot along my nerves. Maybe it was Jamie's fear communicating on the air. We used to be that close. But it had been a long time.

The trail was a faint line in the blackness. I walked carefully, making no sound that would alert men either above or below. I tried to calm myself by resorting to habits—I reviewed the data, starting with Angie.

Morocho, or his men, had killed Jorge, Carla, Hector, Mark Giovanni, a sheriff's deputy, and an elderly woman. Morocho had shot Jamie and was hunting him now . . . and me. But who had killed Angie? Morocho, the man Gallegos-Martínez knew as Reyerto? We knew he'd used at least two aliases, but were he and Dante Montoya—the man who claimed to be Angie's birth father—one and the same? Or was Dante a wild card? Angie's murder, the one that had first drawn me into a web of Tucson violence, was no closer to being solved than it had been four days ago. Yet Angie was the key to unraveling the mystery.

If Angie hadn't met Hector in the support group, she wouldn't have recognized him at school and interviewed him for her articles. That collaboration led to research on *coyotes,* money laundering, the import trade . . . which led to interviews with Miranda. Why hadn't Angie mentioned Dante Montoya's name during her interviews with Miranda?

Because Dante hadn't called her until Wednesday, that's why—after her articles on gambling and money laundering came out. Could Morocho/Reyerto have researched Angie, found the article on birth parents, and posed as her father to learn where Hector was? If Morocho/Reyerto and Dante were one and the same, and Hector recognized him at the amphitheater, had Hector thrown the knife to kill Morocho? Had Angie just gotten in the way?

Or did the Zorya connection get her killed? Did Michael or Cézar or Miranda want to keep her from writing about them or their import-export business? About their family? About the storage facility in Douglas? All were good motives for murder, which is about passion and greed, security and protecting secrets . . . Michael had a knife collection, a motive, and opportunity. Miranda and Cézar had access to his collection, similar motives, and opportunity. Michael loved acquiring beautiful and rare things, without the responsibility of ownership. Because things can own you, he said. Did his clients include Reyerto? Did Reyerto hold Carla hostage until Michael located Hector and killed Angie?

With Hector dead, we might never know. But Angie's murder had scared him enough that he gave me keys, a disk, and a file with the plans of the storage facility. He must have believed he'd be next. He knew too much; he'd talked too much; he was a liability. Therefore, he had to die . . .

I paused where the trail curled into a ravine. Thimble Peak was directly above me. Sheer cliffs shielded me from view. This was better, safer.

I drank some water, chewed jerky. The temperature was approaching its lowest point of the night—low fifties, I guessed. Not bad. Soon the sky would begin to lighten. I moved on, stopping again on a flat ridge that jutted out into the canyon. I edged along the ridge, feeling my way. It had a good view of the road and the western wall, and perhaps a cranny large enough to hide me for an hour or so. I checked for snakes before crawling in. Nothing rattled. Lying on my stomach, I peered over the cliff to the road below.

Back where we'd crossed the stream and climbed up, I saw a flashlight beam sweeping the ground. The confidence of Morocho's men frightened me. Though they'd lost us, they made no effort to conceal their search. What did they know that I didn't? Did they know I was alone?

Coyotes bayed further down the canyon. Above me, on the ridge, a dog howled in answer, making my skin crawl. Below, the beam was moving, crossing the stream to the foot of the gully . . . Where was the second man? I searched the road up to the place where the shuttle turned around, where the Phoneline Trail zigzagged down to meet the asphalt. The second man had just started up the zigzag trail. Soon both men would be on the trail behind me—a pincer's movement designed to flush out prey.

I didn't know how they'd found me. It didn't matter. Staying here was suicide. If they captured me, they could use me as leverage against Jamie . . . or Philo.

I refused to become a hostage. What could I do?

Before daybreak, I had to get down to the road and cross it to the dense growth by the water. Once there, I could work my way up-canyon to the place where I thought Jamie was hiding. I said I'd meet Philo on the road. I couldn't warn him about the change in plans. I just hoped our radios worked when he got here . . . and that the radios Morocho's men carried weren't set to the same frequency.

A deep ravine lay to my left. I moved quickly back to where it intersected the trail, and inched my way down nearly five hundred feet, trying to avoid the cacti, rocks, and thorny shrubs. I was only partially successful. But at least I was hidden from the two men climbing up. I didn't know if the same were true of the man on the ridge.

It took me close to thirty minutes. Night was bleeding from the sky as I reached the road and dashed across.

I looked up, but couldn't see the men. Had they reached the trail? Had they turned around? Were they, even now, closing in?

I worked my way upstream, using every bit of cover. If the men were on the road, they could move more quickly. I didn't stop. I couldn't hear anything but trickling water and the rustlings of animals in the brush. A quail called, a lonely sound in the still air. Thimble Peak glowed red. Sunlight painted the ridgecrests gold, while shadows crawled slowly down the mountainsides and back into their crevices.

Near the shuttle stop, sycamores and cottonwoods wore aprons of yellow leaves. I heard the song of water falling into the first of several pools reflecting an apricot sky—an idyllic setting that hadn't changed much over the years. The hollow was perhaps eighty feet above me. Reaching it undetected was another story.

The canyon walls rose steeply to either side, the topography formed over millions of years as the mountains were uplifted and faulted, and the rushing waters of Sabino Creek cut down toward base level. The metamorphic rocks had been sculpted by water and wind to produce small side canyons and pockets. I paused behind an outcrop of gneiss. A lens of tiny deep-red almandite orbs swirled around white feldspar crystals that were elongated and contorted into augen—almond-shaped eyes that glowed in the early light.

At this hour, I had the place to myself. Or so I thought.

CHAPTER 34

TWO MEN IN JEANS, WINDBREAKERS, AND BASEBALL caps were talking thirty yards away on the road. They each held a radio in one hand, a cigarette in the other. Morocho's men. Were they the same two who'd tried to corner me on the side of the mountain? Had Morocho seen me cross the road and sent them back down? Or were these two others?

I shrank back behind the outcrop and glanced upstream. The road was clear as far as the next bend. I crawled into a protective thicket of brush and trees. Where the hell was Philo?

From the top of a desert willow, a black phoebe fluttered up to catch insects. I heard a plop in the largest pool, as if I'd scared a toad into the water . . . but toads come out at night. I looked up the mountainside where, over millennia, running water had carved a steep, shallow channel. My brothers and I used to climb it to a tiny valley. It had shelter, but no water, except during rainstorms. But Jamie would know that. He'd have scrounged empty water bottles from the trash bin nearby and filled them from the stream. He'd also know that, sooner or later, we'd come for him.

Over by the restrooms, one of the men was speaking loudly enough for me to make out the words. The only trouble was that his Spanish was too rapid for me to follow. I managed to pick out one word in thirty. I resolved to take a refresher course next semester—if I lived that long.

I looked at the sandy ground as I concentrated on their conversation. Garnets, weathered out of granite boulders brought down by floodwaters, had collected in pockets in the rocky wash. They looked like sprinkles of blood.

The speaker paused, and I heard the crackling tones of a radio. I took the gun from the backpack and tucked it into my waistband. I wanted to have my hands free while I slithered up the mountain.

The door to the restroom squeaked open and the men went inside. They and the man on the ridge had lost me again. They didn't know I was a stone's throw away. This was my chance.

I shouldered into my pack and eased myself through the brush. Circling around to the north, I kept a screen of vegetation between myself and the restroom. I stopped just before I reached the bank so I could study the route.

At this point, eroded blocks of various sizes littered the shelves formed by more resistant gneissic layers. No trail led to the spot—just the shallow channel I'd climbed as a child. Above, a V-shaped notch marked the opening into the hollow. More cliffs crowned the slope. Taking the channel route would be quickest, but would leave me exposed. A little to my right, a cactus-choked draw offered a protected approach as far as the notch. I could reach the cliffs under cover. From there I'd have to wing it.

I heard the soft call of the phoebe as the men came out and started down the road. If my luck held, they'd be looking the other way when I crossed the stream. It was now or never.

Crossing the stepping stones at a run, I entered the draw. So far, so good. My boots were still dry and thick grasses and willow provided cover. The air was growing warmer. High cirrus formed a tick-tack-toe board on a denim sky. I took off my sweater and stuffed it in my backpack. My khaki clothes would blend well with the dirt, dusty plants, and talus.

I made my way up the draw as quietly as possible, using every bit of brush for cover. Where vegetation was scarce, I lay down on my stomach and crawled. Unfortunately, the brush was liberally adorned with thorns. My cotton clothing offered little protection, and my mood degenerated with each yard gained, to the point where I'd gladly have shot anything or anyone who crossed my path.

From behind the dubious cover of a chain-fruit cholla, I checked my backtrail. The men had disappeared around a curve . . . I hoped. Any other options scared the hell out of me. But compulsively, I checked the ridge opposite. A flash came from high on Saddleback Ridge. Damn it—I'd been so careful.

Couldn't be helped. If the man on the ridge was Morocho, he'd know by now where I was heading. Had his men taken a more direct route? Were they ahead of me? If Jamie was there, I prayed he was well hidden. I crawled as fast as I could.

I paused at the base of the cliffs. Thirty feet away was the shallow chute leading to the notch. I'd be in the open for at least forty feet.

When I reached the chute, I found streaks of dried blood on the slick rock. Jamie had been here.

I wasn't prepared for the memories that swept over me as I entered Spiny Hollow. The metate-shaped depression was one of those sweet, secret places where memories reside, undisturbed. It was as if no one had been here since the last time I'd climbed the dry waterfall, alone, just after my sixteenth birthday. Yet it seemed smaller, somehow, with fewer hiding places ... Even so, I almost missed Jamie's.

A natural fissure at the base of the rock wall had been expanded through time by running water and frost wedging. After eons of erosion, the undercut portion of the cliff wall had broken away. The huge block now leaned against the cliff, like a rock-hewn altar overturned by an angry god.

I circled the outer edge of the hollow, stepping from rock to rock, trying to leave no footprints, erasing the few Jamie had left. He had improved his den, blocking off all of one opening and most of the other with uprooted bursage and brittlebush. The brush was still green. I pushed it aside. The floor of the shelter was covered with fine silt, sand, and animal droppings. A packrat had nested in the corner.

"Welcome to Casa de Jaime," said my brother. "Or Casa d'Estúpido. Take your pick."

Tears blurred my eyes. I rubbed them away with my sleeve. "I'm just glad to see you're alive," I said.

The shelter was about four feet wide, and barely long enough for Jamie to stretch out. He was reclining against the cliff, his naturally angular face etched with fatigue and hunger. Dust coated his black hair, his blood-soaked clothes, and skin. He looked more like fifty than twenty-eight.

Jamie shifted his long legs and made room for me to sit down as I pulled the brush back into place. When my eyes had adjusted to the gloom, I could see that he favored his left side. He'd torn his shirt into strips that girdled his rib cage and thigh. The strips anchored crudely split and de-spined pads of prickly pear.

I handed him a bottle of water and nodded toward the bandages. "Is it bad?"

He drained most of the half-liter bottle before answering. "Looks worse than it is. One went clean through my flank, the other creased my ribs. They hurt like hell and bleed like a sonofabitch every time I move. But they didn't hit anything vital. I'll live."

I believed him. If he were really in trouble, he'd be whimpering . . . or comatose. "I brought a first-aid kit."

"I'd rather not tamper with success."

I took Tía Miranda's cellophane packets from my pocket.

"What are those?"

"Ground aspirin." I opened the first packet, handed it to him, then held up the second. "And arrowroot balsam, courtesy of Miranda." At the mention of the Carla's aunt, Jamie's face fell. "Charley says to mix the balsam with water—or spit—and use it as a poultice."

"I'll pass on the poultice, thanks. As it is, I'll probably have to deal with giardia from drinking stream water." But he poured the aspirin into his mouth and swigged more from the bottle.

I leaned forward to feel his forehead. No fever. Yet. But his skin was cold. I shrugged out of my backpack and made him put on my sweater. He grunted with pain as the pads shifted against the wounds. There were beads of sweat on his forehead when he finished. I poured him a cup of coffee from a small thermos I'd carried all night. "It's lukewarm," I said. "I'm sorry."

"It's heaven, thanks."

We'd both been talking in whispers. I'd spent the entire night talking in whispers. By now, it seemed natural. I handed him some trail mix and an apple, requesting that he munch quietly, please.

"How many are out there?" he asked, his mouth full of apple. He watched me take the gun out of my waistband and place it next to a little pile of rocks, his only weapons.

I could hear bicyclists and hikers on the road below. Where the hell was Philo? For that matter, where the hell were Search and Rescue, Charley, Kit, and Toni, not to mention my myriad relations?

"Frankie?" Jamie'd finished the apple and was making a dent in the trail mix.

"Three . . . at least. Maybe five."

"Reyerto and his thugs." He dropped the apple core in the empty trail mix bag and handed it to me. "How long before the troops get here?"

"Philo should have been here by now. But, hey, our position's not too bad. We just have to sit tight and wait—unless you have a better idea."

"I'm in no condition to do anything else."

I hesitated, then plunged in. "Do you want to talk?"

"I'd rather talk than twiddle my toes."

"Thumbs."

"Whatever."

"Why did Reyerto bomb Michael's car?"

"The guy was obsessed with Carla . . . You know she was in his house for the last three weeks? Anyway, she refused to go back with him. I thought he was going to kill us right there at the motel, but he stopped . . . and then he smiled. He wanted Michael to see Carla with him, alive, he said, before he killed us. He blew up the car to bring Michael outside . . . and so Michael would know what would happen to Cézar and Miranda if Michael didn't cooperate. I'm not sure what Michael was doing for him. Reyerto didn't say."

"Where did Reyerto take you after the bombing? It was two hours before you showed up here."

"Believe it or not, our captors were hungry. They got takeout from a pizza place down the road, and ate it in the Sabino Canyon parking lot while Reyerto tried to decide what to do with us . . . and the vehicle. He knew he had to get rid of that SUV pretty quickly. So they switched license plates with another car in the lot, which gave them some breathing room . . . Morocho had calmed down by then. He cared jack about me, but he didn't really want to kill Carla—no matter what he'd said before. So he methodically laid out all the reasons why Carla should go back with him, as if they'd been married for ten years. It was bizarre to watch, Frankie . . . When that didn't work, he started with the threats again. He told her he'd seen her dance in Tucson before she went to Spain, that he'd followed her and killed her boyfriend . . . Carla lost it. She started hitting him and screaming, until one of his goons put a chokehold on her . . . 'I treated you like a lady,' Reyerto said to her in Spanish. 'Didn't I treat you like a lady, and not like all the other whores?'"

Jamie ate a Luna bar, though he had trouble swallowing.

"And then?" I prompted.

"The parking lot was empty by then, but it was a little too public. Reyerto ordered the other two to drive down the trail and kill us. I was praying the Range Rover wouldn't make it through the trailhead entrance, but they forced it. A little way along, Reyerto got out to walk his dog."

"His dog?"

"The bastard had his dog in the car the whole time. Part Doberman, part German shepherd. I usually get along with dogs, but this one took after his master . . . Anyway, when Reyerto's men stopped the car, Carla and I managed to break free. We ran toward some rocks." Jamie cleared his throat and took a deep breath. "We didn't get there. They shot Carla—caught the back of her head. I could see she wasn't going to make it, Frankie, but I picked her up and kept running until they hit me . . . They started after me, but they stopped, turned back, and drove away." Jamie shifted, trying to find a more comfortable position. There wasn't one.

"Reyerto and the dog stayed behind?" I asked.

"Yeah. To finish me off. He let the dog loose. Ordered it to kill. So I ran. I made it to the creek and went upstream until I was sure I'd lost the dog. Not far. When I circled back, the men were there with a different vehicle. One watched the parking lot, the other watched the crime scene. They'd have killed me before I took ten steps . . . might have shot someone else, too. I couldn't take that risk. So I waited."

"But they didn't leave," I said.

"No." Jamie sighed. "Reyerto started to work the canyon with the dog. So I just kept moving, making my way up the creek. The dog lost the scent, and Reyerto turned back. But his men took up the hunt. I remembered this place. I could climb up here without leaving footprints."

Just bloody streaks like red tears on the augen gneiss, I thought. "Before you were kidnapped, did you have a chance to talk to Carla about Mexico?" I asked him.

"She remembered waking up one morning two weeks ago. She knew what had happened—she'd had fugues before . . . You know what fugues are?"

"Trancelike states, usually brought on by trauma or stress. Anne Sexton, the poet, had them."

"That's right," Jamie said. "Mom wrote a paper on Sexton. I'd forgotten . . . Anyway, Carla woke up in a house, with no memory of how she got there. Nor did she know who Reyerto was—the man who claimed to be her husband. But she sensed he was dangerous, so she played the part until she could get out of the house. When he left for a meeting on Friday, she talked the housekeeper into a shopping trip."

"Gallegos-Martínez said they caught her on videotape crossing the border with Michael."

"You've talked to him—Gallegos-Martínez, I mean?"

"He's here . . . chasing Reyerto." I gave him the Cliff Notes version of what I'd learned about the man Philo called Morocho. "How did you find out that Carla was at the motel?"

"She called me to explain . . . and to say good-bye. Michael was taking her back to Spain, where she'd be safe." Jamie paused and looked at his hands. "Michael warned her not to use the phone, but . . . I asked her where she was." He shifted again and grimaced. "I led them straight to her, Frankie."

"How could you have known? You didn't have all the facts."

"I had enough. I just wasn't thinking. I . . . needed to see her." He finished the last of the coffee. "Thanks, Frankie—I haven't eaten since yesterday morning."

Yesterday morning he'd eaten the bread for the dead.

I handed him another bottle of water. He drank half and handed it back, then closed his eyes, as if he could block out the memories. "Reyerto's got a lot to answer for," he said.

Jamie didn't know the half of it. I opened my mouth to fill him in when a shadow fell across the opening. I laid a finger over Jamie's lips. His eyes flew open. I lifted my hand and pointed. We both stopped breathing.

I picked up the gun in both hands. *Just point and shoot,* I said to myself . . . *Just point and shoot* . . . But I didn't dare fire, because it could be Philo. The shadow moved away. We began to breathe again.

I heard no sound but the droning of bees in a late-blooming brittlebush. The birds and cicadas were silent. Not a good sign.

Light flooded the hollow as the screen of brush was stripped away. Two men quickly blocked the entrance. They had grins on their faces and guns in their hands—pointed at the ground, thank heavens. Jamie started flinging rocks. I squeezed the trigger again and again and again . . . but they'd ducked aside.

We made ourselves as small as possible. Ricochets could tear us to pieces. The man on the right fired into the shelter. I don't know how he missed, but most shots passed out the back opening. One ricocheted off the wall and took off the tip of my left boot before being deflected outside. I saw a movement to the left and fired again. The bullet whined into the distance.

Jamie wasn't moving. I couldn't tell if he were alive or dead. I had to get him out of this death trap.

I tore the brush from the back entrance, crawled around to Jamie's head, and pulled on his arms. Managed to get him halfway through the opening before his right shoe became wedged under the rock. I leaned across him to work it free. The shoe wouldn't budge . . . How many shots did I have left? I'd forgotten to count. I tried to work his foot out of his shoe . . . Whispers outside. Shadows shifted. We'd run out of time.

CHAPTER 35

I STOOD, FLATTENING MYSELF AGAINST THE WALL
where a bulge in the rock offered a little protection for my
head. The men moved as one. We fired at the same time.
The noise was deafening in that small space. I hit one man
in the chest. He fell toward me with a surprised look on his
face. He landed on his stomach. A hunting knife protruded
from his back, just under his ribs. His companion toppled
backward, missing part of his head. My legs gave out. I
crumpled at Jamie's feet.

One of their bullets had skimmed the back of my hand
and zapped a water bottle in my backpack. Another scar to
add to my collection, I thought, as I watched water pool on
the dusty floor.

I didn't know where the other bullets had landed, but I
was scared to look at Jamie. As long as I didn't look, then
he was still alive and well. It was childish, and Frankie the
child had left this place long ago . . .

The seconds ticked away. I took a deep breath and
turned around. Jamie was breathing. His color was good.

He'd been hit in the outer thigh, but the blood wasn't gushing. The bullet had missed the femoral artery. By dragging him, I'd torn open his previous wounds. Checking the back of his head, I found a knot where he must have banged it on the rock wall. Gneiss is an unforgiving rock, the kind that gives concussions. A nice friable Pleistocene sandstone would have been softer, I thought irrelevantly.

I took out the first-aid kit, found a sterile gauze pad, then maneuvered myself around so I could use my left hand to put pressure on Jamie's thigh. I could feel the bullet's outline just beneath the skin. It must have been spent by the time it hit him.

I drew up my knee to support my right hand. I still held the gun.

I hadn't looked at the man nearest me since he'd landed at Jamie's feet. I peeked, just to confirm he hadn't moved. *Overkill,* I thought, as a shaft of sunlight reflected off the knife blade onto the rock wall above me, picking out a Hohokam petroglyph—a hand. Someone else had been here, long ago . . . just as someone else had thrown that knife. I felt less alone.

Gingerly, I felt for a pulse at the man's throat; felt a faint throbbing—or was that my own heartbeat? It faded. I snatched my hand away. He was bleeding all over my boots. I wished I were on a trail somewhere, with a rock hammer in my hand instead of a gun.

I could hear the sounds made by friendly forces splashing through the pools below. They made no effort to be quiet. Suddenly, a clean white handkerchief fluttered down. Philo's idea of a joke, I guessed. I guessed wrong.

"Don't shoot, Francisca," said a voice.

I didn't reply, but I kept the gun pointed in his direction as a man stepped into view.

Michael Zorya looked different this morning. He blended in with his surroundings as effectively as a cuttlefish. Like me, he wore neutral colors, but it was more than that: his striking features appeared nondescript. But he couldn't disguise those fingers, the slightly longer nails on the right hand. The sun slanted under his hat and caught his eyelashes. His tan cotton workshirt was open at the collar, revealing a thin leather thong pulled taut across his throat, as if something nestled between his shoulder blades. He carried a rifle with a carved wooden stock and telescopic site. On his belt was a radio. He pointed to the dead men and looked at me intently.

"Was there a third man?" he asked.

"Not that I saw. Not here, anyway. But there's one on the ridge over there." I still clutched the gun. I hadn't replaced the clip. That took two hands, and I needed to keep the pressure on Jamie's thigh. But the gun gave me the illusion of control, however unfounded.

Michael prodded each body with his boot, nodded his satisfaction. The shot that had hit the second man hadn't come from my gun, but from the side, I realized . . . from Michael. He looked past me to where Jamie lay, unmoving, in a puddle on the floor. "They shot your brother." A statement, not a question.

I cleared my throat. "They could hardly miss in here. He'll live." My voice didn't seem to belong to me. My body started to shake. "Thank you for what you did," I croaked.

Michael gave me his charming smile. "It was my pleasure." And I knew he meant it.

He listened for a moment. "Your friends are coming." Bending gracefully, he picked up his handkerchief. "Tell your brother I will find the man behind this."

Michael left as quietly as he had arrived. I gently lowered the gun until it rested on the floor, leaned against the wall, and closed my eyes.

CHAPTER 36

I HEARD FOOTSTEPS COME TO AN ABRUPT HALT NEAR the two bodies, then the rustle of brush. I opened my eyes and saw the bleak look on Kit's face. He must have thought we were dead.

I gave him a weak facsimile of my usual grin. "Thank God," he said.

There was just enough room for him to step over the bodies and crouch down beside me. Philo and Toni leaned into the entrance, blocking out most of the light. Kit looked at Jamie. "Is he . . . ?"

"He hit his head dodging a ricochet. Knocked himself out . . . or fainted." I nodded toward where my hand covered the wound. "He's got a fresh bullet in his thigh and wounds along his flank and rib cage from yesterday. No fever."

Kit brushed the hair from Jamie's forehead, felt the pulse at his neck. I saw his face relax. "What about you?"

"Emotionally or physically?"

"Physically."

"My ears are still ringing, and a bullet creased my hand. Burns like hell, but I can still use it."

"How about emotionally?"

"When will Mom and Dad be home?"

He grinned. "Not soon enough."

Toni leaned around Kit and gently pried the gun from my fingers. I thought I heard a collective sigh of relief. She and Kit helped me up and passed me out the back entrance to Philo. I chose to step over Jamie, rather than over the dead men.

The sun felt wonderful on my back. I was still shaking as if with chills. "Ouch!" I said, when Philo wrapped a blanket around my shoulders. "I'm a walking pincushion."

"Sorry," he said. He saw the shadows in my eyes. "We got here as fast as we could."

"I know. You had trouble finding me."

"You might say that."

Spiny Hollow was crawling with deputies, crime scene investigators, paramedics, photographers, S and R, and Forest Service personnel. Gallegos-Martínez stood alone at the edge of the crowd. He nodded his head, and then looked at Saddleback Ridge. His quarry was still out there.

I watched them strap Jamie onto a litter and maneuver him down the mountain, Kit walking by his side.

"Can I go down now, too?" I asked Toni.

She thought about it. "Okay. But stick around. And don't talk to anyone."

Uncles, aunts, cousins, and friends were waiting at the bottom of the hill. My bloody hands told them the news wasn't good. I let Philo fill them in while one of the paramedics checked my wounds. She bandaged my left hand, clicking her tongue and shaking her head the way my mother used to when I was small. But she took one look at all the cactus needles sticking out of my clothes, and handed me her tweezers.

Charley led me to a picnic bench, the only one that offered some degree of privacy. My hands were still shaky, so he spent the next twenty minutes pulling spines out of my skin. A crowd watched from a distance and murmured sympathetically. I put on a stoical face. Inside, I was screaming.

My torture finally ended. Charley returned the tweezers and came back with Philo and a tube of antibiotic ointment. I don't know what Philo said, but my relatives asked me no questions when they kissed me good-bye and headed off down the road.

"How are you doing?" Philo's hands were gentle as they slathered ointment over my punctured skin.

"Have you ever noticed how crystal clear everything seems after shock wears off?" I asked him. "Objects are more defined, colors more vibrant, sounds sharper. The world is reborn . . . That's how it is right now. But I seem to be watching it all from a great distance."

Philo put his arm around my shoulders and pulled my head against his chest. As his body heat gradually seeped into me, I told him what Jamie had said in the hollow. He stroked my hair with his free hand. My skin, clothes, and hair reeked of cordite and the sickly sweet smell of fresh blood. I was fortunate. Most of the blood wasn't mine.

At the next table, Charley took a hunting knife from the scabbard at his belt and scraped it back and forth, back and forth, across a whetstone, repeatedly testing the edge for sharpness. When he was satisfied, he slid the knife back in its sheath. The action had the desired effect: strangers kept their distance.

It was a Sunday like any other to casual visitors to the park. A bicyclist, wearing helmet and gloves, walked her bike down the road. Probably a flat tire. She reminded me of Teresa, training for El Tour de Tucson . . . Hikers traversed the road. A few stopped to ascertain the cause of the commotion. I doubt if they learned much . . .

Toni's partner, Scott Munger, brought me a Mountain Dew. Appropriate. "Toni's on her way," he said.

I watched her come down the hill with Gallegos-Martínez. They both looked tired. I wondered how much sleep they'd had since this started.

Toni and Scott both took notes as I described what had happened after Philo left me. Gallegos-Martínez listened. I kept my answers simple, volunteering no details. They didn't ask me who shot the man in the head or if I had thrown the knife. They didn't know anyone else had been on the mountain. I knew they'd come back to those points later, after ballistics revealed a second gunman, after the knife was tested for prints. Right now, I needed time to think about Michael before I mentioned his participation. He'd saved not only my life, but Jamie's as well. I felt I owed him one.

"Did the paramedics say anything about Jamie's condition?" I asked Toni.

"Vital signs are excellent," she said. "I've asked the hospital not to release any information. Reyerto went to a lot of trouble to silence Jamie. Might buy us some time if he thinks he succeeded."

"Did you find a bomb under Philo's truck?" I asked her.

"A tidy little package," she said. "Bomb squad's taken care of it."

I looked at Philo. "Maybe Reyerto's luck has finally changed," I said.

"Ever the optimist," Philo said. "But we won a skirmish, not the war. He'll try again."

CHAPTER 37

THE ANSWERING MACHINE AT HOME WAS FULL OF messages, mostly from reporters. My parents had missed the plane in Phoenix, but had gotten Kit's message about Jamie. They'd head straight to the hospital from the airport.

I should have gone to the doctor to have my hand checked. It would wait until tomorrow. Everything would wait until I'd washed off the blood . . . and slept. But I didn't want to be alone. I looked at Philo, who was rinsing out the thermoses at the kitchen sink.

"I'm not going anywhere," he said.

He didn't add that Morocho might still be around. I read it in his eyes.

I woke, alone, at four. The shadows were long outside my bedroom window, and the sky was a startling shade of ultramarine. I smelled five-alarm chili. Philo was cooking the owl's-head stew I owed him, and talking with my parents about the media frenzy at the hospital and on the road beyond our gravel drive. The phone rang. I heard my father reassuring someone. I stretched and felt pain stab my injured hand. I wondered how Jamie was doing.

All talk ceased as I walked into the kitchen. My parents looked no older than the last time I'd seen them, but leaner, from walking the mountains of Scotland last summer. The weathering and erosion of years had smoothed their surfaces, softened angles, revealed the silver in their hair. I took after my father—long legged, black haired, gray eyed, most comfortable in denim and boots—though, unlike him, I relished the feel of cashmere and silk against my skin. My mother was my antithesis—five inches shorter, fine boned, naturally fair, and effortlessly feminine, with a kind of flowing grace and intense presence. Amy Tyrrell MacFarlane was poised in any situation. I'd never seen her disconcerted—until now. I must have looked like hell.

"Hi, honey," my father said, filling the awkward silence. "Tough day at the office?"

"Mac." Mother gave the word two syllables, and nudged him in the ribs. "Don't mind your father," she said.

"My life's work," I assured her, hugging both of them at once.

"Her sense of humor's intact," said Mac. "I guess we can leave now."

"At least stay for dinner," I said.

"We already ate with Philo. We're on Greenwich mean time."

Philo was, I noted, very much at home in this kitchen. He'd found all the necessary spices, whereas, after two months, I still had trouble figuring out where my parents had stashed the Tabasco. He handed me a steaming bowl of chili.

"This is great, Philo," I said, adding diced tomatoes, scallions, cheese, and crumbled tortilla chips to the bowl. "It's nice to be waited on."

"It doesn't get you off the hook."

"I'm good for it. How's Jamie?" I asked my father.

"Lucky," Mac said. "The concussion wasn't serious, and they removed the bullet in his thigh. He's on antibiotics and painkillers, but unless there are complications, he can recuperate at home. We'll know more in the morning."

"He was worried about you, though," my mother said.

"I'm fine," I said. "I'll call him later and tell him myself."

"Speaking of later," Philo said, "Toni's bringing Gallegos-Martínez here at seven. Unfinished business."

"The dead men were Salvadoran nationals—mercenaries and known associates of Reyerto, Morocho, or whatever his real name is," said Toni. "They'd been living in Nogales. Jamie confirmed that they killed Carla."

She, Scott Munger, and Gallegos-Martínez had joined the family in the living room. Every few minutes the phone would ring. We let the answering machine pick up.

"They bought the green Range Rover on Friday from a private party in Nogales, Arizona," Toni continued. "Paid cash. It was abandoned in Sierra Vista early this morning. No one saw who parked it at McD's."

"The Lincoln in the parking lot at Sabino Canyon—was that theirs, too?" I asked.

"Two men with Mexican passports bought it in Tucson—cash, again—yesterday."

"The passports were forged, of course," Gallegos-Martínez added. "But the fingerprints in the car match the two men in the canyon."

"As for Reyerto," Toni said, "we've had the ports of entry watched. He hasn't returned to Sonora, at least not through normal channels. He could be anywhere."

"What are the chances he'll cut his losses and disappear?" Mac asked.

"Ramon Reyerto is obsessed with protecting his identity and his privacy," said Gallegos-Martínez. "You have breached both." He hesitated, as if searching for words.

"Señor Dain and your daughter have seen him. Your son witnessed a murder." He left the rest up to our imaginations.

"Don't worry about Jamie," Toni said. "I put an officer outside his door. And he's listed under a fictitious name."

"I'd feel better if we could hide him somewhere until you pick up Reyerto," my mother said.

"My place in the Chiricahuas," Charley said from his chair near the door. "It's pretty isolated—only the one road in."

"Teresa and I can nurse him," Rosa added. "The men will keep watch."

Teresa nodded. She'd said little that evening, as if somber thoughts intruded . . . as if she'd seen what I'd seen on the mountain.

"And I'll take care of the horses while you're gone, Teresa," I said.

"Then you're on, my friends," said Mac. He turned to Toni. "How will you protect Frankie and Philo?"

Kit answered a knock at the door. It was Michael. "Am I interrupting?" His face was drawn, but determined. "I have come to help." He stepped past Philo and set a canvas duffel bag on the floor.

My father and mother looked blank. I remembered, then, that they'd never met. The Zoryas had moved in after my parents left for England. So I introduced them to their next-door neighbor. Michael looked at me. It was a question. He wanted to know if I'd told them about his being in the canyon. I shook my head, just the slightest of movements. He'd have to tell them himself.

"The man who murdered my sister will not stop," he said. "I can help you find him. I can draw him out of hiding."

It mirrored my family's concerns, as if he'd been listening outside the door . . . Maybe he had.

Philo studied him, like Anubis weighing the dead man's conscience against the feather of law. I couldn't tell from his face which way the balance leaned. "Jamie said you're involved with Reyerto," Philo said. "How do we know we can trust you?"

Michael pointed to the duffel bag. "The rifle inside will match a bullet in the head of one of the men on the mountain today. My prints are on it." He handed Toni a cell phone. "Press redial. You will recognize the number. Ask what questions you wish—but in private, please."

"Agent Gallegos-Martínez comes with me," Toni said.

It was Michael's turn with Anubis's scales. Finally he nodded, and Toni and Gallegos-Martínez went into the bedroom. Scott took custody of the duffel bag. No one spoke. Michael spotted my father's old guitar, standing in the corner. Picking it up, he started to tune it.

"How is Cézar?" I asked him.

Michael's face brightened for a moment. "So far, so good. His body has not rejected the heart. He is a fighter."

Bending his head, he began to play, and my world shifted. I was back at La Roca, listening to an artist draw music from the strings—Albinoni and Albéniz, Mozart and Rodrigo, one piece flowing into another to create a lyrical, haunting dirge for his sister. I don't know how much time passed. I didn't notice when Toni and Gallegos-Martínez rejoined us. I don't think anyone else did either.

My mother came in from the kitchen, where she'd been making comfort food. There were tears on her cheeks. Michael's fingers caressed the strings a final time, before he handed the guitar to my mother. "It is a fine instrument."

"Come play it anytime," she said.

"I will remember that. Thank you."

Gallegos-Martínez gave the phone back to Michael. "How can you help us?" he asked, in a respectful, almost wary tone.

"I have a delivery to make to Reyerto. In Douglas."

"CZ-Storage?" I asked.

"How did you know?"

"Hector Ortiz e-mailed the building plan to me before he died," I said.

"The professor who died in the bombing? Why did he have the plans?"

"He also made a delivery there. Material for pipe bombs," Toni said. "Douglas PD searched two units yesterday. They found nothing."

"Of course not. Things are not stored there, oddly enough, and my delivery has not yet been made."

"And what will you deliver?"

"An Aston Martin. Reyerto collects unique and expensive automobiles. He has wanted this one for a long time."

"An automobile?" Gallegos-Martínez asked. "Is that all?"

"No," Michael said, with a wry little twist of the lips. "In the trunk will be rare coins, stamps, and loose gems worth twenty-five million dollars—easily transported or converted to cash. And most important of all, a jade mask. Reyerto is a collector, you see, with a fondness for fine jade, particularly the rare Olmec blue jade. In a short time, he has amassed one of the largest collections of Olmec treasures in Central America, perhaps the world. It has become an obsession. I have what he wants, and this time he will come himself."

"How do you know?" I asked.

"Because before, I met with his representatives, the men who died today on the mountain. He would trust no one else with the mask."

"You're sure he'll be there?" Philo asked. His face was impassive, but his knuckles were blue-white where he pressed his fist into his thigh.

"He is an addict, Philo. He craves four things: certain rare and expensive objects, inflicting pain, creating terror, and . . . my sister. Now that he has killed her, he will get his satisfaction from the other three. Plus," Michael continued, "he needs this last shipment to finance his disappearance."

"What's your plan?" Philo asked.

"Tomorrow night I will drive the car down to Douglas. He has threatened to kill my father and aunt if I do not."

"You've got a passenger, Michael."

Michael stood up, looked from Philo to Toni, and gave a nod. "We leave from my home tomorrow evening."

"I want to ask you something." I followed Michael out to the porch, closing the door behind me. "Are you Alessandro, the guitarist?"

He seemed startled, as if he'd been thinking up excuses to cover up something else—such as which government employed him to do what, and why. But I wasn't interested in his secret life. I preferred to keep abyssal plains between my little world and his clandestine operations.

"There's a poster of you on the wall at La Roca." There also was one on Carla's bedroom wall, but I wasn't going to admit to snooping. "You played some of the same music when we were there. But I didn't recognize you till you started playing tonight. Your hair was long then, and you had a mustache and goatee . . . and you wore dark glasses."

A family of javelinas tromped among the prickly pear, stopping now and then to munch. The porch light reflected from their eyes.

"You are . . . uncomfortably perceptive," Michael said. "I studied guitar long before I took Carla to Spain. That's all I ever wanted to do—play and compose music. But I could not support myself on that alone, and I did not want to teach. So I created a job that would allow me to travel and perform. I give four concerts a year internationally."

"Thank you for playing tonight. It helped."

"It helped me, as well." He turned to go.

"One more thing, Michael. Did you take the tapes from the bunkhouse?"

"Of course. I did not want my family involved in a murder investigation." He smiled. "It was easy. You really ought to get a dog, Francisca." He stopped at the edge of the porch. "I almost forgot. Tía Miranda asked me to give you this. It belonged to her grandmother." Michael lifted a thin-bladed knife in a worn leather sheath from around his neck and handed it to me. "It is a tinker's knife, and very sharp. Don't fall on it," he said, before the shadows enveloped him.

I didn't think he knew me that well.

Toni, Scott, and Gallegos-Martínez came out, touching my shoulder as they passed. Wordlessly, they climbed into their car, their attention focused on what lay ahead. I felt Philo's breath in my hair. Turning, I wrapped my arms around his body, not wanting to break contact, not wanting to start the long journey into tomorrow.

"I have to do this," he said. "I have to finish it."

"I know."

"Toni parked your Jeep by the bunkhouse," he said. "I checked it over. It's clean. Should be safe enough for you to drive it now. Morocho's used up all his pipe bombs. Besides, Toni's put officers around the place. And don't worry, you'll be guarded at school tomorrow." He kissed me, then, a hungry kiss that had nothing to do with the past and everything to do with the future. "I'll call when it's over," he said, and left me.

I stayed there, listening to the night until Charley, Rosa, and Teresa came out. "Thank you for being there on the mountain today," I said, looking at Teresa.

"Did Michael tell you?" said Teresa.

"No. But it looked like the same knife you were wearing yesterday morning . . . and Charley still had his after . . . after it was over. I let Toni think it was mine. No reason to involve you unless she asks."

"Thanks, Frankie. Just don't tell Jamie," she said. "Please—let me tell him in my own way, when the time is right."

"Well, I hope you make the most of the next few days. You're not going to get a better opportunity than this." I turned to her father. "Isn't that right, Charley?"

"I've never been accused of meddling in affairs of the heart," he said. Rosa just laughed.

We said our good nights, and I opened the front door to silence and speculative glances from my parents. So much had happened in the past few months that neither they nor I knew quite where to pick up the threads.

"You and Philo an item?" asked my father. He had reclaimed his favorite leather chair, the one Charley had occupied the night Angelisa died. My mother, shoes off, curled up in a corner of the sofa. The familiar tableau confirmed I was home.

"We'll see," I said. "But apparently the reports of his death were greatly exaggerated."

"Didn't Amy tell you?" Mac asked.

"I thought you told her," my mother said.

"Sorry about that," Mac said. "It must have been a shock."

"That's an understatement, Dad."

"Philo's a good man, Frankie. I always liked him."

Unlike Geoff. My father didn't say it, but it was there between us. I hadn't seen my parents since last year at the Christmas break when I'd brought Geoff home from California to introduce him to the family. They had been their usual gracious selves. Geoff hadn't. It was a strained visit. I served as buffer between my family and my fiancé. He never told me what it was about my family that he objected to. They were just "different," he said. I'd been reticent about discussing it with them. And then it was too late. They'd gone to England; I'd spent the summer doing fieldwork in Nevada.

"She's been in love with Philo since she was twelve," my mother said, setting down her mug of tea. Earl Grey. I could smell oil of bergamot across the room.

Mac lowered the journal he was reading. "Twelve? I never noticed."

"You were working at Chaco Canyon that fall. I was finishing my Alice Corbin manuscript."

This was how it had always been. My parents told time by the books, papers, and projects they'd worked on, rather than by their ages or world events. "We'll see," I said. "How long can you stay?"

"Depends on what happens tomorrow night," said Amy. "We'll go down to Charley's in the morning, and bring Jamie back when it's safe—hopefully by your birthday."

My birthday was four days away. "Why don't I get a sub for Tuesday's classes and meet you at Charley's? We can celebrate my birthday early."

"How old will you be? Twenty-eight?" asked the man who never forgot a carbon 14 or tree ring date.

"No, dear. Jamie just turned twenty-eight. Frankie's turning twenty-nine."

"A prime number. Odd things, prime numbers."

"Odd numbers, you mean." I enjoyed teasing him.

"That, too. Remember Goldbach's Conjecture of 1742?"

"It wasn't on my orals, thank God."

"Every even integer greater than two can be expressed as the sum of two prime numbers. Thirty-two, for instance, is twenty-nine plus three."

My mother and I smiled at each other. "You do know the most arcane bits of trivia, dear."

"Speaking of which," he said to me, "how's the dissertation going?"

I didn't rise to the bait. "I sent it off to the committee last week. I defend next month."

"Good job," he said. "You'll do fine."

I hugged and kissed them good night, the contact immeasurably reassuring. "Thanks for coming home," I said.

"I just wish we could have been here earlier," Mac said.

"Some things are best done alone."

"You've changed," Amy said.

"I'm definitely not the same person I was a year ago."

"Life 401. A graduate course."

"In the school of hard rocks," I said. "I love you. See you in the morning."

I turned at the hall doorway to look at them, sitting on either side of the rock fireplace. He was reading an article; she was writing in her journal. I felt a fierce wave of protectiveness pass over me. I'd allow no one to damage that aura of harmony and balance. No one.

PART VII

Monday, November 3
Southeastern Arizona

Tunnel [mining]: Strictly speaking, a passage in a mine that is open to the surface at both ends.

CHAPTER 38

I DIDN'T SLEEP WELL, AWAKENED FREQUENTLY DURing the dark hours by a nameless, faceless dread. But I got up at my usual time, and had breakfast with my parents. They wanted me to stay home and rest. I couldn't, wouldn't. To begin healing, I needed to immerse myself in the routine and distractions of the campus.

When I drove to school, a shroud of pale gray clouds stretched from the Catalinas to Mexico. The western selvage was so sharp it could have been cut with Miranda's knife. But beyond was a sky of pure, blue hope. By midnight, I thought, the nightmare will be over.

A campus security guard met me in the parking lot. Toni was taking no chances. My name was in the morning paper again—this time with a photo of Charley pulling cactus spines out of my arm. The article was short on details, long on drama. Though Jamie was barely mentioned, Morocho must know that his men had failed on both counts. So I dutifully allowed the guard to escort me to the classroom and position himself in the courtyard.

I was scheduled to teach two lecture classes and a lab. It was the first time we'd met since the day Angelisa was killed. Ernie from the gym was in my first class. He stared at my bandaged hand and asked for my version of events. The rest of the students peppered me with questions. What they really wanted was reassurance that their world made sense, that order was restored. It wasn't—not yet. Instead of falsehoods, I gave them science. I turned my adventures into an exercise.

Copies of the Sabino Canyon quadrangle had been delivered on Friday—after the mop-up, as luck would have it. One day earlier and they'd have been reduced to pulp by the overhead sprinklers. We talked about township, range, and section numbers and Hector's mysterious e-mail. They located the valley with its city streets, the unpopulated mountains, the college, and the trails in Sabino Canyon. They learned about contour lines and intervals, and how to tell ridges from ravines, saddles from peaks, streams from roads. We traced my route, turning my nightmare into a learning experience. They saw that geology wasn't just rocks and minerals and fossils; it also was maps that represented their corner of the world, no matter where that corner might be.

Ernie's class grasped the basics so quickly that I went on to talk about the rocks they'd see in Sabino Canyon on our next field trip. On the board I drew a cross section of a Snickers bar—the nougat at the bottom representing the granite core of the Catalina Mountains; the peanuts and caramel layer in the middle, called a mylonitized zone, where the rocks had been stretched and broken and metamorphosed into banded gneiss while still in a semiplastic state deep underground; and the thin chocolate layer on top that could slide on the plastic caramel until it detached, just as the skin of the mountains had slid, millions of years ago, to where it now rested, under the gravelly floor of the Tucson Basin. But one could map the detachment fault, a line that ran along the foot of the mountains not far away.

I paused, thinking of Carla, whose detachment had been both physical and psychological. Suicide had separated her from her mother, murder from her first love, business from her father. In putting Angelisa up for adoption, her mother had denied all of them a relationship. Carla's fugues had separated her from reality, from her family, and from Jamie, a detachment reinforced by the man Philo called Morocho. And then he'd killed her . . .

"Dr. MacFarlane?"

I started at the sound of Ernie's voice, wondering how long I'd been standing there, staring at the window. I hadn't even heard the bell.

"Class dismissed," I said. "See you Wednesday."

The Sabino Canyon exercise had been so successful I decided to use it for the next two classes. But as the day wore on, tension built behind my upbeat facade. At lunch, I called my parents' cell phone. Jamie had been released to Charley and Rosa's care. They were all on their way to the Chiricahuas. I asked one of the part-time instructors to cover for me on Tuesday. It was easy enough. He could teach tomorrow what I'd skipped today.

The security guard shadowed me all the way to the music hall. I was early. The setting sun stretched long golden fingers across the floor of the amphitheater. Friday's memorial flowers and candles had been removed. I broke off a twig of late-blooming salvia from a bush beside the path and placed the magenta blossoms on the center mark. I still didn't know what had happened that Wednesday night—or who had killed Angie. Perhaps I'd never know.

"Go have some dinner, Fred," I told my guard when we reached the music hall. "I'll be here a while."

Inside, sheet music was stacked on a table near the door.

Gavin Plinkscale was alone, practicing the accompaniment to John Rutter's "Gloria." But at the thought of singing, my throat closed down. I picked up my music and left.

I wasn't worried that Fred had taken me at my word, leaving me unguarded. I was wearing Miranda's knife, suspended from its leather thong. The worn sheath lay nestled between my shoulder blades. Moreover, by this time Morocho would be on his way to meet Michael, roughly ninety minutes southeast of Tucson.

I tried not to think of the setup in Douglas, but it hovered in the back of my mind. So instead of going home to an empty house, I swam laps for an hour. After drying my hair, I dabbed antibiotic ointment on my hand and applied a fresh bandage. I felt immeasurably calmer as I walked through the dark night to the Jeep.

In the almost deserted parking lot I unlocked the Cherokee and climbed in. Unfortunately, I'd forgotten to lock the back end.

"I don't want to hurt you, Señorita MacFarlane," said a voice behind me. "But I will, if you scream."

I turned my head slowly. It was Chuy Desierto, the skipper from Puerto Peñasco. Jorge's brother. Chuy was wearing the workshirt taken from our tack room. He held the point of a filleting knife to my throat. "I listened outside your door last night. I heard your plan."

My mind processed the new information at warp speed, re-arranging the pieces of the three-dimensional puzzle. I thought of the wound in Angelisa's neck. It could have been made by this knife. I had to know. "You killed Angelisa," I blurted out.

"I did not mean to hurt her. I threw a knife at the man who killed my brother. I thought she was out of harm's way. But she ran back to embrace him . . . I could not call it back."

"I can't help you, Chuy."

"If you do not take me there, I will kill one of your family—a brother, a cousin, an uncle . . . or your lover. You cannot protect them all."

This didn't sound like the man who'd taken us fishing for so many years . . . He'd joked with us, laughed with us, told stories. But now his face was as serious as the day he'd discovered Jorge's body.

"But if I drive you," I said, "it will put others in danger."

"That is not the same as dead. You love your family, señorita. At least give them a chance."

A beautiful plan, like a train, can be derailed by a foreign object on the track. I was the foreign object that would wreck Philo's train and kill the passengers—strangers and loved ones alike. "The law will hunt you," I said.

"That is then, this is now. Jorge was not a good man, but he was my brother. He would do the same for me."

"You offer a deal with the devil."

"It is the devil we go to meet. One of us will die. It is in God's hands."

I started the car. How, I wondered, short of throwing myself from a moving vehicle, could I stop Chuy using me as a hostage? It was dark. If he moved to the front seat, I could pull Miranda's knife with my left hand. It would only take a moment . . . Of course, it would take only a moment for Chuy to kill me, too. I might not see my twenty-ninth birthday. A moot debate. Chuy stayed behind me.

I drove south through town, passing no police cars. Why is it that they're never around when you want them, even when you're purposely going twenty miles over the speed limit and running red lights?

"Slow down," said Chuy. "We do not want to attract attention."

Speak for yourself, I thought, but I did as he asked. I sped up again as I merged onto I-10, but everyone else was going faster. Just past Benson, I turned south again on highway 80. Cars occasionally passed us going north, none going south. Maybe in Tombstone, Bisbee, or Douglas, where there were lights and people, I could open the door and fall out on the pavement.

No one was expecting us at the storage unit. No one knew I was missing. My parents and Teresa were at Charley's ranch in the Chiricahuas. Philo and Toni were with Michael.

"The police will be there—why not let them arrest him?" I asked.

I looked in the rearview mirror. Passing headlights caught the look on his face. He thought I was simple, or at least naive. "You do not understand what it is like in Mexico. Where there is so much money, the *policía* protect the criminal. The evidence goes away. The witness disappears . . . No, I do this my own way. No one will mourn him."

I tried a different tack. "You'll be outnumbered."

"No matter. I will do what I came to do. *La bruja* at the house next to you told me so."

"You saw Miranda?"

"She read the cards for me. Jorge's murderer will die."

"Did she tell her nephew Michael?" I asked.

"Alessandro? The man who plays the guitar at La Roca? That is this Michael?"

"Yes," I said. "Does he know you're coming? Did his aunt tell him so?"

"I tell you, it does not matter. Now, no more talk."

It mattered to me. It mattered very much. Philo was there. Toni was there. Gallego-Martínez and Michael were there, as well as others I didn't know. Chuy's knife had missed the mark once before. I couldn't let that happen to someone else. To protect my family, I had to keep my end of the bargain and allow Chuy to reach the storage site. Then I'd have to find a way to disarm him.

We each had a knife. I knew where his was. He didn't

know I had one. I just needed to be patient. I needed to out-think him.

We drove through quiet St. David, past the lighted cross of the Benedictine monastery; through Tombstone, "The Town Too Tough To Die," with its Boot Hill and OK Corral. A few miles later, we wound down into Bisbee. Lights shone from the bed-and-breakfast inns. Here, in the Queen Mine, I'd gone deep into the earth for the first time. The guide had turned off the lamp on his hard hat. We'd all followed suit. In the darkness that was blacker than death, I'd felt the rocks press down, eloquent in their silence.

The last time I'd been to the hills around Bisbee was on a trip with my high school geology class. We'd collected fossils from the Paleozoic limestones, beautifully preserved corals, sea lilies, bryozoans, and brachiopods—detritus shed to the floor of an ancient seabed more than a quarter of a billion years ago. I could remember the roughness of the gray carbonate, the smell of broken rock, the excitement of finding, bagging, labeling, and identifying the fossils. It was as if I'd come full circle, found the place where the seed had been planted that germinated into a passion for deciphering Earth's story from clues locked in stone. This was, in a sense, my other home, the place where I had been reborn. Odd that I should remember this now, at a time when it looked like that life might come to an abrupt end. But I'd be damned if I'd go quietly.

This was an uncompromising land with a violent history both above and below the surface, from the ancient volcanoes spewing lava, to the mineral-laden waters invading fractured rocks and depositing ores; from the roving bands of Apaches stealing cattle and horses, to the frontier justice of rope and tree limb; from the gunfights and saloons of boomtowns, to the drug wars and *coyotes* of the present—a rough land, a beautiful land, a dangerous land, where guns were as plentiful as scorpions, and citizens still made arrests.

That was it—I could arrest Chuy for the accidental killing of Angelisa and the planned murder of Reyerto. Chuy was guilty by his own admission . . . but it was my word against his. I didn't have him on tape, and there were no other witnesses. I had to come up with another plan.

A sheriff's car approached me. My left hand tapped the high beams on, then off. He did the same, and waved as he passed. Shit.

I felt the knife sting the back of my neck. Blood trickled down between my shoulder blades. Clearly I'd underestimated Chuy. He wasn't simple either.

I saw the lights of Douglas in the distance. The end of the trail.

People have to have a reason to go to Douglas—copper mining, geology, border crossing, or a history lesson. This was Texas John Slaughter's corner of Arizona back in the late nineteenth century. Cattlemen wrested the land from the Indians, then protected their hoofed investments from rustlers. A silver strike created Tombstone. When copper and silver were discovered further south, Bisbee and Douglas sprang up, their fortunes and populations waxing and waning with the demand for ore. Douglas was a company town, the copper smelter and mine within shouting distance of Agua Prieta, Sonora. But the railroad cemented the town and kept it viable.

In recent years, the city had become a major port of entry from Mexico, for legal goods, such as produce, and illegal ones, such as drugs and people. Whenever the Border Patrol clamped down further east and west, the smugglers shifted to this isolated corner of Arizona.

I turned off highway 80 onto Pan American Avenue. Straight ahead to the south was the Douglas Port of Entry.

To the east was the old city itself, surrounding the marble-floored and gilded Gadsden Hotel. A billboard directed us to CZ-Storage. It sat on a strip of land within shouting distance of the border. Across the street to the north, set well back from the road, was a strip mall with big-box stores. To the west, a dirt road led into the dump. The border itself was defined by two high, curved, metal fences enclosing a deep ditch. Powerful lights exposed every square inch of no-man's land.

An electrified hurricane fence, designed to discourage thieves, transients, and border crossers, surrounded the storage facility. *Don't even think about it,* the razor wire proclaimed in international sign language. Within its wire-mesh cocoon, the complex was box shaped. Only one way in—or out. A lone guard could watch the interior and the single gate, which meant you had to overcome only one man to gain access.

We drove by once, then turned around and parked at the shoe store across the street. The CZ-Storage parking lot was empty. A cigarette glowed from behind the tinted windows at the right side of the guardhouse, which was large enough to contain a computer station and a small restroom. Unless he made regular rounds, he never had to leave that booth. I wondered if the company screened its employees for claustrophobia.

The rear units blocked the guard's view of the back fence. That would be where Toni, the local authorities, and maybe DEA would cut their way through the fence, I decided, while Michael and Philo used the gate. I said as much to Chuy. He nodded, but made no move to leave.

"I think this is where you get out, Chuy."

"*Lo siento,* Señorita MacFarlane, but I must take you with me."

I turned to face him, my left hand going up in a nervous gesture to gather my hair at the base of my neck where a thin crust of dried blood marked Chuy's cut. I reached for Miranda's knife in its sheath that nestled between my shoulder blades . . . Stopped. Light from a blinking neon sign above us glanced off a revolver. It was pointed at my head.

CHAPTER 39

I SUCKED IN MY BREATH. HE WANTED A HOSTAGE. "I brought you here. I kept my word."

"Who knows? This could be any place. I see no one but the guard. When I see the man I search for, you may go."

Maybe, if I'm still alive, I thought. I left the knife in its hiding place. Taking a rubber band from the stash wrapped around the door handle, I trapped my hair in a pony tail. My watch showed 9:45.

"Get out." Chuy pointed across the dusty road. No streetlights there, only long, inky shadows. "If you scream, someone will be killed, someone in your family. I swear this on my brother's head."

He had a way with words. I gave it one last try. "We could both be killed in there."

A flash of white in the darkness of the car, the grin I remembered from the old days of fishing in the Sea of Cortez, eons ago. "I feel lucky tonight, Señorita MacFarlane. Do you?"

I used up my luck yesterday, I thought, and stepped out of the car. He was beside me. I hadn't seen or heard him move. If he was that quick, maybe there was hope yet.

He made me go first into the shallow, rocky wash that paralleled the western fence. It was a corridor for javelinas and border crossers, used recently. Litter showed white in the starlight. The brush-choked, dry watercourse smelled of urine, and worse. I stepped in things I didn't want to think about. My Ariat slip-on boots weren't made for this. I decided to live in field boots from now on. Expect the un-expected. Who cared about fashion? Who cared if my students were taunted that their teacher wore combat boots?

At least I was wearing jeans and socks that offered some protection from the thorny brush. My Harris Tweed jacket picked up every burr it encountered. I stumbled, banging my wounded left hand and bruising my shins. Chuy, of course, was surefooted as a desert bighorn. I resented it. But I didn't speak, except for a muttered mix of prayers and curses.

The fence was above us, lit only by powerful lights at the corners. Chuy lifted his head until he could see over the edge of the wash. For a moment, light glinted off his eyes, his hair. In profile, he reminded me of Charley. I wished he were here. If wishes were silver dollars, we'd all be rich . . . What would Charley do if he were in my place? *Play along,* I heard him say, as if he were standing next to me. *You're only a means to an end. Stay low. Keep your head down. Wait till he's distracted.*

When we came to the southwest corner, we went a little way further, out of the range of the floodlight, before turning east. I was watching for sentries. Not that I'd see one till it was too late. Chuy was looking for the break in the fence that I'd said might be there. *I could use a little help here, Charley,* I thought.

Help's inside. Philo and Toni and Michael . . . Stay calm . . . Stay low . . . Be patient.

Patience was never my strong suit, Charley.

I could hear his soft laugh. *It's never too late to learn.*

Chuy spotted what he was looking for about halfway along, just beyond the light from either corner floodlight. He prodded me toward the gash, where a loop of narrow wire conducted the current around the break. I hung back. He shook his head and pointed. I crawled, careful not to touch the wire. I felt a hand on my ankle and turned my head. Chuy was through. Then he was beside me. Our shoulders touched. The gun was hidden away somewhere. The knife was in his teeth.

He pointed to a pool of blackness ten feet away—the back wall of the storage complex. I got into a sprinter's stance, let my eyes sweep no-man's land. I smelled dog feces. I hadn't thought of dogs, didn't know whether the faint smell came from inside or outside the fence. I sprinted, hoping he'd eat Chuy first.

No dog, at least not at the moment. Chuy had his knife in his right hand, gun in his left. Oh great—he was ambidextrous. Exhaustion and hunger were making me giddy. Nothing about this night or this situation was real.

Whoever had cut the fence had scaled the wall and was on the flat roof of the complex. A knotted rope dangled down invitingly. Chuy nudged me away from it. Imagine that. I led the way along the wall to the east, then turned north again. I tried to be noiseless. I'd had a lot of practice lately. I had no idea what we'd do when we got back to the front. Maybe the guard would be watching TV. That's what guards did in the movies.

We reached the northeast corner of the building. The windowless back of the guardhouse was toward us, poor planning on the builder's part . . . I'd forgotten—Cézar's company had built it.

It was ten degrees cooler here than in Tucson. The wind was blowing from the southwest, covering any night sounds and sending the temperature tumbling into the forties. I shivered in my thin silk sweater and blazer.

The front gate was shut. A car turned into the parking lot across the street. The road was empty. Without looking to see if Chuy was behind me, I ran along the front wall toward the guard's hut, crossed the exit lane, and crouched under the window. If I could alert the guard . . .

I held my breath and stood up. No one home. I'd have to come up with Plan C.

Chuy pointed to the left. We entered the lion's den.

CHAPTER 40

IT WAS ONLY 10:20. I FELT AS IF YEARS HAD BEEN sliced off my life.

The units all opened onto a central courtyard. They were twelve feet deep. I paced it off as we crept along the wall beside the guardhouse. There were numbers painted above each garage-style metal door. Once at the interior edge we could see all of the units except the first twelve, the row to our left. Number 13 was in the northeast corner, facing west; unit 12 was at right angles to it, facing south.

The door to 13 was up, but the light was off. I could just make out the gleaming bumper of a silver car—the Aston Martin. The unit looked a little wider than 14, which was odd. I remembered the architectural plan Hector had e-mailed me. Now I understood his cryptic note. A twelve-by-twelve-foot corner space between units 12 and 13 was enclosed by the outer wall, the wall I'd just run around. I'd seen no exterior door. To access that space, there must be a door in either 12 or 13—or both. Or perhaps a trapdoor on the roof. My money was on 13, though the local authorities had found nothing. So there couldn't be an obvious door. Perhaps the whole interior wall moved up or down . . .

Where were Philo and Michael? Toni would have seen me by now if she were up on the roof with her cohorts. I scanned the roofline, saw a head bob down on the northern wing. I hoped it was Toni.

I pointed at 13. Chuy poked me in the ribs with his knife and pointed with the gun. I'd gone only ten steps when I heard voices from 12. Its door was also open, its light flicked on. I could think of no place to hide except the dark hole of 13 . . . where Michael was to meet Reyerto.

Chuy nudged me forward. I shook my head and pointed behind us, made a circling motion with my forefinger. It would be better to circle the courtyard and slip into 13, if we could—anything but cross that patch of light pouring out from 12. I took off my boots and ran the perimeter until I could see directly into 12.

Two men stood there—the guard, in uniform, and Michael, laughing as if he hadn't a care in the world. They were eating burritos. I salivated at the thought.

The interior walls of 12 looked solid. There were boxes inside, brown shipping ones stacked against the walls, and a few wooden boxes. Michael pointed to a box, and they both turned to look. They had their backs to us. I sprinted for the black hole of unit 13.

Hands grabbed me, pulled me inside. No words, but I knew those hands. Philo's hands. Chuy must have sensed something as he rounded the corner, because he dropped to a crouch. But his eyes were not as accustomed to the dark as Philo's were . . . They grappled. I heard a soft grunt . . . Philo ended up with the knife and the gun. Chuy lay motionless on the floor.

"Is he . . . ? Please tell me you didn't kill him," I whispered in Philo's ear. I had mixed feelings about my kidnapper.

He shook his head as he pulled plastic strips from his pocket and cuffed Chuy's hands and feet. "Who is he?"

"Chuy—the skipper of the fishing boat at Puerto Peñasco. Reyerto killed his brother, Jorge. We found him the day Carla disappeared."

Philo carried the much smaller Chuy to the near back corner and dumped him next to a stack of quilted moving blankets. I draped one over him.

"Sorry to crash your party," I said. "He said he'd kill someone in my family if I didn't bring him here. He wants Reyerto."

"Don't we all? But so far he's a no-show."

I looked at my watch. "He's only thirty minutes late."

"Not like him. It worries me."

"Did you find the tunnel?"

"Not yet. I didn't want to turn on the light while the guard was socializing with Michael."

"Where's Gallegos-Martínez?" I asked him.

"On the Mexican side of the border," he said, "hoping that Morocho will lead him to the other tunnel entrance."

"Did Michael mention the inner room?"

"What inner room?"

"Someone finished off the northeast corner to make a room." I said. "It's not on the plans, but it's fair sized— about a hundred and forty-four square feet. Doesn't look like the entrance is from unit 12, so it must be from here . . . or the roof."

"Or both." Philo detached infrared glasses from his belt. We edged past the front of the car, then ran our hands over the far wall, feeling for any kind of opening. Nothing. The only breaks were at the corners themselves. What about the floor? Was there a trapdoor?

The laughter and talk in unit 12 dropped off. "Don't you have to check in?" Michael asked.

"Shit." The guard ran toward his hut. Michael turned off the light in 12.

"Can you stop him, Philo?"

He gave a soft owl's call, barely audible above the sound of the door closing. Not very original, but it worked. The door stopped. Michael turned and stepped into the darkness of unit 13. "We've got company," Philo whispered.

"Reyerto?"

"Frankie. And she brought a friend."

"Female, I hope."

"Sorry," I said. "It's Chuy, the skipper from Puerto Peñasco."

"Jorge's brother?"

"He came for Reyerto. He dragged me along."

"Dragged you?" I saw his teeth flash in the dark. He seemed almost lighthearted. "Impossible."

"He's a brave man," said Philo.

"He's Seri," I said, as if it explained everything.

"Where is this terror?" Michael asked.

"Under a blanket at the back. Unconscious," I said.

"Or playing 'possum," said Michael. Light from outside caught the thin blade in his hand. Philo was already at the blanket.

"Damn," he said.

"You're slowing down, amigo," said Michael. "Must be time to retire."

Philo flipped him off. Apparently three hours together had turned acquaintances into friends.

We checked the cubicle, under and in the car, looked round the courtyard. Came up empty. He'd escaped while we talked.

I flashed on the opossum card that I'd dealt in Miranda's shop . . . an odd coincidence.

"What's wrong?" Philo asked.

I looked at Michael. "Tía Miranda and I talked about her healing cards. I dealt the coyote, 'possum, antelope, lizard, and badger."

"Badger?" Philo chuckled softly.

"What's so funny?" I asked.

"That's what my middle name, Graevling, means in Danish."

Michael smiled. "Never underestimate my aunt," he said. "Now, Philo, why did you stop me putting down the door?"

"Ask Frankie."

I went to the door of 13, where a little yellow light from a courtyard flood found its way into our dark space. Using my finger, I drew a plan on the floor—units 12 and 13, doorjamb meeting at right angles, and the doorless square between them. "Where's the entrance to this room? We've checked this unit. It's solid. We need to check 12."

"If there is a tunnel large enough for cars, and it heads due south from under the room with no door, then the entry angle would be much easier from unit 12," Philo said. "Especially if the whole wall could move. You could back the Aston Martin out of 13, still hidden from the guardhouse, and whip it in there. Perhaps Reyerto's late because you and the guard were talking on the other side of his door."

"If there *is* such a door," said Toni, dropping down beside me. I wondered how long she'd been dangling like a spider, listening to us.

Philo and Michael were already ducking under the half-closed door. Toni was close on their heels. Which left me alone. I backed to the rear of the unit and sat on the pile of blankets, wrapping one around my shoulders. Like Chuy, it smelled faintly of fish. I couldn't see anything beyond the dark outline of the Aston Martin.

Slumping back against the wall, I felt, rather than heard, the building vibrate. Stale smells of concrete and rock swept over me. Noiselessly, the whole wall had gone down. Not five feet away stood someone who reeked of tobacco smoke and sweat. I wondered if he smelled me, too . . .

CHAPTER 41

REYERTO. MOROCHO. DANTE MONTOYA. I KNEW IT without being told. Knew it by the way he ran a caressing hand over the car's left front fender. *"Bueno,"* he said, so softly it sounded like a sigh.

This was the man from La Roca, the man who'd killed six people in Tucson and set off a half-dozen bombs; the man who'd hunted Jamie, and sent men to kill us. . . . I clamped my jaws together to keep them from chattering, and moved just enough to take the knife from its worn leather sheath. Tía Miranda's knife. An old blade, Michael had said. Her grandmother's. Had it killed people?

And then I saw the gun in his hand, the dark barrel catching a ray of light as he stepped to the entrance. A knife, at least in my unpracticed hand, was no match for a gun.

I needed to warn the others without alerting Reyerto. The men on the rooftop would have seen him perhaps, if they had on their night-vision goggles. They'd warn Philo and Toni, who were wearing earphones. But no one could see me.

Reyerto moved around the rear of the car to get a better view of the courtyard. Could they see him now?

I moved noiselessly along the back wall to my right, felt for the side wall. It wasn't there, just the shadow of an interior room lit only by a skylight. I inched across the threshold, my fingers feeling the slot where the wall had slid downward, out of the way. Ingenious.

The concrete floor, wide enough for a one-ton van, sloped downward into a tunnel that resembled a parking garage ramp. Above, the skylight gave enough moonlight to show me a ladder leading to a trapdoor in the ceiling—a way out across the rooftop. A border crosser would only have to wait until the gate was open and the guard distracted.

Reyerto reached inside the car from the right-hand driver's door. I heard the brush of cloth against the steering wheel, the faint rattle of keys. He had a dilemma. If he opened the trunk, a light would go on, revealing his presence, blinding him, making him a target. But he could just drive away. What was he waiting for?

The knife in my hand seemed to burn. Reyerto wanted to kill Michael. Reyerto must not need him anymore. He wanted what was in the car, and then he'd move on, leaving no witnesses behind . . . except Jamie, Philo, and me. Reyerto probably had plans for us, too. I had to warn Michael without getting shot.

I didn't have a pebble to toss. Throwing my knife would give me away and leave me without a weapon. I crawled next to the car, yanked the rubber band from my hair, looped an end around the steel haft of the knife, stretched the band, sighted, and leaned against the tire to wait for Michael. I was sure Reyerto could hear my heart beating as loudly as the cricket that started singing near my left foot. My boots . . . Where had I left them? What if Reyerto tripped over them?

My feet, chilled by the concrete floor, were going numb. *Come on, Michael, come on, Michael . . . What's taking you so long?*

They could see Reyerto from the rooftop, could see the gun. Why didn't they just wing him? Because they knew I was somewhere within, hiding. A stray shot could kill me.

Philo must be going nuts. His nemesis was between us. I was a potential hostage—again. How long before Reyerto found me? Was he alone?

After I let fly with my rubber band, what then? I'd have to get out of the way. Not down that tunnel—nothing would get me to run that direction. At one end was Gallegos-Martínez, who wouldn't be expecting me; at the other, Reyerto . . . I could roll under the car, but I'd be exposed when he backed it up to turn into the tunnel—or worse, be dragged by the car. Not a pleasant thought . . . That left the ladder. How did the trapdoor open? I'd have to figure it out in the dark. I could do it. I'd have to do it. And Reyerto wouldn't be looking for someone up near the ceiling.

My hands were getting tired from holding my impromptu slingshot at the ready. The stress of keeping the haft vertical tore open the furrow ploughed by the bullet. Was that only yesterday? Blood seeped out from under the bandage and slid down my arm. My hands shook with fatigue. *Come on, Michael* . . .

I saw Reyerto straighten up. Michael stepped silently into the doorway in front of me. "Señor?"

I let fly with my puny alert system.

CHAPTER 42

THE RUBBER BAND GLANCED OFF MICHAEL'S NOSE.
I'd been aiming for his body, but at least I'd found the target.

"*¿Qué paso?*" Reyerto's voice.

"It's nothing. An insect bit me. The gun—is it necessary?"

"Show me the mask."

"Patience. It is in the trunk."

"So open it."

Michael walked to the passenger door. He saw me, plain as day, crouching in the darkness against the front tire. I pointed at the ladder. He winked at me. I offered him the knife, haft first. His left hand discreetly waved me off as he casually leaned into the car, took the keys, and walked back to the trunk.

I knew that as soon as Reyerto saw the mask, he'd want to be out of there. I heard trial scrapes as Michael searched for the lock. "Do not scratch her," Reyerto said.

"You worry too much." There was a soft *snick* as the key

found the lock. The trunk lid swung up, blocking their view of me and the ladder. The light went on. I put the blade in its sheath so I wouldn't drop it, jumped for the ladder six feet away, and climbed like a spiny lizard. I reached the deep shadow at the ceiling in two seconds flat. When I looked down, Reyerto had put away the gun. The mask was in his hands. He held a penlight to the curved edge of the chin—the blue jade glowed like the glacial waters of Lake Louise, seen through a rising mist.

I forced my eyes away from the mask. My fingers found the outlines of the trapdoor. It was three feet square, the catch a simple sliding bolt. I prayed the bolt would be well oiled.

My prayers went unanswered. The action was stiff. My fingers worked it back, but the scraping sound was loud as a raven's call.

Reyerto quickly put down the mask and closed the trunk. "What is it?"

"A packrat in the tunnel, perhaps."

"Turn on the light."

"No. The guard will see the tunnel."

But Reyerto was already coming to investigate. I pushed—the door didn't budge. I heaved at it with my shoulder. Nothing. Frantic, I shoved harder. It moved a fraction. The last rain must have swelled the wood.

Reyerto was below me now, his gun pointing down the tunnel. I stopped breathing.

"Come down," he said, in Spanish. "You may use the front door." He must have thought I was one of his border crossers who'd followed him through the tunnel.

"No, no señor. *Yo tengo miedo,*" I said in a high, breathy voice, grateful that my twin brothers had taught me to say "I am afraid" in five languages. They'd also taught me how to say "I want your body," so I prayed I wasn't mixing up my phrases.

"I won't hurt you." Jorge's killer put one hand on the ladder and offered me the other. "Here, let me help you," said the spider to the fly. Behind him, Michael shook his head.

I felt a rush of air as the trapdoor above me opened. A head blotted out the starlight. Michael grabbed Reyerto's gun hand and twisted. The gun clattered to the floor and slid down the ramp. Reyerto hit a button beside the ladder. Hands pulled me onto the roof, and Chuy took my place on the ladder. As the wall rose slowly to close off the tunnel, I heard Philo and Toni running in from the front. They switched on the interior light. "Frankie," Philo called.

"Up here," I said. Our eyes met for a moment before the wall closed.

Below, they were fighting, illuminated only by the skylight and trapdoor opening. There were grunts and curses and thuds. Someone found the light switch. Reyerto was strong and muscular as a bull. He flung Michael against the wall, knocking the wind out of him. He lay, gasping for breath, while Chuy and Reyerto faced off.

Reyerto circled to get close to the gun. Chuy didn't know it was there. If I could open the wall-door, Chuy would have help. I heard men running over the rooftop. They wouldn't get here in time. I took out my knife, swung my legs over, and went back down the ladder. I couldn't see Michael anywhere.

Reyerto's eyes met mine as I hit the switch. I saw no fear there, no hatred, nothing but a feral excitement. The wall slid slowly down. Reyerto lunged for his gun as I tossed the knife, haft first, to Chuy. I scrambled for the trapdoor.

This time Philo pulled me out and handed me off to Toni before dropping through to the tunnel. He didn't bother with the ladder. Neither did Toni. She jammed a crowbar in the track of the door to hold it open.

Below me, Reyerto stood with his back to the wall of unit 12. His left hand held the gun. Blood dripped from a cut on his right hand, and ran like a lifeline down into the tunnel. Toni and half a dozen officers in flak jackets, guns pointed at Reyerto's chest, blocked the open door to 13. I couldn't see Philo or Chuy. They must have gone a little way down the ramp. Somewhere deep in the tunnel, a dog barked wildly, and then was silent.

"Drop the gun, Reyerto," Toni said.

Reyerto ignored her. "I should have killed you quickly," he said to Philo, "instead of taking my pleasure."

Philo didn't respond. Reyerto kept his eyes on the tunnel.

"It's blocked at the other end," Toni said.

Reyerto took a step toward Chuy. "Shall I tell you how Jorge screamed as I killed him? I made it last a long time. I let his blood drip into the sea to call the sharks, and then I left him for you to find . . . He was not a brave man, señor."

"It's no use, Morocho." Philo's voice echoed in the tunnel. "Put down the gun."

Reyerto continued to bait them, knowing he'd run out of options. I could feel the hatred and desire for revenge boil up out of the tunnel toward this lone figure. But they refused to be drawn. The tunnel was blocked by three men, unit 13 by six. Three more crowded around me on the roof, all trying to peer down at once.

"You will not allow me to take the honorable way out?" Reyerto asked at last.

"Arizona has the death penalty," Philo said. "That is your honorable way out. And you'll have years in a cramped prison cell to think about it before they finally give you the needle."

Reyerto shrugged. "I think not." His eyes flicked up to meet mine before he swept his arm across his chest and gave a stiff little bow of farewell.

He straightened, raised the gun, and fired at my head.

I'd flinched instinctively when his arm came up. The bullet creased the helmet of the officer behind me. I lost my balance and fell backward as gunfire exploded in the room below. The smell rose up to dissipate into the night sky.

"Son of a bitch," said the officer on whose lap I came to rest.

"Sorry," I said.

"Anytime, ma'am. My pleasure."

I looked down into the windowless room. Reyerto lay sprawled in an awkward pose. Blood seeped from multiple wounds in his body. Part of his head was missing. A knife protruded from one eye socket; another from his groin. Michael and Chuy walked up to the body, retrieved their weapons, and disappeared into the depths of the tunnel. No one tried to stop them.

CHAPTER 43

**On the road to Charley Black's ranch,
Chiricahua Mountains, November 4,
2:00 A.M.**

FROM DOUGLAS, CHARLEY'S RANCH WAS A SHORTER
drive than Tucson. It didn't make sense to go home and
drive back again in a few hours. I called my parents there to
tell them it was over, and to alert them to our early arrival.

Philo drove, cradling my left hand in his right. With his
help, I'd rebandaged Sunday's wound. It throbbed now, in
time to the slow, steady, reassuring beat of my heart.
Though we'd rinsed the blood from our skin, our clothes
still smelled of gunpowder residue and the sickly sweet
scent of dried blood. Worse, I couldn't seem to erase
Chuy's presence from the car. He'd sat behind me for two
hours, holding a knife to my throat . . .

For most of the way the highway paralleled the eastern
face of the mountains, a vast pile of volcanic rocks, homeland of the Chiricahua Apaches. Moonlight bleached the
flesh-colored ashflow tuffs of the summit. At one point the
highway jogged into New Mexico before curving back into
Arizona. The night creatures were out. A lone coyote trotted beside the ribbon of road. A great horned owl took off

from a fence post, just missed the Jeep, and snagged a jackrabbit mesmerized by the headlights.

We were alone on the road. I looked at Philo's profile, illumined by the dashboard light. A frown creased the skin around his eyes; his hand clenched the steering wheel, then relaxed. He sighed.

For me, tonight had brought answers. Chuy, seeking an eye for an eye, had accidentally killed Angelisa. But he'd had his vengeance in the end. And we'd both looked into the face of a man who had killed, maimed, or tortured our loved ones and friends—Jorge, Philo, Jamie, Carla, and Hector. Morocho had had a quick death, an easy death. He'd do no more harm. That was enough for me, enough for Chuy, I thought. But did Philo feel the same?

He turned his head and looked at me for a moment. "What is it?"

"Stop the car, please."

He screeched to a halt in the middle of the road. "Are you sick?"

"I'm okay. I just wanted to ask you something, before we reach Charley's."

He smiled. "I'm capable of multitasking, Frankie. I can drive and talk at the same time."

"But then I can't see your eyes."

The old guarded look slid over his face. "Frankie—"

I stopped him with a finger against his lips. "What did Morocho do to you?"

He sat back in his seat, his eyes following the centerline into the night. I hadn't a clue what he was thinking, but I noticed his left hand went instinctively to his thigh in that now-familiar gesture. Finally, coming to a decision, he pulled the Jeep off to the side of the road.

"You'll find out soon enough anyway. It's not something I can hide," he said, and turned off the engine.

Silence settled over us like a warm blanket. I could hear crickets singing in the cold night air.

"Morocho wanted information. But more than that, he wanted to produce exquisite pain. He used a paring knife— small cuts, you know, and buckets of salt water. I lost a lot of blood. When that didn't work, he resorted to cigarettes." Philo's tone was carefully controlled, neutral, but his fingers tightened on mine. "I have part of his name burned into the skin of my thigh—a permanent reminder . . . not that he thought I'd live. He just wanted to frighten whoever found the body . . . I'll never forget the stench of my flesh burning. M-O-R-O . . . The bastard finished four letters before . . . Anyway, when Gil and the others crashed the party, Morocho left me for dead and disappeared into the jungle."

Shaking, I wrenched open the door, stumbled into the brush beside the road, and was violently ill. I felt Philo's hand rubbing my back. When there was nothing left, and the dry heaves subsided, he handed me a bottle of water to rinse out my mouth, then sat with me in the dust. He pulled me against his chest and rocked me like a child, trying to replace the ugliness with that soothing, primitive rhythm.

"He's dead now, Frankie. He can't hurt us anymore," Philo whispered.

"You're at peace with it?"

"I'm at peace with it."

He helped me up and back into the Jeep. The rumble of the engine, and even the final miles of washboard road, soothed me. Charley was waiting on his veranda when we parked in front of the old ranch house in the wee hours of the morning. I sat for a moment, spent, letting the cold stillness of the moon-drenched hills wash over me. The stars were close enough to kiss, but I still felt no joy, no satisfaction, in surviving.

When Charley opened my door, the interior light revealed everything I wanted to hide. The deaths of others, loved ones or not, he'd once told me, should leave some mark on us. It seemed that now, even my scars had scars.

"Do you have any more of that godawful tea?" I asked, as he helped me out. "I think Philo and I could both use a cup."

It was the most reassuring thing I could have said. Jamie grinned at us from the doorway. He had one arm casually slung across Teresa's shoulder. I wondered if he knew that Teresa had helped save our lives on the mountain, or whether it would remain a secret. Behind them, her brothers stood with my parents and Rosa, a family united.

"Tough day at school?" Jamie asked, sounding so much like Mac I wanted to cry.

The experiences of the last few weeks had lent a firmness to his mouth. His blue-gray eyes showed a raw understanding. A few silver strands had appeared in his hair. I hadn't realized how important it was to me to see him standing, to touch him. The last time I'd seen him, he'd been covered by a sheet.

I hugged him fiercely. "You have no idea."

"Easy, easy—remember the rib cage." Jamie examined me just as closely—the bandaged hand, my filthy, burr-covered clothes. I must have looked as if I'd crawled all the way from Douglas.

"I've looked better," I said.

"No, you haven't," said my brother.

PART VIII

Speak to the earth, and it shall teach thee.

—JOB 12:8

EPILOGUE

THE NEXT MORNING, I CALLED TONI AND TOLD HER OF Chuy Desierto's confession. Though she notified Gallegos-Martínez, she had no hope the Mexican authorities would arrest and extradite Chuy. Unofficially, the case was closed. I sent a note to Joe and Rebecca Corday, relating the facts of Angie's death. I signed my own name. I said I was her teacher.

A few days later, on my twenty-ninth birthday, my parents drove Jamie down to Puerto Peñasco. Unlike me, he was ready to put his ghosts to rest. Chuy's boat was gone. He'd returned to his village, said one skipper. Another said he'd crossed the Sea of Cortez to Baja California, and was living in San Felipe. There were many places where a resourceful Seri could hide.

Back in Tucson, Hector's family located his possessions in a storage unit not far from the school. They took his body back to New York for burial. The college held a memorial service for him on the morning after the first frost of fall. The sandstone benches of the amphitheater retained the night's chill. I gave the eulogy.

Carla's funeral mass was held at the Church of Saint Pius X, a modern structure on the east side of Tucson. Philo, Jamie, and I arrived early and settled into the last pew. Teresa and Rosa joined us a few minutes later. Carla's flower-draped casket was center stage.

The church was not as large as old St. Augustine's downtown, nor as gilded and quaint as Mission San Xavier del Bac. This church was only thirty-five years old. The ambience was one of clean lines and spaciousness, without overtones of pomp. Great dark beams supported a white ceiling. Light came through tall, narrow side windows, a skylight over the altar, and from inset ceiling lights. Water fell over stone, creating a soothing melody; green plants and candles filled niches. *Sanctus, Sanctus, Sanctus*— Holy, Holy, Holy—was carved into the golden wood behind a plain altar draped with fringed, woven cloth. It reminded me of the shawl covering the table in Tía Miranda's store.

As if sensing my thought, she turned in the front row and glanced back at me. I nodded. She looked wizened— a carved-shell lamp in which the light had gone out. In a short time she'd lost not one niece but two, one of whom she'd raised as her own daughter. And she'd almost lost Cézar, the man she loved, the man she'd dedicated her life to. She met my eyes, nodded in return, and leaned toward Cézar, who sat in a wheelchair parked in the main aisle.

Floral arrangements covered the two steps before the altar. One, with red and white roses, was from the MacFarlane family. The flame-colored roses were from Jamie. Their scent drifted back as a classical guitarist, hidden from me by a grand piano, began playing hymns softly.

"Ave Maria" followed "Panis Angelicus." When the artist slipped easily into Albinoni, I recognized Michael's touch. I thought of Carla. Water, stone, fire, plant, soil, air, light, music—all the elements were here, within these walls, bearing witness to her life. Soon she'd be returned to earth.

"Speak to the earth, and it shall teach thee," my father used to quote to me. I'd taken it to heart in my choice of professions. But had I learned anything from Carla's life and death? I knew only that my own life had changed from the moment that she crossed my path. I would remember her, glowing like a Mexican fire opal. Opals fracture easily, as Carla's psyche had fractured. It is water molecules, bound within the opal's silica lattice, that weaken the structure as they create a rainbow of color. But that combination of fire and delicacy makes them precious and special, as Carla was special.

People continued to file in quietly—business associates in suits, taking time away from work to attend; friends and customers dressed in Tucson casual. Each stopped to shake hands with Cézar and Miranda. The door next to me opened and Gavin Plinkscale hesitated just over the threshold. I asked Philo and the others to make room for one more, then touched Gavin's arm and gestured for him to sit. He looked as if I'd saved his life.

"You knew Carla?" I asked him in a soft voice.

"No. But I knew Angelisa." He picked at a hangnail on his thumb. "I lied to you about that. She'd started taking private voice lessons from me. She was quite good. I read in the paper that she and the Zoryas were related. I just came to pay my respects to the family." He looked around at the throng of faces, many, like Tía Miranda, crying. "I don't belong here," he said, and started to rise.

I put my hand on his arm. "Stay," I said. "This is as much for Angelisa as it is for Carla. It's for the entire family."

He stayed.

* * *

Outside, after the service, I found *agente de policía* Gallegos-Martínez waiting. I hadn't seen him since the night in the tunnel. Gallegos-Martínez had walked from the Mexican side to view the body of Reyerto/Morocho. But he'd gone back by the time I climbed off the roof.

"Hello," I said, holding out my hand. "I didn't see you inside."

He shook my hand. "I was on the opposite side, with Officer Navarro and her mother. You are well?"

"Doing better," I said. "Tell me—will you go after Chuy for killing Angelisa Corday?"

He looked past me into the side courtyard where children hopped and skipped within the painted black lines of a maze. "Her death was unfortunate, but it is a problem for your local authorities. There is nothing I can do."

"Nothing you *will* do, you mean."

"As you say."

"One thing still bothers me—and I'd rather not ask Michael."

"I'll answer if I can," he said.

"Carla's bracelet, the jade-and-silver one she gave to Jorge on the beach—was she involved in Michael's . . . business?" I looked around to see if anyone was within earshot. Philo and Jamie were talking to Cézar; Teresa and Rosa were with Miranda.

"I asked Michael, of course," said Gallegos-Martínez. "He said that when he learned Carla was going to Puerto Peñasco for the weekend, he asked her to give the bracelet to the man on the beach in exchange for a few things for the shop. She did not know the history of the bracelet or that Jorge represented Reyerto. That was Michael's business. He told her he would be playing that night at La Roca and to give him the tennis bracelet as a tip. That also was for Reyerto. Jorge picked it up after Michael's performance that night."

"So Carla was an innocent victim."

"Yes. The jewels you described her wearing when she disappeared, the pendant and earrings, were rare coins in special settings. They were in the plastic bag Jorge gave her on the beach. Jorge had served as middleman for all Reyerto's transactions with Michael. Michael had never met Reyerto, only spoken to him on the phone. If Michael had known Reyerto would be in the restaurant that night, Michael would have prevented Carla from going there."

"And Jorge?"

"His wife told me he had been skimming some of the money he transported for Reyerto. We found it hidden in his home. Reyerto dealt with him that night and left him for Chuy to find. It was a threat that Chuy understood—a sample of what would happen if he or anyone in the family spoke to the authorities about Jorge's activities."

"What happened to Reyerto's dog? I thought I heard it in the tunnel that night?"

"He was adopted by one of my men."

"That's it, then," I said.

"Not quite." Gallegos-Martínez took two folded sheets of paper from his pocket and handed them to me. "I told you we would speak later. You have seen these?" he asked.

The first page was a police report with a California driver's license photo of a missing person—one Bernard Venable. He'd disappeared from an apartment complex near the UCLA campus last December, just after moving there to attend graduate school.

"I know Bernie," I said. "He was an undergrad at my school. Finished last fall. I hadn't heard he was missing."

"Look at the second page."

It was a photocopy of a Mexican police report, translated into English. Bernard Venable had been arrested in Tijuana, Mexico, after an altercation following a minor traffic accident. He paid a fine and was released. The accompanying photo was not the same as the one with the first report. This was a booking photo of Geoff Travers, my former fiancé. It was dated last Memorial Day.

The papers slipped from my grasp. I scrambled to recover them. Gallegos-Martínez stayed out of the way.

"So Geoff's alive," I said, feeling emotionally scattered.

"It would appear so."

"Was it Bernie's body they found in the ravine?"

"I do not have any more information than this. I expect you will receive a phone call soon."

"It was kind of you to warn me."

"It was the least I could do," he said, and handed me his card. "This has my numbers. Please contact me if I can assist you in any way. *Adiós,* Francisca MacFarlane."

I heard my name called, and turned to find Philo behind me. When I looked back, Gallegos-Martínez was climbing into Toni's car. They both waved as Toni pulled out of the parking lot.

"What was that about?" Philo asked, noting the papers I was slipping into my purse.

"Trouble. I'll tell you about it later."

"I've paid our respects to the Zoryas," Philo said. "Jamie's going with them to the graveyard." He paused, waiting for me to decide what I wanted to do.

"I want to go home," I said, echoing the words Carla had spoken in Puerto Peñasco, the day the nightmare started.

A week after the funeral, Michael took off on one of his trips. When he stopped by the house to say good-bye, he had the pinched, driven look of a man on a mission. But I saw a gleam of hope in his eyes.

"Tía Miranda wanted you to have this. Chuy returned it in the tunnel that night," he said. Michael held out the beautifully crafted blade that I'd last seen buried in Morocho's body. I didn't want to touch it.

"Knives have a way of finding their owners," he said.

"You used this to warn me. You loaned it to Chuy. It helped us pay a debt. It belongs to you, now." I still hesitated. "She purified it," Michael said, and grinned.

"I can just imagine," I said.

"And she said it could protect you from badgers."

I took the knife. One never knows when a badger might drop by.

Early on Thanksgiving morning, I stuffed a twenty-five-pound turkey with piñon-nut dressing. Philo helped me maneuver the bird into the oven. Though my parents had returned to England to finish their sabbatical, Kit and his family, Toni, Elena, Charley and Rosa, and Cézar and Miranda were joining Jamie, Teresa, Philo, and me for dinner. We'd finally gather again around the banquet tables we'd left standing on the patio the night Jamie was kidnapped—the night Carla died. It was time.

I answered a knock at the back door. Michael stood there. Gone was the haunted look. He radiated a zest for life.

"I just flew in," he said. "Would you have room for two more at dinner?"

"Of course," I said. "Who are you bringing?"

From the look on his face, I half expected him to produce a wife or girlfriend, but he motioned me outside to where an old man sat at the picnic table next to the porch. The family resemblance was strong.

"I know my father is here somewhere," Michael said. "Would you mind very much finding him for me? I have a surprise."

Cézar stood just inside the corral fence, crooning softly as he curried the dapple gray. Cézar's body had accepted the new heart. His color was good and he'd put on weight, but a perpetual sadness clouded his golden eyes.

"Michael's here," I said, resting my arms on the top bar. "He's helping Philo peel potatoes in the kitchen. He asked me to find you."

"And you did his bidding?" Cézar's eyes crinkled at the corners. "That boy has golden hands and a devil in his smile . . . He got them from his mother." He fed an apple to the mare and gave her a final pat. " 'You cannot harness happiness or children,' my father used to say. 'They must be free as the wind flying over the steppes.' I miss him still, my father, and it has been more than sixty years. I wonder if my son will miss me?"

"More than you know," I said. "He brought you a present."

"A present? For me? What is it?"

"Not what, who." And I stepped aside.

He looked beyond my shoulder to where the old man waited with Michael and Philo in the shadows by the house. "Mikail?"

Cézar opened the corral gate as if in a dream. I closed it behind him and joined Philo and Michael on the porch. Philo slipped his arm around me, pulled me into the curve of his body, and kissed the top of my head. Michael said nothing, but he smiled as he watched the two men, one frail, one robust, meet in the middle ground. Cézar's hand trembled as he touched the stubbly cheek, fingered the shabby coat, shiny with wear.

"Like Papa used to say: 'The coat is new—only the holes are old,'" said Mikail Zorya, in heavily accented English. "You see, it has taken such a long, long time to find you, brother." The two men embraced, laughing and crying at the same time.

"You have a fine son, Cézar."

"I do," Cézar said, smiling at Michael. "He did not give up searching for you." Cézar took his brother's gnarled fingers in his own. "Come, meet my horse."

"The spotted gray?"

"I used to have a white one . . . and a lovely wife. They brought me no end of trouble."

Wanting to give them privacy, we left them. When I glanced back, they were speaking a language I did not understand, and holding hands like small boys walking along a railroad track.

From *New York Times* bestselling author
Nevada Barr

DEEP SOUTH

Park Ranger Anna Pigeon stumbles upon a
gruesome murder with frightening
racial overtones.

0-425-17895-1

BLOOD LURE

Anna Pigeon is sent to the Waterton-Glacier International
Peace Park to study grizzly bears,
but all is not well.

0-425-18375-0

HIGH COUNTRY

It's fall in the Sierra Mountains, and what awaits Anna Pigeon
is a nightmare of death and greed—
and perhaps her final adventure.

0-425-19956-8

**Available wherever books are sold or at
penguin.com**

LYN HAMILTON

ARCHAEOLOGICAL MYSTERIES

"Hamilton's archaeological mysteries [are] sure
to have armchair travelers on the edge of their
settees. At once erudite and entertaining."
—*New York Times Book Review*

The Xibalba Murders	0-425-15722-9
The Maltese Goddess	0-425-16240-0
The Moche Warrior	0-425-17308-9
The Celtic Riddle	0-425-17775-0
The African Quest	0-425-18313-0
The Etruscan Chimera	0-425-18463-3
The Thai Amulet	0-425-19487-6

Available wherever books are sold or at
penguin.com

Also available from
BERKLEY PRIME CRIME

Dead Men Don't Lye
by Tim Myers

Benjamin Perkins thought he had his hands full taking care of his family's specialty soap store and keeping his quirky clan in line and out of trouble. But he's about to learn that when it comes to murder, there's no such thing as a clean getaway.

0-425-20744-7

Death at Blenheim Place
by Robin Paige

Kate Sheridan is at Blenheim Palace to research King Henry's mistress Rosamund, said to have been poisoned there by Eleanor of Aquitane. But her visit takes a strange turn when her hosts unwittingly begin to relive the legend.

0-425-20237-2

Theft on Thursday
by Ann Purser

A friend has asked working-class mother and house-cleaner Lois Meade to help crack a case. It looks like the handsome new choirmaster may have been poisoned. Soon, Lois finds herself untangling a web of secrets, bigotry, and intrigue—and can't let the culprits get away clean.

0-425-20747-1

Available wherever books are sold or at penguin.com

Also available from
BERKLEY PRIME CRIME

Chamomile Mourning
by Laura Childs
This sweet serving of the bestselling *Tea Shop* mystery
series takes us to Charleston's Spoleto Festival, where
Theodosia Browning's Poet's Tea is forced indoors by
rain—which is the least of her problems after a local
auction house owner plummets from the balcony to
his death.

0-425-20618-1

Blondes Have More Felons
by Alesia Holliday
There's nothing like December in Florida—especially
when it's attorney December Vaughn showing a drug
company and its ruthless lawyers that some blondes
are smarter than they look.

0-425-20892-3

Final Fore
by Roberta Isleib
Cassie is steeling her nerves for the U.S. Women's
Open when a rival is poisoned. And strange e-mails
and messages prove to Cassie that competition can
truly be murder.

0-425-20896-6

Available wherever books are sold or at penguin.com